Praise for the *New York Times* Bestseller The Littlest Bigfoot

"Young readers who have ever felt too big or been made
to feel small will feel just right in the cheerful glow
of Weiner's contemporary fairy tale."
—*New York Times Book Review*

"A charming story about finding a safe place to let your
freak flag fly." —*People*

"Enchanting right up to the sequel-beckoning end."
—*Kirkus Reviews*

"A heartwarming tale about friendship and belonging that will
resonate with those young readers who have ever struggled to fit
in or find their place in the world." —*School Library Journal*

"Weiner makes a winning children's book debut with
this witty story of outcasts coming together."
—*Publishers Weekly*

Praise for Little Bigfoot, Big City

"Fast-paced and full of questions, answers,
more questions—and heart."
—*Kirkus Reviews*

"Fans of a good mystery and sweet endings
won't be able to put it down."
—*Booklist Online*

Find out how the adventure began in

The Littlest Bigfoot

# Little Bigfoot, Big City

## jennifer Weiner

**ALADDIN**
New York London Toronto Sydney New Delhi

ALADDIN

An imprint of Simon & Schuster Children's Publishing Division

1230 Avenue of the Americas, New York, New York 10020

First Aladdin paperback edition May 2018

Text copyright © 2017 by Jennifer Weiner, Inc.

Cover illustration copyright © 2017 by Ji-Hyuk Kim

Interior illustrations by Sara Mulvanny copyright © 2017 by Simon & Schuster, Inc.

Also available in an Aladdin hardcover edition.

All rights reserved, including the right of reproduction in whole or in part in any form.

ALADDIN and related logo are registered trademarks of Simon & Schuster, Inc.

For information about special discounts for bulk purchases, please contact

Simon & Schuster Special Sales at 1-866-506-1949 or business@simonandschuster.com.

The Simon & Schuster Speakers Bureau can bring authors to your live event.

For more information or to book an event contact the Simon & Schuster

Speakers Bureau at 1-866-248-3049 or visit our website at www.simonspeakers.com.

Book designed by Laura Lyn DiSiena

The illustrations for this book were rendered in ink, pencil, and Photoshop.

The text of this book was set in Calluna.

Manufactured in the United States of America 0418 OFF

10 9 8 7 6 5 4 3 2 1

The Library of Congress has cataloged the hardcover edition as follows:

Names: Weiner, Jennifer, author. | Mulvanny, Sara, illustrator.

Title: Little Bigfoot, big city / by Jennifer Weiner ; illustrations by Sara Mulvanny.

Description: First Aladdin hardcover edition. | New York : Aladdin, 2017. |

Series: A littlest Bigfoot novel ; [2]

Identifiers: LCCN 2017012319 (print) | LCCN 2017037180 (eBook) |

ISBN 9781481470797 (eBook) | ISBN 9781481470773 (hc)

Subjects: | CYAC: Sasquatch—Fiction. | Friendship—Fiction. | Talent

shows—Fiction. | Families—Fiction. | New York—Fiction. |

BISAC: JUVENILE FICTION / Fantasy & Magic. | JUVENILE FICTION / Social Issues /

Friendship. | JUVENILE FICTION / Humorous Stories.

Classification: LCC PZ7.1.W433 (eBook) | LCC PZ7.1.W433 Lg 2017 (print) |

DDC [Fic]—dc23

LC record available at https://lccn.loc.gov/2017012319

ISBN 9781481470780 (pbk)

To David Reek

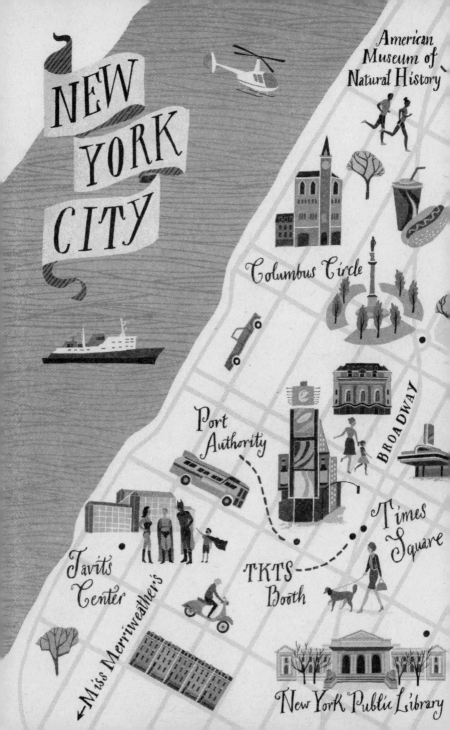

Central Park

Alice's Apartment

Carnegie Hall

FDR Drive

Rockefeller Plaza

# Little Bigfoot, Big City

# PROLOGUE

THE NEXT STAGE

THERE WERE THREE JUDGES ON *THE NEXT Stage*, the top-rated televised talent competition in which singers and dancers, comedians and magicians, acrobats and ventriloquists all competed for a million-dollar prize. At nine o'clock on a Saturday night in New York City, the head judge, whose name was Benjamin Burton, was standing onstage.

Benjamin Burton was over six and a half feet tall, with long, lean legs and a thick head of glossy black hair. A mustache and a neatly trimmed beard covered his face from lips to neck; dark sunglasses concealed his eyes. There was something faintly menacing about his posture,

1

about the way he moved and, even more, the way he held still, with his head perfectly motionless, his body angled like a knife; posed like a wolf ready to spring at its prey.

A girl who played the accordion and sang country songs stood to his left. A break-dancing boy was at his right. Above them were nets filled with barrels of silver and gold confetti, and in front of them was a crowd of five thousand people, all of them breathlessly waiting for the winner's name to be announced.

"Devon," said Benjamin, indicating the little girl. "Jaden," he said, and gave the boy's shoulder a squeeze. "Both of you have performed brilliantly tonight. But only one of you can go on . . . to the next stage."

The girl looked up at him hopefully. The boy stared straight ahead, like he was too terrified to move. Benjamin Burton waited, his body coiled and still, looking out at the audience, examining each face, like a man looking for lost treasure, like he had all the time in the world.

The judge who sat to Benjamin's right at the table that faced the stage was a singer/dancer/actress named Julia Sharp, who was famous for her glamorous good looks and long, honey-highlighted brown hair. On Benjamin's left was Romy Montez, a laconic country singer who was rarely seen without his western boots and cowboy hat.

The two of them had worked with Benjamin Burton for three years, but neither one of them could claim to know him or call him a friend. Neither one of them knew what Benjamin Burton did when he wasn't onstage or in the judging room. They didn't know how he spent his time, who he spoke to, or where he went as they made their way across the country, holding auditions. Benjamin Burton was as much of a mystery to them as he was to the rest of the world, which knew him as a successful music producer who ran an enormously profitable record label and served as a tough but fair judge on the talent show that he'd created.

He appeared to be in his thirties, although no one was sure. When reporters asked him where he'd grown up, he'd tell them, "Here, there, and everywhere," with a smile that showed his teeth and held a hint of menace that made further inquiry feel risky. He had never been married. He'd never appeared with a date on the red carpet or waved to a special someone in the audience. He kept an apartment in New York and a house on the edge of a cliff, high in the Hollywood Hills. At night, when the show was done taping, he would go home alone, lock the doors behind him, and stay there, until he was needed at the set or on the road.

When the show was in production, the morning was devoted to meetings, and the auditions began in the midafternoon. During their free time, Julia tended to her hair and her fans and her athleisure-wear business and Romy worked out with his trainer. Benjamin went to his trailer . . . and then, ten minutes later, when no one was watching, he'd slip out the door, disguised in jeans and a sweatshirt and a pair of run-down sneakers, with a base-ball cap pulled down low, its brim casting a half-moon of shadow over his face.

Every afternoon, in every city that *The Next Stage* held auditions, he would prowl the waiting hopefuls, a clipboard in his hand. As he moved swiftly down the crowds, slipped onto escalators, or cut through the crush of bodies crammed into hotel conference rooms, his gaze would touch on every face. He paced and scribbled and stared, sometimes for so long that he'd make someone uncomfortable, but he seemed to be able to sense the instant when his presence would become noticeable, and he'd move on, sometimes walking so swiftly that puzzled mothers would end up staring at the space where he'd been, then wonder if he'd been there at all.

Five minutes before showtime, he would emerge from his trailer, dressed in an impeccably crisp blue suit, with his thick black beard neatly trimmed, his hair carefully combed, and his big, dark sunglasses obscuring his eyes. He would nod at Romy, offer Julia his arm, escort them to the judges' table, then walk onto the stage.

"Welcome . . . ," he would begin. The room would go quiet. The silence would stretch for a long, tense moment, while Benjamin Burton stood in the spotlight, a microphone in his hand. His head never moved, but close observers could see his eyes, behind the glasses, passing over the crowd, from the balcony to the seats up front, left to right, row by row, taking in what felt like every face until finally, he'd say, "to *The Next Stage*!"

The audience would start cheering, clapping, and whooping. The spotlights would sweep the auditorium, alighting on the faces of the hopeful contestants, who filled the first three rows. The orchestra would start to play the theme song, and the taping would begin.

"He's looking for his lost love" was how Julia explained Benjamin's ritual. Julia was a great reader of romance novels, and she liked the idea of cool, distant, polite Benjamin Burton having a lost love somewhere and searching the crowd for some woman who'd broken his heart long ago.

Romy did not agree, even though he'd nod and smile

when Julia unfurled her theories. He'd seen the set of Benjamin's jaw, the way he stood with his shoulders rolled back and his hands curled in loose fists at his sides, as if he was ready to pounce or hit somebody.

So he kept quiet when Julia talked, but he didn't think that Benjamin Burton was looking for a lost love at all. He thought that his fellow judge was, instead, scanning the crowd in every city they visited for someone who'd hurt him, who'd stolen something he treasured, someone who'd done him wrong.

And when Benjamin Burton found that person, Romy Montez knew, for sure, that he didn't want to be anywhere near what happened next.

# CHAPTER 1

## Alice

As much as she hated school, Alice Mayfair had always hated school vacations even more. At least while she was at school, there was always hope, a glimmer of a chance that some kid might like her or some teacher would befriend her, a tiny bit of hope that her life could turn around.

Time with her parents offered no such possibility. They didn't like her. Worse, they were ashamed of her. And nothing Alice could do or say would change it.

Mark and Felicia Mayfair had arranged her life so that they saw as little of her as possible. When she wasn't away at one of the eight different schools she'd attended, she was at camp. When she wasn't at camp, she was spending a week with her beloved granny in Cape Cod, the only place she'd ever felt happy. It was only for the handful of days that she wasn't in one of those three places that she stayed with Mark and Felicia, whom she'd learned, long ago, not to call Mom and Dad.

Her mother was elegant and slender, always in a dress or a skirt and high heels, her hair sleek and glossy, her mouth always painted red. Her father was handsome in his suits and polished shoes, with a newspaper or an iPad tucked under his arm and a look on his face that let the world know he was important.

Then there was Alice, tall and broad, her hair a tangly mess, all stained clothes and clumsy hands and big feet; Alice, who resembled neither of her parents; Alice, who didn't fit.

Now that she had learned the truth about herself—that she wasn't human and that her parents weren't really her parents and that her home was not really her home—for the first time, Alice didn't feel ashamed or like she wanted to make herself smaller. Alice felt free.

She'd left her boarding school, the Experimental Center for Love and Learning, on a chilly morning in December, to start her winter break. It was early after-

noon when Lee, her parents' driver, dropped her off at her apartment building on New York City's Upper East Side. Alice waved at the doorman, took the elevator to the penthouse, and found her parents waiting for her at the door. She hugged her mother, flinging her strong arms around Felicia's narrow shoulders, feeling Felicia's body stiffen, seeing the startled look on her face.

"Look at you!" said Mark, and instead of slumping or slouching or trying to rearrange the curls that had escaped from her braids, Alice stood up straight and met his eyes. And did her father flinch a little when she looked at him? Was Felicia looking a little sneaky and strange as she stroked Alice's hair with a fragile hand?

It didn't matter. They weren't her parents. She didn't belong with them, and that knowledge, a secret tucked up and hidden, like a butterscotch in her cheek, let her smile and say, "I thought I'd make us dinner."

Her parents exchanged a surprised glance. "You can cook?" asked Mark.

"She took a cooking class at school," Felicia said, letting Alice know that at least one of her so-called parents had glanced at the "narrative assessment" the Experimental Center for Love and Learning sent home instead of report cards.

"I'll go grocery shopping," Alice announced before her parents could object. "We'll eat at seven."

After a moment of startled silence, her parents agreed and handed over a credit card. Alice found her apron in her suitcase and went to the apartment's airy, immaculate, rarely used kitchen to get started on the meal she'd imagined, and planned on serving at the small table in the kitchen instead of the enormous one in the dining room, where they typically ate on the rare occasions when all three of them dined together.

*They tested your blood, and it isn't human.* That was what Jeremy Bigelow, the so-called Bigfoot hunter who'd been hot on her friend Millie's trail, had told her that morning. At first Alice had been shocked and scared— Was she a space alien? Some kind of mutant?—but almost immediately she realized what this could mean.

If she wasn't human, she might be Yare—what humans called Bigfoot. She might be part of the same tribe as Millie, her best friend. Which would, of course, be wonderful. Maybe that was why being Yare was the only possibility she'd considered, the only thing that she thought might be true. Also, as far as she knew, being Yare was the only possibility. During one of their early conversations right after Alice had learned the truth about her friend, she'd asked Millie whether, if Bigfoots were real, then other things might be real too.

"What other things?" Millie had asked.

Alice felt uncomfortable. She'd caught the way Millie's voice had gotten a little louder when she'd said "*things*," as if Alice had implied or meant to suggest that the Yare were in a different, less-important category than humans.

"I don't know . . . vampires? Hobbits? The abominable snowman?"

Millie had thought, then shaken her head. "I am not hearing of those ones," she said. "Probably they are stories that the No-Furs tell their littlies, to keep them behaving. Like the Bad Red-Suit No-Fur, which is, of course, Santa Claus."

Alice had smiled, remembering how Millie had told her the Yare legend of a No-Fur in a red suit who snuck down Yare chimneys each December and stole the toys of bad Yare boys and girls and gave them to the No-Furs, and how Alice had explained how the Yare had twisted the story of Santa.

"How about the Loch Ness Monster?" Alice asked.

"Oh, she is real," Millie said immediately. "But very shy. Also, she does not like to be called 'Monster.'"

Alice's mouth had dropped open, and Millie had

giggled, and Alice, knowing that Millie was teasing her, but not in a mean way, started laughing too.

Alice probably had real parents, Yare parents, out there, somewhere, who were looking for her and who would love her when they found her. Being Yare would explain all the ways that she was different: bigger and taller than other girls her age, with big hands and big feet and a wild tangle of unruly hair that she called the Mane. She would find her parents, and she would find her people, and everything would make sense, and, most of all, she wouldn't be lonely anymore.

Alice opened the refrigerator. There was a quart of almond milk that she recognized from her last visit home, two sad-looking apples, a container of bean sprouts and another of tofu, a tub of fat-free Greek yogurt, and a jug of maple syrup that, Alice knew, had never been poured onto pancakes but had instead been mixed with lemon juice and cayenne pepper when her mother did a cleanse.

Felicia was hovering, practically wringing her hands. "I'm sorry," she said. "If I'd known you were going to cook, I would have had some staples on hand."

"It's all right," said Alice, who was feeling generous. She'd planned a dish that Kate, the school cook and

Alice's instructor, had served in the dining hall: butter-nut squash baked with honey and maple syrup, stuffed with a mixture of rice, black beans, and goat cheese. *Any kind of squash is okay,* Kate had told her, *and you can put anything you've got into the stuffing. It's a very forgiving rec-ipe.* Of course, Kate hadn't told her what to do when you had nothing. Kate had probably never even imagined a kitchen as bare as this one.

Alice walked to the grocery store on the corner. There, she took her time, picking out the firmest squash, the sweetest-smelling onion, the biggest head of garlic. She bought nutmeg and cinnamon, selected a cylinder of goat cheese, and scooped rice into a paper bag. At home she washed her hands and located a knife and the cut-ting board, as well as a pot for the rice and a baking dish for the squash, both of which looked brand-new. For a while Felicia watched from the doorway, balanced lightly on her high heels, slim as a blade of grass in her skirt and blouse, asking Alice if she needed help turning on the oven, telling her to be careful with the knife. Alice shook her head. "I'm fine," she said. She was thinking of the sweater that was draped neatly over Felicia's shoulders. The sweater, Alice knew, would never dream of slipping, and the skirt's hem would never be crooked, and not a strand of her mother's long, straightened hair would dare to fall out of place.

Alice settled the squash on the cutting board and used a knife almost as long as her arm to slice it open with one strong, exact stroke. "Look at you go!" said Felicia.

If her mother was slim as grass, then Alice was sturdy as an oak tree. She was strong and fast. She could run for miles, she could leap over fallen logs, she could swim across a lake and tow another girl to safety. She had saved Millie, and saved the entire Yare Tribe, and now, finally, Alice knew the truth about herself, and now, finally, she was going to find out where—and to whom—she really belonged.

Felicia was still watching. She watched while Alice smashed cloves of garlic and diced an onion, while she cooked the rice and toasted the spices and crumbled a fistful of cheese. Eventually, Felicia drifted over to the breakfast bar, where no one had ever eaten breakfast, and sat on one of the stools, which had never held anything but a newspaper or a purse or a stack of fashion magazines.

Alice drained the golden raisins that she'd plumped in a mixture of cider and vinegar.

"That looks delicious," said Felicia.

"I can make lots of things," said Alice, offering her

mother a spoonful of stuffing. "Lasagna. Curried tofu. Persian rice."

Her mother nodded, then looked at her. Alice readied herself for the usual scrutiny, for the way her mother's mouth would get tight and her nostrils would flare, like she'd smelled something unpleasant, when she inspected Alice's midriff or her hips. There was always something wrong with Alice's appearance—a sweater that had gotten too tight, a hank of hair that had slipped out of the braid, a rip or a stain or the dread horizontal stripes that, Alice had been told again and again, were not "slimming." "Slimming," of course, was Felicia's highest praise for a piece of clothing.

"I like your"—Felicia paused, looking at Alice, groping for a word, finally settling on—"outfit."

"One of the girls at school made it for me. Her name's Taley. She likes to sew," said Alice. Taley Nudelman, her roommate and her not-quite-friend (but not-quite-not-friend, Alice reminded herself) had made her the jumper as a holiday gift. The Experimental Center welcomed learners of all religions, while observing no holidays, but before the winter break the students were allowed to exchange handmade holiday gifts. With Millie's help, Alice made her bunkmates rosemary sugar scrubs and lavender-infused honey, and baked them each a tin of cookies to take home. Taley had sewn them all jumpers, soft corduroy dresses that you could wear over shirts and tights or leggings. Alice's was a golden brown color, and its straps fastened with bright orange buttons.

Felicia opened her mouth, preparing to say something, then closed it without a word. Alice bent, sliding the pan of squash into the oven. Seventeen days, she told herself. Seventeen days, ten of them in Hawaii, and she could go back to school.

Alice's father set the table, and Alice sliced the cranberry nut bread that she'd baked at school and brought home in her suitcase. There were bottles of sparkling water, candles, little dishes of soft, salted butter, and, on the sideboard, a cake box tied with pink twine.

"Ladies," said Mark, holding out first his wife's chair, then Alice's. He took two slices of Alice's bread, then grinned at his wife. "C'mon," he said, poking Felicia's arm with the bread basket. Felicia looked predictably horrified as she murmured something about an upcoming black-tie gala and how she wouldn't fit into her ball gown, before selecting the smallest slice and setting it on the very edge of her plate.

"Wow," said Mark. "You're really going crazy." He gave Alice a conspiratorial grin.

16

Alice smiled back, and wondered. Maybe Mark was her real, actual father. Maybe he'd met a Yare somewhere in the world and fallen in love. Except she couldn't imagine where on his travels her father, who had spent his entire life in suits, in big cities, might have come across someone from Millie's Tribe. Nor could Alice imagine her father in the embrace of a woman like the Yare she'd glimpsed during her one trip to Millie's village. The Yare women were large, and they wore simple homemade dresses and were typically barefoot, with the tops of their feet covered in fur and their calloused soles impervious to twigs or thorns or cold weather. Their eyes, framed by long, curling lashes, looked startlingly lovely in their faces, which, Alice thought, were regular lady faces, underneath the fur.

She smiled at the thought of Mark in a suit with his arms around a woman with a wild tangle of hair and fur covering her arms and legs and face.

"Something funny?" Mark inquired.

Alice shook her head. She served each of her parents a portion of the squash and dug in, enjoying the richness of the cheese, the sweetness of the honey, the texture of the perfectly cooked rice on her tongue. It was the kind of thing Millie could be eating, right at that moment.

Except Millie wouldn't be at a table in a fancy apartment with parents who seemed to have very little to say to each other and nothing to say to her. Millie would be deep in the woods, sitting at a fire in a cozy little house tucked under a hill, snug between parents who loved her, surrounded by her Tribe.

"Honey, what's wrong?" Felicia was looking at Alice from across the candlelit expanse of the table.

"Nothing," said Alice. She made herself smile and buttered another bite of bread.

"Was this school really all right?" asked Felicia. Her plucked eyebrows were hoisted high, and there was a single black bean speared on the tine of her fork. Her tone suggested that she could hardly believe it. Which wasn't surprising, Alice thought, given the seven schools she'd been kicked out of or whose administrators had politely asked that she not re-enroll.

"It was," said Alice. "It was weird at first—everything's got funny names. Like, students are learners, and teachers are learning guides. And the food was mostly vegetarian. But I liked it. Some of the kids were okay."

She felt, more than saw, the look that her parents gave each other, and tried not to feel insulted by their obvious pleasure and their just-as-obvious surprise.

"Did you miss me?" she asked, her voice innocent.

There was only the barest pause before her mother said, "Of course we did. You're our sunshine." Her father nodded, trying to say something around a mouthful of squash and stuffing, finally settling for a wordless thumbs-up.

Alice doubted that either one of her parents had actually even noticed her absence. Felicia's social schedule, her roster of balls and luncheons and party-planning sessions and Pilates classes, would roll on, unimpeded by the occasional demands that Alice made on her time, and Mark was away so much, either at his office all day or flying off to China and Japan, that Alice knew he went weeks without seeing her mother and even longer without seeing her.

"I'm just glad we're all together," said Felicia, reaching to take Alice's fingers in her cool, bony ones. It was strange. Alice had always envied her mother's tininess, her fragility, had thought—and had been taught—that women could never be too thin. Now she could see things differently. She wondered what the Yare would make of Felicia and thought, a little smugly, that if her mother had to run through a forest or swim across a lake to save one of her society-lady friends, she probably wouldn't be able to make it more than a few hundred yards without collapsing. Those slender arms and fingers would never be able to haul a heavy log out of the way; that slim body wouldn't be able to hide a friend from view. Alice knew that she would never look right to Felicia, but her body could do things. She could run for miles, maybe not fast, but steadily. She could save a life.

She smiled at the thought, aware that her mother was looking at her strangely as her father continued to decimate the loaf of bread, lavishing butter on each slice like a man who knew he might never taste it again.

"Tell us more about the school," said Felicia, who appeared to be picking each black bean out of her portion of stuffing before spearing them on the tines of her fork and popping them, one at a time, into her mouth.

Alice took another bite of squash. "I liked being near the forest," she said. "I went running. And I liked the school. I learned a lot about myself." She cut another bite, watching her parents closely. Mark's eyes were on his plate, but Felicia was looking at Alice with what seemed to be a mixture of curiosity and fear. "By the way," Alice said, "we're doing family trees, so I'm going to need to ask you both some questions about my relatives."

"They do that project at every single school you've

been to, right?" said Mark, giving her a good-natured smile through a mouthful of rice and beans.

Instead of answering, Alice imagined that she was Riya, one of her cabin mates and almost-friends, who was a nationally ranked fencer. Riya practiced in the Center's gym, a ramshackle building constructed as an afterthought by administrators who were obviously not big on the idea of sports. A single court was used for everything from basketball to dodgeball to kickball to tennis . . . and, of course, there was no scoreboard, as the Center did not believe in winners and losers. Riya used the court in the late afternoons, when it was empty, and Alice would watch her, with her silver épée slashing through the air, advancing and retreating, her feet pattering against the ground in a dizzying dance. Sometimes you'd press an opponent, trying to score points, Riya explained, while other times you'd just try to keep your opponent moving until they were exhausted. Alice decided that the second tactic might be in order with her parents. She'd bombard them with questions, keep them off balance, then find out what she needed to know.

"What kind of baby was I?" she began.

Mark looked puzzled. Felicia's face had been rendered

largely inexpressive due to the injections she got every month, but she still seemed to be afraid.

"The regular kind," Felicia said. Alice could hear the effort it was taking for her mother to keep her tone light. "You slept, you cried, you ate . . ."

"What were my favorite foods?"

Felicia tapped her fingertips against the tablecloth. "Oh, sweet potatoes, I think."

"Avocados," Mark supplied. "You liked avocados." He smiled. "I used to slice one of those suckers in half and feed you the whole thing with a spoon." Felicia's mouth pursed.

"That was too much avocado for a baby," she said. "Avocados are very high in saturated fats." She looked down at her plate, the tines of her fork shredding the squash, as if she were checking to be sure that no one had hidden any saturated fats underneath it.

"Was I a good baby?" Alice asked. "Did I cry a lot? Did I like other kids? Did I have friends?"

Another uneasy glance traveled across the table, almost like a shadow or a wind. Alice nibbled a raisin. If her theory was correct—if she'd been born to a Yare family, then stolen somehow or given away—her parents wouldn't have any idea of what she'd been like as a baby, because they wouldn't have been around to see it.

"You were fine," said Felicia, her tone firm, clearly eager to change the subject.

"Do you have any pictures?"

This time her parents made no attempt to hide their surprise. Alice had never in her life asked to see a picture of herself and usually tried to hide when they were being taken. She'd pose for school pictures because she didn't have a choice, and there were a few family pictures taken at Thanksgivings and vacations, where she'd try to camouflage herself behind a convenient grown-up. In most of them, she was frowning; in a few, when she was little, she'd actually tried to cover her face with her hands, knowing, even then, that she looked wrong.

Felicia collected herself. "I'll see if I can find some," she said.

Alice had nodded serenely, knowing that her mother would come up with some excuse, and that no photographs would be forthcoming, because they didn't exist.

Mark, beaming, clapped his hands. "Who's ready for dessert?" he asked, and untied the paper box to reveal a cake with white buttercream frosting and pink spun-sugar flowers and the words "Welcome Home, Alice" written on top. Felicia cringed. "I'll cut it," said Alice, and she helped herself to a thick slice with a pink frosting rose and a big glass of milk.

That night Alice sat on her bed, in her favorite plaid pajamas, waiting for her parents to go to sleep. Her plan was to scour the house, every desk drawer and cabinet, trying to find pictures of herself as a baby. She was checking her email—she'd lent Millie her laptop for the vacation, hoping they could stay in touch—when her mother knocked on her door.

"Come in," Alice called. Felicia wore a lacy nightgown and a matching robe. Her pedicured feet were bare and there was a book in her arms, with gold-leaf pages and pale-pink leather binding.

"I wanted to give you this," she said, handing Alice the book. Alice saw her initials and the date of her birth, all rendered in scrolling gold-leaf cursive on the cover. "It's your baby book," she said, unnecessarily, as Alice flipped to the first page and saw a picture of her mother in a hospital bed. "It's important, I think, to know where you come from." Alice was so busy studying the first shot that she almost didn't hear. In the photograph, Felicia looked frail and exhausted. Her hair—not the bright, sleek blond with

which Alice was familiar, but instead an unremarkable reddish-brown that looked more like Alice's own hair—was matted and curling around her cheeks. Her eyes were shiny and her face was flushed as she clutched a blanketed bundle in her arms. Her face was fuller than Alice had ever seen it, her cheeks plump and rosy and without the fashionable hollows underneath. Her lips were chapped and lipstick free, and her gown clung to her, damp with sweat. There were IV lines in both of her arms, and Alice counted the figures of half a dozen people gathered around the bed.

"It was a very long birth," said Felicia, as Alice continued to scrutinize the picture. "And, of course, you can't color your hair when you're pregnant."

Alice nodded, even though she wasn't sure what hair dye might have to do with a pregnancy. "Was this Mount Sinai?" she asked, naming the hospital in their neighborhood, the one where most of her Upper East Side acquaintances had been born.

Felicia shook her head. "Upland, Vermont."

"I was born in Vermont?" This was new information for Alice.

"Your father and I were up there for a ski trip. Well, your father was planning on skiing, and I was going to keep him company. Then he was called away for business."

Alice nodded, remembering the dozens, possibly hundreds, of times that her father had gotten a call from his boss in the middle of a vacation or a sleepy Sunday or a meal.

"And then you decided to make your debut a month ahead of schedule. It took a while for Mark to make it back. There'd been this huge snowstorm. It was days before they got the roads cleared and they let me go home." Felicia flipped the page. There she was in a wheelchair, her hair marginally neater, drawn back in a ponytail, holding a bundle that was probably her baby, and wearing—Alice blinked, looking more closely—sweatpants and a loose plaid button-down shirt and thick wool socks and . . .

"Are those hiking boots?"

"Snowstorm," Felicia reminded her, and Alice nodded. Except she'd seen how Felicia dressed for the snow. Her winter clothing typically involved a coat of the stitched-together pelts of small, dead furry animals, and fur-trimmed gloves and high-heeled leather boots that matched.

Alice turned the page, and there was the mother she knew, in a picture she'd seen before in a silver frame on the table in the apartment's entryway.

"Your christening," said Felicia. In that shot, Felicia's hair was blond and shining, as she stood in front of their

apartment's floor-to-ceiling windows with the baby in her arms. Alice, in her mother's arms, was wearing some kind of stretchy yellow garment, patterned with ducks, that covered her from her neck to her toes, and she looked like she had doubled in size since the first picture. She had three chins and no hair, but Felicia had put a head-band of fake flowers around her head. There was no fur anywhere that she could see. She looked, Alice thought, with her heart sinking, entirely human.

"Dinner was delicious," her mother said.

Alice, who'd been studying the picture so closely that she'd almost forgotten that her mother was there, gave a little jump. *You didn't eat any of it,* she thought.

"I'm proud of you," Felicia said, and bent down in a cloud of perfume to brush Alice's cheek with her lips. Once her mother had departed, in a swish of silk, Alice resumed her study of the photo album, flipping slowly through the pages, feeling her heart sink with each shot that documented the first hairless Yare-less year of her life. There was Felicia feeding her a bottle, and Felicia giving her a bath, and Felicia and Alice, asleep on the couch, with Alice tucked up against Felicia's shoulder.

*Maybe it was a fake baby,* she thought, and checked her phone again, hoping for a note from Millie. Maybe Felicia and Mark had faked all of these shots, just waiting for this very occasion, the day when Alice would ask to see proof that she was theirs.

Except the baby in the pictures had a heart-shaped birthmark underneath her left ear, the same as Alice. And even though she didn't want to, Alice could see herself in that pudgy-faced, squishy-limbed baby: the arch of her brows, her full lower lip, even the shape of her fingers.

In her pajamas, cross-legged on the down comforter on her bed, Alice frowned, leaning so close to the pictures that her breath fogged the plastic that covered them as she flipped back to the very first shot of Felicia in the hospital and newborn Alice in her exhausted mother's arms.

She was about to close the book when something in the assembled figures around the hospital bed caught her eye. All of them—doctors? Nurses?—wore scrubs and surgical masks and most of them were men. But one of the figures toward the back was short and round and female, with merry blue eyes that seemed to twinkle with some secret knowledge.

Alice squinted and held her breath. Unless she was mistaken, or her educational consultant had a twin, she was looking at Miss Merriweather, the small, kindly, white-haired woman who'd been responsible for sending

Alice to all eight of the schools she'd attended . . . the one she'd first met when she was six years old.

But why had she attended Alice's birth? What would an educational consultant from New York City be doing in a hospital in Vermont with a brand-new baby? Had Felicia and Miss Merriweather known each other before Alice was born? And if that was true, why had her parents introduced Miss Merriweather to her as if she were someone they had just met, instead of someone they were already acquainted with?

Alice looked more carefully, wanting to be sure. Her heart was beating so hard that she could hear it, and her mouth felt cottony. *Millie,* she thought. *I have to tell Millie.* But of course she couldn't. She could write an email, but Millie would have to find time and privacy to check it . . . and of course the Yare did not have cell phones, so there was no chance of a call.

"Nyebbeh," she muttered, which was a Yare expression, before padding, barefoot, out of her bedroom and into the living room. Her parents kept a dictionary on a stand next to the bookcase full of fancy leather-bound books that Alice didn't think had ever been read. On top of the opened dictionary was a magnifying glass. Alice carried the magnifying glass back to her bedroom, then used it to peruse every bit of the baby picture. She was almost positive—almost, but not entirely sure—that the masked figure at the very edge of the shot was, in fact, Miss Merriweather. She was smiling down at baby Alice, like one of the good fairies in the story of Sleeping Beauty, one who'd come to give Alice a gift, not of grace or beauty or a lovely singing voice, but maybe the gift of strength, of resilience, the patience to wait and the courage to keep trying until she'd found her place in the world.

She looked at her mother again, her messy hair and flushed, freckled cheeks; her plaid shirt and her flat-soled boots; and, after she closed the book and fell asleep, she dreamed a dream she'd had a thousand times, a dream of running to her real mother, a mother who'd want her and who'd love her. Only, the thousand other times she'd had that dream, she'd never seen the woman. She'd always been some far-off figure in the shadows, too far away for Alice to see her face.

This time, for the first time, as she ran toward the woman, along an endless, shadowed hallway, she thought she could see hair that looked like hers, freckled skin, chapped lips that smiled, and she could hear a voice that echoed in her bones, a voice that said, "I love you. You're my girl."

# CHAPTER 2

## Millie

"Darn it," Millie muttered as she glared at Alice's top-lap—the laptop, she reminded herself—and waited for its screen to bloom into life. "Darn it" was one of the No-Fur expressions she had picked up in her time with Alice and her friends, and she'd started to say it when things weren't working out, which, just lately, felt like all the time.

"What's wrong?" asked Frederee, her Tribe mate and, for the day, her partner in crime.

"The Wi-Fi is very slow," said Millie, which was also something she'd learned from the No-Furs, who were forever complaining about how long things took to appear on their various devices. Finally, the website loaded, and the space for Millie to type in her password appeared. Alice had shown her how to use the computer and how to sign in to the Experimental Center's Wi-Fi, which was accessible even across the lake and miles into the forest, where the Yare village was hidden. That made things go faster, but faster was still not fast enough for Millie. Any minute her mother might go walking through the woods to try to find her, or Tulip or Florrie, the other Yare littlies, might come running through the snow and see Millie doing a forbidden thing and get her in all kinds of trouble.

Frederee peered over her shoulder, frowning and chewing on his fingernails and looking, the way all Yare did these days, a little unsettled to be in Millie's presence. He'd known Millie for her entire life, just as the rest of the Yare in the village had, but ever since she'd gone swimming across the lake and been rescued by Alice, ever since she had almost exposed the hidden Tribe to human eyes, and then been part of the plan that had saved them, everyone—from Old Aunt Yetta to Ricardan and his wife, Melissandra, to Tulip and even Millie's parents—had started treating Millie with a kind of fearful reverence, as if she might burst into flames if they said something wrong. Or, she thought, make *them* burst into flames. They thought that she knew things she didn't know; that she'd seen things she hadn't seen; that, just by having a No-Fur friend and spending time out in the No-Fur world, she'd become someone different.

The littlies asked her for stories from the No-Fur encampment. They wanted to know about cars and airplanes and elections. Was it true that they only ate three times a day? And did they mind being naked all the time, without any fur beneath their clothes?

Millie explained that they were untroubled by their furlessness, and that airplanes were safe and that No-Furs did, indeed, vote on their leaders. She let them admire the friendship bracelet that Alice had given her, and she taught them how to make fortune-tellers out of folded paper and how to sing "Ninety-Nine Bottles of Beer on the Wall." The other young Yare all acted as if she were a hero, crediting her for saving the Tribe, and they all seemed to have forgotten that if it hadn't been for her curiosity, the Tribe would never have been in danger in the first place.

The truth was that it had been Alice's plan that had saved them, once they'd learned that a bad No-Fur boy named Jeremy Bigelow had seen Millie and had announced a plan to gather hundreds of No-Furs on the shores of Lake Standish to lead a search into the woods. On the night of the search, Alice had put on a fur vest and let her thick, curly hair out of its braids. Alice had run right into the crowd, looking, even Millie had to admit, enough like a Yare that the No-Furs all started to chase her. Instead of leading them to the Yare village, though, Alice led them to her school, where all the learners and learning guides and even the school's founders had been lined up outside the gates. They'd shamed the No-Furs for chasing after a girl just because she looked different, and when Millie stepped forward to claim that she was just a No-Fur with a skin condition, not a Bigfoot at all, the other No-Furs hadn't looked suspicious or like they wanted to throw her in a cage. They'd looked ashamed of themselves and had gone slinking off into the darkness, abandoning their search, leaving the village still safe and hidden, and Millie a hero.

Mostly, Millie didn't mind the special treatment, the way that Aelia would slip her extra hand-pies on her way to school, bowing her head, too shy to even meet Millie's eyes, or how Teacher Greenleaf no longer got angry if Millie hadn't finished her readings or if she wanted to spend extra time in the Lookout Tree, from whose top branches she could see the Center. She especially enjoyed the way Tulip, the largest of the Yare littlies—and, for years, Millie's sworn enemy—would flinch and cringe if Millie even looked her way, as if Millie might have learned some secret new fighting tricks during her time across the lake. But it made her sad when Frederee, her old friend, did the same thing.

Millie had always felt different from the other Yare. Most of her Tribe mates would have been more than content to live a safe and quiet life, to know that when they were grown they would live the same lives as their parents. They were happy in their village, content in their snug and hidden homes dug into the sides of the hills, pleased to spend their days sewing and mending and cooking, chopping wood and gathering healing herbs, tending to the goats, preserving foods for winter, or making crafts or clothing or all-natural soaps and scrubs to sell on Etsy.

Not Millie. Millie wanted more. Millie wanted to taste every treat that the No-Fur world had to offer. She wanted to shop in a No-Fur store, not just wear the dresses her mother sewed and the shoes her father bought her on-the-line. (She had tenderfoot, a condition in which her feet never developed the fur and thick calluses that allowed the rest of the Yare to spend even the coldest, snowiest winters without shoes.) She wanted to go to concerts and see a movie in a big soft seat in the darkness of a theater, with other No-Furs laughing at the funny parts and crying when the story got sad, instead of watching them on Old Aunt Yetta's television set all by herself because no one else was interested. She wanted to ride a train and a boat and a subway; to visit a beach and a desert and a mountaintop; to live in a big city and sleep in a partment like the one Alice came from, high above the busy streets.

More than any of that, though, Millie wanted to sing. She wanted to perform, on a stage, in front of an audience. She wanted to be on television, like the people in her favorite show, *Friends*. Her fondest wish was to win the TV talent competition *The Next Stage*, to stand in the spotlight next to Benjamin Burton while gold and silver confetti rained down and the crowd shouted her name.

The other Yare had always known these things about her. Before she'd crossed the lake they had treated her like she was strange but amusing; eccentric little Millie with her skimpy fur and tiny little feet, who would some-day grow up and be their Leader. Now that she'd actually gone out into that other world and come back with a human friend, they treated her with something closer to awe . . . as if all of her strange dreams might actually come true.

Frederee tapped her shoulder, then pointed at the laptop. "What do we do now?"

Millie looked at the screen. Before she'd met Alice and gone across the lake, Frederee had never been shy about telling her no or when he thought something was a bad idea. Now he would agree to help even before Millie had promised him all of her sweets for a month, but he didn't look happy about it. He kept turning around, peering over his shoulder, even though they were down by the lake, on the first day of the First Month, standing underneath a pine tree's snow-laden branches. Old Aunt Yetta was off attending to Ricardan, who had fallen through the ice while ice fishing and broken his arm. Millie's and Frederee's fathers were both deep in the forest, cutting down trees and dragging them back to the village for firewood, and Millie's mother, Septima, was hosting the other ladies of the Tribe to finish a wedding quilt for Aelia, who would fasten hands with Laurentius come the spring thaw.

"'Submit Information Here,'" Millie read. She'd already filled in the entire form, putting in whatever she could that was true, making up the rest. She had already convinced Alice to let her use her address at the Center so she'd have the required mailing address, and Alice had agreed to collect any mail that might arrive. All the other pieces were in place. Millie had an email address. She had faked her parents' signatures in the electronic signature boxes and had promised that, indeed, she'd be available for an in-person audition in New York. All she needed— she smoothed her best blue dress, the one she'd been glad her mother hadn't noticed her wearing—was to submit an audition video by five o'clock on January 15. Which was why she'd convinced Alice to let her borrow her laptop and had talked Frederee into coming with her into the forest.

"What do I do?" asked Frederee as Millie located the app for the camera and clicked it into life. The laptop looked like a toy in his big hands, and he held it as if it were a bomb that might explode if he loosened his grip.

"Hold the top-lap."

Frederee fumbled with the computer.

"No, you need to turn the screen so it's facing me," Millie said, and tried not to sound impatient. If she could have asked Alice to help or, really, any of the No-Fur kids just across the lake, they'd have known what to do without being told. All of them had computers and tablets and phones; some of them even read their books on slim electronic screens. Millie just had Frederee, a laptop that she didn't entirely understand, and two weeks to complete her audition and submit it. She squirmed with impatience as Frederee fumbled with the keyboard, then the screen.

"Look!" Frederee sounded delighted as he peered down. "Millie! I am seeing me!" He grinned at the screen, then reached up to fluff the fur on top of his head, and dropped the laptop into the snow. Millie shrieked. Frederee apologized. Thankfully, the laptop wasn't broken, and Millie was able to figure out which button to click so that the camera was shooting out instead of in.

"Good. Now you have to move it so you can't see my face."

Frederee frowned.

"Just lower it down, until you're looking . . ." Millie gestured toward her midsection, which was covered by her dress and looked like it could belong to a normal No-Fur girl. In other words, it did not display any fur.

Frederee frowned at the screen as he rocked back and forth on the snowy ground. "It says on the form, 'Contestant's entire face must be visible.'"

Millie felt her temper rise. "We will tell them that it slipped."

Frederee shrugged and held the screen still. Millie

breathed in the icy air, straightening her shoulders and curling her toes, in their fur-lined boots, more deeply into the snow. She'd thought for hours about which song to choose, one that would show off her voice and her personality, and had finally settled on "Defying Gravity," from *Wicked*. Every word of the song, and the story of a green-faced girl who wanted to make friends and fit in and change the world, could have been her story, if you substituted "fur" for "green" and "get famous" for "change the world." She pulled in another breath of the sharp wintry air, and began: "Something has changed within me / Something is not the same."

"Um, Millie?" Frederee was holding up one hand, gesturing for her to stop. "Sorry," he said, sounding sheepish. "I jiggled."

"Try not to jiggle. We do not have much time!"

Frederee nodded and adjusted the top-lap. Millie started again, and this time she got through the entire song, then trotted up to Frederee to review the video. There was her midriff, centered in the snowy outdoors, and there was her voice, clear and pure and sweet, and it was perfect.

Only, instead of hitting "upload," Frederee's thick finger accidentally pressed the key for "delete."

Millie trotted back, took another deep breath, and sang it again, maybe even better than she had the first time, and Frederee managed to upload it correctly. Millie was about to declare the day a triumph when a notice appeared on the screen. "'We are SORRY,'" Millie and Frederee read together as a frowny-face emoji appeared beneath the words. "'It appears as though something in your video has gone wrong! Please try again.'"

So they did, with Frederee aiming the camera at a point just below the fur of Millie's chin. That way, Millie reasoned, whoever was looking at these videos would assume it was an honest mistake, and then of course once they'd heard her voice they would send her through to the next round. Except, almost as soon as they'd uploaded that attempt, the same message reappeared.

"I think," Frederee said carefully, "that it knows it is not seeing your face."

Millie made a frustrated snort. They tried posing with her face in shadow. They shot her singing with the camera aimed at the back of her head. Both times, the system told them no. And, then, even though her voice was getting hoarse, and Frederee was making noises about being so hungry he could drop, Millie asked for one more try.

Frederee shook his head, his gaze moving anxiously

toward the sky. "It is getting on sundown," he said, as if Millie hadn't noticed the sliver of moon that had appeared over the black mirror of the lake.

Millie's shoulders sank, and she slumped against a nearby tree. "I will never figure this out," she said.

"There's always next year," said Frederee. He handed Millie the computer and went hurrying away through the snow, back to his parents, his dinner, a few games of checkers or Scrabble, and then his cozy bed, back to the only life he'd ever wanted, a life where he'd never known a minute of discontent.

And where could Millie go? She would never be happy here, in the Yare village. She could never be content with a life spent in hiding, a life lived in whispers, a life where the simple act of singing could put all their lives in danger.

Alice could help her, but Alice was gone, to New York City, and then to Hawaii with her parents. The night before, Alice had written, saying that she had big news— "the biggest!"—but that it was a secret that she could only tell in person. Millie had written back, a long letter detailing all the trouble she'd had getting the laptop up and running and how she kept getting bounced off the Wi-Fi and how she'd struggled to make her handwriting look different for Maximus's and Septima's signatures.

After realizing that she'd written two pages' worth of complaints, she'd deleted it and hadn't written back at all. *I will write when I am less grumpity,* she promised herself. Meanwhile, she needed to figure out how to make her fur disappear, at least temporarily. There was, she thought, smoothing down her arm-fur with her fingertips, such a lot of it, and while it wasn't thick, like most Yare fur, it was abundant, a silvery white that covered her body and fell in tangles around her face and lay like soft, almost invisible down along her cheeks and her chin.

Old Aunt Yetta had a potion that could do the trick. Millie had found it on a shelf in her friend's kitchen. She had sniffed it, blinking back tears at its bracing, peppery scent, and she'd slipped a vial of it in her pocket the night she'd run away and tried to swim across the lake. The night she'd almost drowned. The night she'd met Alice. Her plan had been to gulp down the potion once she was on the other side of the lake—the No-Fur side—before any of the No-Furs could see her, but the vial had slipped out of her pocket during her swim and was probably lying on the bottom of Lake Standish, and Millie would never have a chance to find out of it worked. Probably some fish had sucked it up by now. Millie wondered if the sharp, minty-smelling stuff had made its scales fall off.

With the laptop tucked under her dress, Millie crunched through the snow, making a list in her head:

*Try to get more of the potion*

*Ask Alice for ideas*

*Practice song*

*Plan for in-person audition*

*Figure out a solution, because time is running out.*

She walked on, lost in thought, sometimes murmuring to herself, sometimes singing snatches of her audition song. She never noticed the sound of footsteps behind her; never felt the eyes that were staring at her back; never had any idea that someone had been watching her in the forest and that the same someone was following her, almost all the way home.

# CHAPTER 3

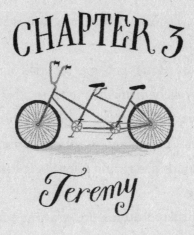

*Jeremy*

JEREMY BIGELOW WRAPPED HIS SCARF AROUND his neck and the bottom half of his face and pulled his wool hat down tight over his ears before working his bicycle helmet down on top of it. The streets of Standish were still icy in places, the lawns still covered in dingy gray snow, but not even a blizzard could have kept Jeremy inside.

When he'd woken up and gone downstairs he'd found his mother hunched over the kitchen counter, still in her bathrobe, with a pile of bills spread out in front of her and the telephone tucked beneath her shoulder. Dirty dishes stood in stacks beside the sink; the table where they ate breakfast was covered in crumbs and piled high with folders.

"No, please don't put me on hold again," Jeremy heard her say as he helped himself to a banana, a jar of peanut butter, and a spoon. "I have been the victim of identity theft. Someone in Arizona is trying to take out a mortgage in my name, and I need to speak to an actual human being."

Jeremy gathered up his breakfast and hurried away, down the hall, until a wash of red and blue lights against the wall froze him in place. Two cop cars pulled up to the curb. His father's car was between them.

Swallowing hard against the lump in his throat, Jeremy listened as a voice from the first car blared, "COME OUT OF THERE WITH YOUR HANDS UP!"

Jeremy's father looked sheepish as he exited his station wagon. Worse, he looked scared. "Is there a problem, officer?" he asked, and then attempted a chuckle. "I guess there must be, if I got a police escort home."

The police officer wore sunglasses and a hat whose brim kept his face in shadow. "License and registration, sir."

Jeremy watched as his father fumbled the documents out of the glove compartment. A radio crackled as the officer from the other car called in his father's license plate. His father had a cringing kind of smile on his face and new lines around his eyes. Jeremy knew—because his father liked to make a big deal about it, especially to Jeremy's oldest brother, who'd be taking his driver's test soon—that he'd never been in an accident, never gotten a speeding ticket. "Not even a warning," he'd say, and glare meaningfully at his boys until all of them promised that they too would be cautious drivers.

"What now?" asked Ben, who emerged, yawning, from his bedroom, rubbing at his head with one muscle-bulging arm. Jeremy nodded toward the window. Ben blinked.

"I don't get it," Ben muttered, before helping himself to Jeremy's jar of peanut butter and going back into the bedroom that looked more like a home gym than a place to sleep.

Unfortunately, Jeremy did get it. His parents, who were completely law-abiding—such straight arrows that they would never even use the express line at the grocery store if they had thirteen items instead of twelve—had been the target of some kind of governmental action for weeks. And Jeremy was the reason why.

Every day since Jeremy had led half of Standish on a chase through the woods that had ended at the gates of the Experimental Center for Love and Learning, every day since he'd been exposed as a fraud and discovered that what he'd thought were Bigfoots were just kids, a little girl with a skin condition and a big one with wild reddish hair, there had been some new aggravation or shame visited not on him, but on his family.

Jeremy had been warned. A letter had arrived at his friend Jo's house, instructing them both to turn over all of their Bigfoot-related research, warning that there would be consequences for "you and your parents and/or guardians" if they failed to comply. The letter had been from something called the Department of Official Inquiry, a government organization that neither one of them had ever heard of, one that didn't show up on Google . . . but it was real. He'd learned that soon enough.

First his mother's credit cards had stopped working. Then Ben had lost a wrestling match, his first one in three years, after the lights mysteriously went out in the middle of the match and the referee had failed to notice his opponent elbowing Ben in the nose. They'd come home to learn that his parents were being audited, which Jeremy knew had something to do with their taxes. And now this.

He felt like a ghost as he ate his peanut-butter-less banana, pulled on his warmest gear, slipped into the garage, collected his Christmas present for Jo, and started to walk to her house. He waved at his father, who didn't seem to notice him because he was busy talking to the police officers ("I know it says the policy's expired, but if you'd just give them a call"). Nobody had said good-bye to him. Probably none of them even noticed he was gone.

He made it to Jo's house in less than fifteen minutes and pulled off his hat and mittens while he waited for her to come to the door. She grinned when she saw him, amused by his surprise.

"You look different," he said.

"You've never seen me standing up," Jo said, looking pleased, and Jeremy nodded. For a long time he'd thought Jo preferred to scoot her wheeled desk chair across the floor of her Batcave—the back porch she'd filled with computers and maps and whiteboards and corkboards— because it was faster than walking. He'd known her for months before she'd let him see her wheelchair, before she'd told him about the hip condition that her doctors had misdiagnosed, the surgeries she'd had, and how nobody was sure if she'd ever be able to walk again.

But here she was, on her feet, leaning on an old-lady walker made of metal and gray plastic, with wheels so that it could swivel.

"So it worked?" Jeremy asked. Jo nodded, her smile widening.

Six weeks ago, Jo had been accepted as part of a clinical study at a children's hospital in Philadelphia. She'd be undergoing an experimental surgery that would use some new high-tech compound to repair her joints. Both Jeremy and Jo had found the timing highly suspicious; both of them strongly believed that the Department of Official Inquiry had done something to get Jo accepted into the trial.

Jeremy had been afraid that it was a plot to separate the two of them, to keep Jo in Philadelphia while he was stuck in Standish. He'd even worried that the study might not be a real thing and that the surgeons might get Jo on the operating table and hurt her instead of helping her.

But his friend had promised that the clinical test was real—"my own doctor's been trying to get me into it forever"—that a bad outcome would reflect poorly on the surgeons, and that it was her best chance at ever being able to walk.

"And I want to," she'd said. "I know it means I'll be gone for a while, but if I can walk when I come back, it'll be worth it."

So she'd gone off to Philadelphia. For six weeks they'd

communicated by brief emails and even briefer texts. Jo believed that the Department was intercepting all of their communication and had probably found a way to track exactly what they were looking up on the Internet. "I will address that situation when I am home," Jo had written, trusting that Jeremy would know what the situation was.

Now she was back, in her familiar jeans and long-sleeved T-shirt and baseball cap. On her feet, she was exactly as tall as Jeremy. She had a piece of paper in her hands, which she'd shoved at him as soon as he'd started to unwind his scarf.

"ROOM IS BUGGED" she'd written. Jeremy felt his eyes go wide as Jo reached into her pocket and pulled out a tiny microphone, smaller than a fingernail, then pointed up at the smoke detector on the ceiling. She raised one finger to her lips. Jeremy nodded, then tilted his head toward the door. "Come see your Christmas present."

After Jo had warned him that the Department was monitoring his email, Jeremy had been afraid to use his own computer for anything but homework. He'd started going to the library to browse his favorite sites, the ones that tracked UFOs and Loch Ness Monster sightings and, his favorite, Bigfootisreal.com, and always he was careful to delete his history and use a different computer every time.

He'd gone old-school to find Jo's present. Instead of the Internet, he'd perused the *Standish Shopper*, a magazine-shaped gazette delivered to every house in Standish once a month, until he'd found a classified ad for what he'd wanted. The seller turned out to be an old man, with white hair and sad eyes and a garage so crammed with junk that Jeremy could have stayed there, happily, for days, just sorting through the piles. "I used to ride it with the missus," he'd said, leading Jeremy on a narrow path between a love seat and something that Jeremy thought was either an ashtray or a spittoon, "but then . . ." Jeremy braced himself for a sad story about how the missus had died or left him or fallen and broken her hip, but the man had smiled and said, "She liked it so much that she wanted her own bike."

The man gestured at a tandem bicycle leaned against the garage wall. It was a Schwinn, painted blue, with blue-and-white seats and a sturdy steel frame. It was heavy, but that meant it was solid, hard to tip over, easy to ride.

The listed price had been fifty dollars, but Jeremy was able to talk the old guy down to twenty-five, including two new tubes for the tires. An afternoon at Standish Cycles, a little grease for the chain and a new basket for the handlebars, and the bike was in perfect working order.

"Can you ride a bike?" Jeremy asked as Jo bundled herself into her winter gear and made her way carefully down the porch steps to examine the bike. "Because if you can't, you can just leave your feet on the pedals, and I can pedal us both."

"I can pedal," Jo said. "They had me doing it for my physical therapy." She settled herself onto the backseat. A few wobbles, one near miss of a mailbox, and they were on their way to what Jo had decided would be their first destination. Jeremy thought that would be the Experimental Center for Love and Learning, where Alice the not-human girl went to school, or maybe the forest, from which Alice's furry cousin—quote-unquote—had emerged on Halloween, but Jo just shook her head and pulled a map of Standish out of her pocket when they stopped at the corner.

"To go forward, we must go back," she said. It was another one of her riddles—Jo loved riddles—and Jeremy knew better than to ask her to explain.

Pedaling steadily through the slap and sting of the icy January morning, they made their way through downtown Standish, up Harley Hill, along a street called Wedgewood, then up Blossom Road, until they came to the Overlook, a neighborhood of grand old mansions that brooded on top of Mount Standish, peering down at the town from behind wide, shaded porches and gingerbread lattices. A few of them even had towers, like castles, and dormer windows that looked like suspicious eyes.

"Thirty-Nine Overlook Place," said Jeremy, who was sweating underneath his layers of fleece and wool. Jo nodded and directed him toward the woods, where they leaned the bike against a tree.

"What is this?" Jeremy asked, standing on his tiptoes to get a good look. The house was enormous, three stories of brick and glass and stuccoed timber that sprawled behind a six-foot-high brick fence.

"Take a guess," said Jo, unfolding her walker from where they'd bungee-corded it to the back of the bike. By then Jeremy had seen the letters engraved on a stone square that was set into the gate. "Carruthers House," it read. "Constructed in 1837 by Milford Carruthers, Patriot, Statesman, and Founding Citizen of the Town of Standish."

*Patriot, statesman, and exploiter of Bigfoots,* thought Jeremy. He was remembering the illustration he'd seen of Milford Carruthers, posing next to a fur-covered creature in a cage. "The captive 'Lucille,'" the caption had read. The Bigfoot—because that's what she was—had worn an old-fashioned dress. One hand had held a parasol. The other rested on the lock of her cage.

Except that illustration had appeared in 1912, more than a hundred years ago. Milford Carruthers had looked to be about forty years old, which meant he'd probably been dead for at least fifty years. Along with "the captive 'Lucille.'"

"Don't be so sure," Jo said, mysteriously as ever, after Jeremy had told her as much. They made their way cautiously up the walk, which had been shoveled and salted, and climbed the steps to the front door. There, Jo straightened her hat, pulled off one fleece-lined glove, and rang the doorbell. They waited . . . but there was no answer. Jo rang again, then knocked at the door, three firm raps. Still nothing.

"Does anyone even live here?" Parts of the mansion looked perfectly spiffy—the front door looked freshly painted, the brass knocker recently polished, and the driveway newly resealed—but Jeremy could see the way the vines had grown up over the first-floor windows and how drifts of rotted leaves were piled on the lawn. *It's a disguise,* he thought, and shivered, wondering who'd take the time to try and make a house look haunted while they were living there.

Jo held up a single finger—*wait*. The door swung open.

Jeremy wasn't sure what he'd been expecting, but it wasn't the woman who stood there. She was old, maybe the oldest person Jeremy had ever seen. She'd probably been short all her life, and she was bent over a walker—a fancier one than Jo had, all metallic-blue tubes, with a cushioned chair to sit on. She had a head of fine white curls and watery blue-gray eyes, and she wore a down vest over a wool sweater and the kind of pants he'd heard his mother call "slacks." There was a heavy gold ring on her right hand, and a wedding band hung loosely from her left ring finger.

"Children!" she said, in a voice that was cracked and high-pitched and cheerful. "Come in!" Jeremy found himself thinking of the witch from "Hansel and Gretel," the one who enticed a boy and girl into her house made out of candy because she wanted to eat them.

"This is Priscilla Landsman," Jo said, and the old woman gave Jeremy her hand, which he shook, very gently. It felt like a collection of Popsicle sticks wrapped in skin.

"To the point, I am Priscilla Carruthers Landsman," said the lady.

"She's—" Jo began.

"Milford Carruthers's youngest daughter." Leaning

on her walker, Mrs. Landsman scooted down the hallway at a surprisingly brisk pace. Jeremy had the impression of high ceilings and dark wood, painted portraits on the walls, the smell of smoke and old candle wax. The house seemed to grow warmer and brighter as they moved deeper inside of it.

They ended up in what Jeremy thought might be called a sitting room, with fancy fringed rugs on the floor, deep leather couches, and tables made of patterned, polished wood, wedges of light wood alternating with sections of dark. *Antiques,* Jeremy thought. His mother would probably know what this kind of table was called, and what wood it was made from, and how much it cost. A fire burned high in the fireplace, flames licking at fresh logs, and candles were lit on a mantel still draped in boughs of evergreen. A clock with golden hands inside a cylinder of glass stood at the center of the mantel. Jeremy could hear it ticking.

"Such a pleasure!" Mrs. Landsman was saying. "It's so rare that I get visitors these days!" She rang a small brass bell on the table closest to her chair. Jeremy spotted a pile of large-print books on the table and an iPad on top of them. Almost immediately a young man in loose-fitting scrubs came into the room carrying a tray with three mugs and saucers, two pots, and a plate of cookies.

"This is Warren, my companion," Mrs. Landsman announced. "Cocoa or tea?"

Warren poured the cocoa. Jeremy was careful to use his saucer and keep his napkin on his lap. Next to the fireplace were a dozen logs, neatly arranged in a circular iron holder. Above it hung a portrait of a man in old-fashioned breeches and a vest, with a bushy mustache that extended from his lips down to his chin. He had a rifle in his hands and his foot rested on a dead lion's back.

Priscilla sipped her tea and saw where Jeremy was looking.

"It was a different time," she said. "My father was a great hunter. He traveled all over the world, looking for exotic things to kill. Lions, boars, rhinos . . ."

"Bigfoots?" Jeremy's mouth felt dry.

"Lucille," Priscilla said, and sighed. "After all these years, I am finally going to talk about Lucille."

Jeremy's skin was prickling. He opened his mouth, but Jo was there with her question first.

"Did you see her?" Jo asked.

Priscilla gave a gentle, sad smile. "Yes." She closed her eyes, set down her teacup, and stretched her hands toward the warmth of the flames. "I knew her. She lived with us, for a time." Her voice cracked. "She was my friend."

Bit by bit, with pauses for sips of tea, Priscilla told them the story. She'd been a little girl, maybe five or six, when her father had gone into the woods one morning and come back with a large, furry something slung behind his saddle.

"We thought it was a bear at first," she said. "Father took it in the stables, and he locked the door behind him, but I knew how to sneak into the hayloft. I could look down at him . . . at them."

Priscilla Landsman closed her eyes and resettled her hands in her lap. Her face softened, and her voice got higher, until Jeremy thought that if he shut his eyes he'd believe that he was listening to a little girl. "I saw that the creature—whatever it was—had a human face. It had hands—claws, really—and enormous feet, but a face like ours, underneath its fur, and I could tell that it was a she. He'd shot her in the side, but it looked like more of a graze than a dangerous wound. I watched as he lifted her off his horse and tied her hands and feet together, and then cleaned and bandaged her. Her eyes were closed, and I could hear her crying . . ." Priscilla's voice broke off. She paused, sipping at her tea. "Her voice was all squeaks and snarls at first, but if you listened, you could hear the words. She was saying that she had children, and to please let her go."

Jeremy could barely breathe.

"'Who are you?' my father asked. 'What are you?'

"She told him a name, but I couldn't hear it. She said that she'd been in the woods looking for evening primrose and mayapple. He asked her the name of her tribe—you know there were Native Americans, Lenape, that used to live here—but she didn't answer. She just kept saying that she had children." Mrs. Landsman gave a shuddering sigh. "I'll never forget that."

"And your father sold her," Jeremy said. Mrs. Landsman's eyes blinked open. "He trapped her," Jeremy said, remembering the picture. "He trapped her and he sold her." Jo gave him a stern look.

Mrs. Landsman shook her head. "He meant to," she said. "He meant to do just that. But before he could, she had to heal." Her lips formed a thin line. "He couldn't sell damaged goods. That would have ruined his reputation. So he kept her in the stables, hidden from my mother and my sisters and the servants. And then one day, after he left . . ." Priscilla shut her eyes, and she was quiet for so long that Jeremy was sure she'd fallen asleep.

"I slipped through the back door and climbed up into

the hayloft. I could hear all the horses, stomping and snorting in their stalls," she finally said. "'Little No-Fur,' the creature was saying. She was calling to me; calling to me from down below. She knew I was there. She could smell me. 'Little No-Fur,' she said. 'Come down. I won't hurt.'

"So I crept down the ladder. He'd tied her to a post, with her hands and feet still bound. Her fur was still matted with blood above the bandage, and her teeth were so big, and her claws . . ." Priscilla drew a shuddering breath.

"'Let me go,' she whispered, 'and I will bring you a chest of gold.' But I was too afraid. She had claws, and teeth, and I thought she might be angry—it was my father who'd shot her, after all."

Priscilla went silent again. A tear slid down her wrinkled cheek.

"I had an apple in my pocket. I always put an apple in my pocket when I went to the stables. I'd feed it to my pony. I rolled the apple toward her, even though her hands were tied, and I knew she couldn't pick it up. She closed her eyes, and I could hear her crying, and I ran out of the barn."

She sipped more tea. "For ten days, father kept her there, while she healed, and he sent telegraphs to every circus on the East Coast, telling them what he'd found, asking them to make their offers. He built a cage for her, like a giant birdcage. To this day, I can't imagine what he told the blacksmith. He had clothing sewn, and he bought a hat, but no gloves or shoes. So the buyers could see her claws and feet, I suppose." Mrs. Landsman stretched her gnarled hands toward the fire.

"Every night, after dinner, Father would carry a bucket out to the barn, full of our leftovers. Table scraps and chicken bones, potato peelings and apple cores. He'd have her stand with her back against the cage, and he'd tie her hands and feet before he'd unlock the door. He'd give her food and fresh water and check to see how her wound was healing and clean her chamber pot. For the first few nights, I'd hear her begging him, but then she must have decided it wouldn't do her any good, because she stopped. But she talked to me." Mrs. Landsman sighed. "She asked me my name, and how old I was, and had I always lived in Standish, and was I big enough for school. I started bringing her real food: loaves of bread, honey, and apples." She gave a rueful smile. "She loved anything sweet. She asked, 'What will become of me?' I didn't want to tell her, even though I knew what my father had planned. I thought that maybe I could tell my father she was gentle, that she wouldn't hurt anyone, and she'd be able to stay with us—

with me—as sort of a pet." Another tear slipped down Mrs. Landsman's cheek. "She said, 'I am not a pet. I am being a person. I have a family, and a home.'"

With one trembling hand, Mrs. Landsman reached for her teacup. She sipped, then set the china gently down in its saucer. "I didn't know what to do," she said. "I'd always been my father's favorite, and I knew that this was his biggest find. But I couldn't stand to think of her in that cage, carried from city to city, even across the ocean, and never seeing her children again."

"What did you do?" asked Jo.

Mrs. Landsman shut her eyes again. "The next time I saw her was when the men from the circus came. Father fed them dinner and probably made sure they'd had a few drinks before he took them back to the barn. He'd put her in her dress and hat, and I remember . . ." Mrs. Landsman's throat convulsed as she swallowed. "How they stared. How they laughed at her. How they said she was the eighth wonder of the world, and that she'd make them all a fortune. The newspapermen took pictures, and Father and Giles Sanderson—the man from the Sanderson Traveling Circus—shook hands on the deal. Sanderson said he'd hire a wagon and draft horses and come get her in the morning, and my father . . ." Her lips quirked, like she was trying not to cry. "My father said he'd throw in her cage for free. They'd agreed to call her Lucille and give her some story about how she'd come from some exotic land, Malaysia or some such. I suppose that sounded more mysterious than the woods in New York. Then they all left. She must have known that I was up there—must have smelled me or something—because as soon as they were gone, she started calling. 'Little girl,' I heard her calling. 'Little Cilla.' Because that was my nickname back then.

"Her hands and legs were free, because she was in a cage. 'Please,' she said. 'I won't hurt you. Please don't let them take me. I just want to go home.' I told her that I'd save her. That night I went back to the stables with the key and one of my father's guns.

"She started shaking when she saw it, shivering all over. I said, 'I won't hurt you if you don't hurt me.' I threw the keys into her cage, and I ran away as fast as I could, knowing that she could have chased me down if she'd wanted to, easy as a cat catching a baby mouse. But I heard her cage door open, and then I heard her running, the other way, past the horses, toward the front of the barn. Out into the night, and into the woods. I put the key back on my father's desk and put the gun back in

64

the cabinet where he kept it and went back to my bed."

Jeremy had to remind himself to breathe. "What did your father do?" he asked.

"Oh, he ranted and raved, when he found out his treasure was gone. He tried to tell Sanderson that the creature—whatever it was—had used some kind of magic to escape. He never suspected that I'd been the one to free her. He had to give the circus its money back, of course, but that wasn't the worst." Priscilla shut her eyes again. "My father died two years after I let Lucille get away, and he spent almost every minute of those two years in the forest. In the rain, in the snow, in the heat of summer, in the dark of night, he was there, on his horse, on foot, going over every inch of the mountain, climbing into every cave, looking for her." Another tear slid down her face. "He even hired men to dredge Lake Standish. He would come home to eat and change his clothes and sleep for a few hours, but it was as if the rest of us had vanished. Like nothing mattered anymore. Only her. He was obsessed. He was . . ." She paused, and her eyelids slid down over her eyes. "Broken," she whispered, and it sounded, to Jeremy, like the word broke something inside of her to say. "He stayed in those woods, even after he caught pneumonia, even after his doctors ordered him to bed. He couldn't stop looking, and he never saw her again. Never so much as a footprint." She pressed her lips together. "And now my tale is told."

"Your father never saw her again," said Jo.

Mrs. Landsman nodded.

"But what about you?" Jo asked. "What did you see?"

"Oh, you're a sharp one," said Mrs. Landsman as the young man in the nurse's uniform came into the room.

"Time for your nap, Mrs. L.," he said in a gentle voice.

Priscilla lifted one hand. "A moment, please," she said. She stood up, grunting softly, her veiny hands clutching the edges of her walker. She scooted toward the fireplace, stood on her tiptoes, reaching for the frame enclosing the portrait of her father, then swung the portrait aside. There was a safe behind it, and her fingers were slow and careful as she spun the wheel left, then right, then left again.

The safe opened with a click, and Priscilla reached inside, carefully removing a wooden chest. "Help me with this," she said, and Jeremy leaped out of his seat and carried the chest back to the table beside Mrs. Landsman's green chair. When she lifted its lid, it breathed the scent of cedar into the room, and Jeremy and Jo could see that it was full of bars of gold and thick gold coins with ragged milled edges. There was a note on top, three words in a pretty script, one that suggested that the writer was no stranger to pen and paper.

"Thank you," it read. "From your friend Yetta."

"She's out there," said Priscilla. Her eyes had drooped shut, and her chin was sagging toward her chest, like her neck could no longer support the weight of her head. "Sometimes . . . at night . . . when I can't sleep, when the wind is blowing . . . I think I hear her. Calling me. *Girl . . . girl . . . little Cilla.*"

"How can we find her?" Jo asked. "Where should we look?"

*She can't still be alive,* Jeremy wanted to say . . . except Priscilla herself was alive. But Priscilla was ancient, and she'd only been a little girl when she'd met Lucille, while Lucille had been an adult, with kids.

"Where?" Jo was asking.

"That's enough," said the nurse. His voice was gentle but firm.

Priscilla raised her head. "The biggest heart," she murmured. Jeremy and Jo exchanged a glance. "Look inside . . . the biggest heart. Ask . . ." Her chin dropped to her chest. Jeremy could see the blue veins in her lids as they slid shut.

Jeremy was prickling with excitement after he dropped Jo off at home, but as he pedaled the bike to his own house, he found his good mood fading. First, a pickup truck full of teenagers pulled up alongside him, and one of them yelled, "Hey, you're such a loser, you're riding a bicycle built for two all by yourself! Don't you have any friends?"

He ignored them, trying to focus. What had he and Jo learned that they didn't already know? That there were Bigfoots in the woods around Standish. That they could talk. That one of them had been captured, then escaped back into the woods, almost a hundred years ago. That she'd given an old woman a chest of gold. The gold part, he supposed, was exciting, but that stuff about "the biggest heart" was a million miles from helpful, and they'd already known about Bigfoots in the forest. He'd been all set to prove it too, when everything had gone so horribly wrong.

He still cringed when he remembered the story the *Standish Times* had run: "Hoaxers, Hucksters, Pranksters, and Lies: A History of Standish's So-Called Bigfoot Tribe," illustrated with a picture of Jeremy, standing on the back of someone's pickup truck, begging the crowd to remain calm. Of course, in the picture, you couldn't tell what he was saying, only that he was yelling, which meant that he could have been saying anything at all.

Jeremy still dreamed about that night, and in his dreams, it all went right. He'd be walking through the forest, the crowd far behind. He imagined the smell of wood smoke, of curing meat and maple syrup, and how the leaves would crunch beneath his feet as he walked, slow but unafraid, into the midst of the Bigfoot village, with his hands open, held at his sides. *I come in peace,* he would say, and at first they'd try to hide, but then the bravest one—in his imagination, that was usually a boy Bigfoot, around his age—would step forward and congratulate him and say, *In all their years of seeking, no human has ever come close to finding us. You are the first.*

They'd invite him to stay, and they'd tell him the whole history of how they'd gotten there and why they'd left the human world. He would listen, and they would know that Jeremy wasn't like the other humans, that he would never hurt them or exploit them, that he would be their friend. Maybe they'd offer him a bed in one of their houses, or even a house of his own, and then, after some time had gone by, the Bigfoot boy would accompany him out of the forest, to Channel 6's offices on Old Maple Road. Donnetta Dale's shift started at three in the afternoon (Jeremy had checked). He could imagine the way her beautiful brown eyes would widen when he walked through her office doors, side by side with a real live Bigfoot.

But that, of course, was not how the story had ended.

Jeremy's house was much as he'd left it, only someone had moved the piles of papers off the table and replaced them with a stack of plates and place mats.

"Jeremy, set the table," his mother called. Jeremy's nose crinkled as he smelled something burning. His mom was an indifferent cook in the best of times, but over the past month their meals had gone from unremarkable to inedible.

His father was in his office, on the phone. His brother Noah was in his bedroom, typing. In the basement, Ben was doing a set of wall slams, hurling a weighted ball into the wall and catching it as it bounced back.

*The biggest heart,* he heard the old woman saying in her whispery voice. Look inside the biggest heart. Did that mean finding someone who was especially kind and generous? Someone known for doing good deeds?

He was still wondering what it meant later that night, in bed, when sleep took him. He dreamed of Bigfoots and a woman in a cage and racing through the woods, only this time he was the hunted one instead of the hunter. He ran as fast as he could, until his breath burned and his throat tasted like blood, and then he tripped over a root and went sprawling on his face. When he looked up, Priscilla Landsman's nurse was there, looking down at him, holding his coat, telling Jeremy that it was time for him to go.

# CHAPTER 4

*Alice*

On her fourth day of winter break, after promising her mother that her suitcase was all packed for Hawaii—that yes, she had her swimsuit and her sunscreen and the running shoes for the race she'd signed up for—Alice went to the library, the main branch in the middle of New York City, where two marble statues of lions flanked the front doors. The city streets were decorated for Christmas, with twinkling lights and wreaths hanging from the streetlamps and all the department-store windows done up with holiday displays. Alice walked past the windows, taking in the wrapped and ribboned piles of pretend presents, the Christmas trees dusted with fake snow, the mannequin families rejoicing at their bounty. The air smelled like roasted chestnuts and sugar-glazed almonds, and it was full of cheerful conversations in a dozen languages.

Alice found an empty chair in the library's high-ceilinged reading room, where patrons sat at long wooden tables, at workstations lit by individual reading lamps. She threaded her scarf through the chair to claim it, then went in search of a librarian who could help her. She located a man whose nameplate announced that he was Dr. Ettman; he had a soft pink face and wore a bright green bow tie underneath a trio of wobbly overlapping chins. His hair had once been red, but there was only a fringe left, circling his bare skull. He frowned when Alice told him what she needed.

"They gave you that project for your Christmas break?"

"It's more of an independent research kind of thing," Alice said. In preparation for the morning's request, she had combed her hair, then bundled it as neatly as she could into a bun at the base of her neck. When she did her hair like that—especially when she pulled it back when it was still wet—Millie told her that her curls looked like an angry squirrel trying to burrow their way into Alice's brain, and now Alice thought of that hairdo as the Angry Squirrel.

Dr. Ettman looked down at her list. "Standish, New York," he said. "That's upstate, right?"

"Near Putnam County," Alice said. "We have to do a project about a place—to write about the people who lived there in the past, all of their customs and languages and beliefs. I know there's been a lot written about New York City, but I haven't been able to find out much about Standish."

Dr. Ettman's eyes opened wider, and his chins seemed to quiver in anticipation. "You just said the magic words," he said.

Alice felt stupid. "I did?"

"*I haven't been able to find out much about something*," Dr. Ettman repeated. "Like catnip to a librarian!" He leaned forward happily. "Now. Does this Standish of yours have a local newspaper?"

Twenty minutes later Alice was back at her workstation with a stack of oversize, musty-smelling books, each one bound in green cloth hardcovers, each containing a year's worth of issues of the *Standish Times*.

"We're in the process of putting a lot of these smaller local papers online," Dr. Ettman said, "but for now . . ." He opened a binder to 1987. Alice saw a story about President Reagan doubling the import price on goods from Japan,

74

alongside a headline that read "Standish High Baseball Team Prepares for Upcoming Season." "At least this will give you a sense of what was going on."

"How far back do they go?" Alice asked.

The librarian consulted the card he'd pulled from the catalog. "All the way to 1906. That's when it looks like the *Times* was founded. Happy hunting!" he said, and told Alice where to return the binders when she was done.

Alice sat down and opened her notebook. The pen felt clumsy in her hand. She'd gotten used to typing her notes, but it hadn't felt like much of a sacrifice to lend Millie her laptop over the break, although it was a little troubling that she hadn't gotten a single response to any of the emails she'd sent. Was Millie all right? Had the laptop been discovered? Or—Alice's stomach lurched unhappily—had Millie made another friend somewhere or just gotten too busy to remember Alice?

Alice looked at her phone to make sure that Millie hadn't written. The only mail she'd received was an email from her bunkmate Taley.

> I am spending my break at an allergy clinic
> at an alternative health center in Lenox,
> Massachusetts. They are making me eat an

> eighth of a teaspoon of yogurt at a time
> and say a mantra beforehand. Three times
> a day they make us rinse out our sinuses
> with a neti pot. Please send help. Except
> they will probably confiscate your help
> when it arrives here because we aren't
> allowed to have mail that might have been
> contaminated with mildew or pet dander.

Instead of a signature, Taley had ended her note with four sad-faced emojis and a tiny teapot. Alice smiled, thinking of something Felicia liked to say: *No matter how bad you think you've got it, someone's always got it worse.*

Riya had written a short note from the fencing clinic she was leading in her hometown of Tampa, and Jessica had sent a picture of herself on a yacht in St. Barth's. She had a bikini top and a towel wrapped around her waist. Alice wondered if Jessica could even wear bathing suits, given her unique anatomy, the secret that Millie had literally sniffed out that terrible night at the Center, when she'd forced Jessica to reveal that she had a tail.

Alice squared her shoulders, opened the first binder, and began to read. It took her a while to get the hang of flipping from one front page to another, and even with that trick mastered, it was almost three hours before she found her first useful headline.

"Military Men Arrive in Standish on Mysterious Mission." The article was from 1982.

> On Monday morning, diners at the Standish Café might have noticed a few new faces. Men in sharp suits with short haircuts, driving cars with Washington, DC, license plates. The men declined to tell this reporter what brought them to Standish or if their arrival had anything to do with the recent reports from hunters about strange creatures in the woods. "We're not at liberty to discuss that," said one of the men, who acknowledged that he and his compatriots were in town "on government business," while refusing to give his name or even say which branch of the government employed him. "For the time being, this is a classified mission," he said. When this reporter asked if he too had heard rumors that the creature was a Bigfoot, the man said,

"No comment," and when this reporter tried
to ask further questions, the man said, "Are
you trying to get yourself arrested?"

*Hmm,* thought Alice. There were no other reports of
the men or what they might have been looking for, but,
three weeks before their arrival, she found the story that
might have brought them to Standish. "Hunters Tell of
Night of Terror," Alice read. The same reporter who'd
spotted the men in the diner had written about how six
men had gone into the woods "for a weekend of hunting, fishing, and camaraderie." They'd been swimming
in Lake Standish when an enormous, hairy creature had
appeared on the shore where they'd made their camp.

"The men shouted at the creature, asking it to iden-
tify itself," Alice read. She wondered if the swimmers
had shouted or if they'd actually screamed. "The creature did not answer. Instead, it lifted the cooler they'd
packed with steaks and baking potatoes and beer, hoisted
it onto its shoulder—'Like it weighed nothing,' said Doug
Broussard, 42, of Standish, 'and it had to be at least fifty
pounds, with all the meat in there'—and walked back
into the forest, pausing only to steal the L.L.Bean jacket
that Broussard had left hanging from a tree branch. 'I tell

you what,' said Broussard, 'I'm a big guy, but that jacket's going to be a tight fit. That monster had to be seven feet tall, at least, and three hundred pounds, easy.'"

Alice made a note of Doug Broussard's name, reminding herself to see if he still lived in town. Then she went through every page of the paper for the next year to see if there were any other stories, either about the hunters or about the government men. She found nothing . . . but, as she kept going through the binders, she found other hints, other clues, other signs that the Yare tribe was thriving in the forest around Standish, nearby but invisible.

From a 1987 paper's "Good Morning!" column, a collection of neighborhood announcements (usually about tag sales) and requests (usually about who was parking in front of a neighbor's driveway).

> A BAKER on BELLEFONTE LANE politely requests that whoever is stealing the pies from her windowsill on Thursdays please cease and desist. "If whoever it is wants a slice, they can knock on my door," the baker said, "but the pies are for elderly shut-ins, and I'm losing four at a go."

From the "School News" page in 1991: "The Case of the Stolen Sneakers."

> A sixth-grade class that constructed a Japanese tea house in its classroom as part of a unit on Asia wanted everything to be authentic, which meant that, on the day the tea ceremony was held, the students took off their shoes and left them lined up outside the school. By the time the tea was gone, so were the shoes—all twenty-three pairs belonging to the students, plus the shoes that Mr. Hallas said were his favorites. "My guess is that it's just a prank, but I hope that whoever took them realizes sneakers don't grow on trees," Mr. Hallas said. "And neither do Florsheim loafers."

In 1994, a sub shop reported that its daily delivery of rolls was being stolen from its doorstep, some time between the five a.m. drop-off and the six a.m. arrival of the manager.

In 1996, another "Good Morning!" item claimed:

> The Laundry Thief of Lowery Lane is at it again! The families of Lowery Lane say they've

seen everything from bedsheets to T-shirts to ladies' unmentionables go missing. "I thought it was just kids playing pranks, but whoever it is, they're pretty picky," said Tina Ferriman, whose husband lost his favorite plaid shirt in the latest raid. "They don't take everything. Only the good stuff."

In 2001, high school seniors Brian DeVeaux and Courtney Long said that someone had stolen a valuable set of tools out of the back of Brian's father's pickup truck while Brian and Courtney were parked by the lake at eleven o'clock on a Saturday night.

In 2004, fishermen said that eighteen cans of beer they'd left cooling in a stream in Standish Park had gone missing.

In 2007, a woman wrote to "Good Morning!" to ask if anyone had seen the gold-rimmed reading glasses she'd left on a picnic table by the lake.

Alice stood, stretched, walked outside, and ate on the library's marble steps the sandwiches and apples and squares of chocolate she'd packed, glad that it wasn't too cold out and that she had a thick down coat to keep the chill away. She drank her water and wondered what it would be like to have fur, to carry your coat with you everywhere you went.

Back inside, she checked the papers all the way through 1970, then decided to change tacks. She put the binders in a neat stack and went to use one of the public computers.

She began by typing her mother's maiden name into a search engine, looking for anything, any scrap of information that would tell her what her mother had been like as a girl and young woman, where she'd lived and what she'd done before she'd married and had Alice. She found nothing. Not when she typed in "Felicia Wolf" and the name of every college and university in Vermont, not when she combined her mother's maiden name with any relevant words she could think of—"New York City" or "Atwater School," where her mother had told her she'd gone, and where Alice had lasted for just one grade. As Felicia Mayfair, her mother was everywhere— on charitable committees, at parties, and at galas, her blinding smile shining out from the society pages of newspapers and magazines—but Alice could find no trace of Felicia Wolf, the woman her mother had once been. It was as though, before the wedding announcement that told the world that Felicia Wolf would marry Mark Mayfair, her mother hadn't existed at all.

Strange.

Back outside, Alice sat down on the steps again. This was the part she had been dreading, the call she'd been putting off. She had always thought of Miss Merriweather as a friend, someone who looked out for Alice and wanted what was best for her. It would hurt to learn that Miss Merriweather had lied about who she was and when they had met . . . and what if Miss Merriweather was worse than a liar? What if she was one of the Bigfoot hunters Millie and her Tribe were so afraid of, the people who'd treat the Yare like they were freaks to be displayed or animals to be caged? What if . . .

Alice shook her head. There was no point wondering. Not when she could know for sure.

She had Miss Merriweather's number on her phone. Her thumb on the button that would connect the call when she changed her mind. Calling, announcing herself, making an appointment—all those things would give Miss Merriweather a chance to come up with a story. *No, that's not me. I have a twin sister; she's a doctor in Vermont,* she could say. Or, *Yes, that was me, but I wasn't an educational consultant back then, and your parents and I didn't know each other that well, so it didn't make sense for them to tell you that we'd met.*

Alice put her phone back in her pocket after looking up Miss Merriweather's address. The subway took her right down to Greenwich Village. From there it was just a five-minute walk to the carriage house at the end of a narrow, cobbled street where it turned out Miss Merriweather lived. The building had a red-painted door, a curved panel of windows at its center, and an elm tree spreading its branches over the roof, which probably kept things shady and cool in the summertime.

Alice pressed the buzzer. "Up here!" a familiar voice called. She climbed a narrow flight of stairs to the second floor and opened the door to Miss Merriweather's apartment.

In spite of the sunshine, the apartment was dim, the windows covered by curtains, the rooms lit with pools of lamp or candlelight. Colorful woven rugs, all in shades of red and sapphire and gold, were layered on the floor, the corner of one overlapping the edge of another. The furniture was worn and soft and comfortably squishy, as if Miss Merriweather had spent long hours curled up in each couch or chair. It felt cozy, with low ceilings and the scent of tea and baked goods, cinnamon and vanilla and the old-fashioned kind of hairspray that Miss Merriweather used. It reminded Alice of something, some place she'd been, but she couldn't remember what or where.

"Hello, Alice!" Miss Merriweather took her coat and boots and invited her to sit at a small wooden table in front of windows that overlooked a small bricked garden. If she'd been surprised to see her or worried that Alice had shown up unannounced, she'd hidden it well. Miss Merriweather looked the same as ever, small and plump and pink, with white curls, and was dressed in a high-necked blouse with lace at the sleeves underneath a suit jacket paired with a matching skirt. She wore a pearl necklace and low-heeled pumps, and looked like she was on her way to meet with a student or had just come home.

"What a lovely surprise! How are you? Can I get you something to drink? A snack?"

Alice had never seen the inside of a Yare house, but Miss Merriweather's place was exactly what she imagined they'd be like. The kitchen, for example, had everything a normal kitchen had, only everything was smaller. The stove had two burners instead of the four that a regular stove had, and the eight that Alice's stove boasted; the refrigerator was waist-high, and instead of cabinets, there were two plain shelves, which held a neat if limited assortment of plates and mugs and glasses.

Built-in bookcases that lined the living-room wall held books about how to take aptitude and admissions tests and stacks of brochures for boarding schools all over the country, along with dozens of romance novels and what Alice's mother would have called objets, decorative items set out in pleasing arrangements. There were two birds made from pale blue glass and a little wooden birdhouse, a pink-and-gold antique plate on a stand, a jade elephant, and a polished teak family of bears, each one the size of Alice's thumb. Bud vases held single blossoms: a pink peony, a cluster of pale-pink hydrangea, an apricot-orange rose. The apartment reminded Alice of a bird's nest, if the bird had lived there long enough for her belongings to form layers, with each piece having a history, and all of them telling a story. Maybe Miss Merriweather had been to India and gotten her jade elephant there. Maybe she went to the flower market and bought her blossoms every morning. Maybe a grateful family whose kid had finally found the right school had given her the glass birds. Maybe . . .

Alice froze. She'd been standing in front of the bookcase when she saw a woven basket on the floor. It didn't look very special—just a regular basket, made of straw, round, with a handle you could loop over your arm—but

Alice had seen a basket just like it before. She'd seen four of them, in fact. Millie had given one to her and one to Jessica and one to Taley and one to Riya before they'd all left for their break. She'd made them herself, she'd said, looking pleased and a little flustered when Taley had asked, and she'd filled them with . . .

Alice bent down, checking to see whether Miss Merriweather's basket contained honey or tea or the salt scrub that Millie had made, but before she could get a good look, she heard Miss Merriweather's cheerful voice behind her.

"Come sit," Miss Merriweather instructed. "Tea?" she asked, setting a small plate of miniature éclairs and cream puffs on the table, along with a pair of folded napkins and a pitcher of water. Alice's heart was beating hard, but she took her seat and accepted a thin china cup with a gold rim and roses on its side, which Miss Merriweather filled from a steaming pot of Earl Gray.

"So we finally found the right school for you!" Miss Merriweather said.

Alice nodded, swallowed her tea, and said, "I'm working on a project, and I need to ask you some questions."

"Of course," she said. Her expression was serious but not frightened and not, Alice noticed, surprised. "I'll do my best to help."

What am I? Alice wanted to blurt. Who am I? Where did I come from? What do you know about me? Are Mark and Felicia my real parents? Why don't they want me? Why can't I be where I belong? And who are you? Why were you at the hospital where I was born? Why is there a Yare basket on your shelf?

But she had to be more careful than that. Pulling a notebook out of her backpack, she began, "Was I adopted?"

She waited for Miss Merriweather to counter with a question of her own, to ask Alice why she thought that she, a hired consultant, would know anything about Alice's personal life or early childhood, or whether this was an appropriate topic for the two of them to discuss. Instead, she answered.

"No," Miss Merriweather said. Her voice was firm, and her gaze was steady. She didn't blink or fidget or pull at the lace of her sleeve. She just looked right at Alice as she spoke. "No, you were not."

"My mother showed me my baby book," Alice said, pulling the book out of her backpack and holding it on her lap. Miss Merriweather nodded and made a go-on gesture with one hand. "Your picture is in it," Alice said. "At the hospital when I was born. You were there." Alice opened to the right page, pointed at the picture, then held her breath, praying she was right. In the quiet, she could hear the tap-tap-tap of Miss Merriweather's toe against the floor. "That's you, right?"

"I've known your mother a long time," Miss Merriweather finally said.

"Then why didn't she say so? Why didn't she say that you're her friend? Why did she tell me that all you are is someone she hired?"

"It's complicated," said Miss Merriweather, her toe tapping faster as she shifted in her seat. Which, Alice knew, was grown-up-speak for *You're a kid and I'm not going to tell you*. Miss Merriweather circled the rim of her teacup with one finger. "It has to do with your father. It was easier for him to accept me in your life—easier for your mother to explain who I was—if I was the person helping you find the right school, and not an old friend from even before you were born."

"I don't understand," Alice said. Her thoughts, and her tongue, all felt tangled. She'd imagined Miss Merriweather immediately acknowledging that yes, she'd been at Alice's birth; that yes, she knew about the Yare and that, in fact, she'd been the one who had taken Alice away from her Yare mother and father and given her to Felicia and Mark. She'd explain why Alice had to leave the Tribe and tell her when she'd be able to go back, and be reunited with the Yare parents who surely missed her.

Instead, Miss Merriweather looked at her from over her teacup. "Sometimes," she said, "people have things in their past they would like to forget. Things that would be hard to explain. Things that are embarrassing."

Alice, who knew about embarrassing, nodded, even though she couldn't imagine her beautiful, elegant mother being embarrassed about anything or having something in her past she'd try to hide.

"And you're happy, aren't you? Happy there in the woods?" Miss Merriweather gave her a sunny smile. "Your mother tells me you've made friends."

Alice felt as if an electric current had rippled over her skin. Was this Miss Merriweather telling her that she knew about Millie, telling her without saying the words?

"Of course, I'm happy to try to help you," Miss Merri- weather said. "What else would you like to know?"

Alice looked down at her lap, wishing she'd made notes. "Why haven't I ever seen a picture of Feli—of my mother when she was pregnant, then?"

"I imagine," said Miss Merriweather, "that maybe if there aren't any pictures, it's because your mother didn't want there to be a record. Maybe she was uncomfortable."

Alice settled herself more deeply in her chair. She knew how vain about her figure Felicia was; how her mother would scroll through her phone looking at pictures of herself, one long-nailed finger swiping, swiping, her painted lips pursed as she'd hit "delete," until there'd be not one single shot left to commemorate a family trip or a birthday party.

"So I wasn't adopted."

"You were not. I met you when you were a baby. You don't remember—of course you couldn't—but I was there, and you were beautiful." Miss Merriweather's gaze took on a far-off, longing look. "With your pretty little face and your sweet little nose. Ten perfect fingers, and ten perfect toes."

Alice knew she needed to redirect the conversation.

"Is Mark my father?"

"Mark has loved you since the day you were born," Miss Merriweather said. As she spoke, Alice saw her gaze flick up and to the left, a motion so swift that she almost missed it. *She's lying,* she thought. Except maybe she wasn't. Saying that Mark had loved Alice since the day she was born was not the same thing as saying that Mark was her dad . . . but it wasn't proof that she had a different, real father.

Miss Merriweather pushed up the lace-trimmed sleeve of her blouse and peered at the round gold face of her little watch. "And now, as lovely as it's been to catch up, I have several appointments this afternoon—"

"Miss Merriweather," Alice interrupted, her words coming in a rush, "am I human?"

Miss Merriweather set her teacup down on her saucer. "Are you human?" she repeated in a tone that gave nothing away.

"There was a boy," Alice said. "This boy who was interested in Bigfoots and things like that, he thinks that there are Bigfoots in Standish, and he got some of my hair, and he sent it to a lab to be tested, and right before I came home, he came to the Center and he told me that I'm not human."

"What a terrible thing to say." Miss Merriweather lifted her chin. "Human is as human does."

Which, again, was not quite the same as telling Alice, emphatically, that she was, indeed, 100 percent human being.

"I want," Alice began, and then stopped. Because it wasn't just about what she wanted—friendship, love, a sense of belonging, a true home. It was also about what she didn't want. She didn't want Mark and Felicia to be

her parents. She didn't want to be human. She wanted to be Yare. She wanted to live in the forest, with her friend Millie, where no one cared that she was tall and clumsy and broke things or that her feet had been bigger than her mother's since she was six and she had to order her school uniforms from the special-size section of the catalog.

Miss Merriweather's voice was quiet. "Your parents have done what any parents do. They have loved you to the best of their abilities. They have tried to make you happy. More than that, they've tried to raise you to be strong enough to deal with adversity. Because no one's life is perfect. And, of course, they've always kept you safe."

Alice nodded, knowing it was true. Or, at least, not untrue. She wasn't starved, wasn't beaten; she hadn't been thrown out of her house, the way some of the other kids at the Center had been, for liking boys instead of girls or girls instead of boys. Her parents cared for her, even if she'd never felt like they loved her or even liked her very much. She'd never wanted for food—even if it was all low-calorie, healthy stuff—or for clothing, even if it was constricting and uncomfortable. They had certainly done their best to find her good schools and summer camps, even if they did it so that she'd hardly ever be home.

"It's good that you're asking questions," said Miss

Merriweather, looking at her seriously. "But, Alice, you must understand that the answers might not always be the ones you want to hear."

Alice nodded again. The words *Do you know about the Yare?* were buzzing in her brain, but she couldn't say them. She couldn't decide what would be worse: Miss Merriweather looking puzzled and shaking her head, or Miss Merriweather saying that yes, indeed, she knew all about the Yare, and Alice wasn't one.

"I belong somewhere else," she blurted, when she couldn't think of anything else to say.

Miss Merriweather smiled. "Well, isn't it a good thing that school starts up soon?" she said. "I imagine that you miss your friends."

*Friends,* thought Alice, remembering how Taley and Riya and even mean Jessica Jarvis had all hugged her good-bye before break. She did have friends—or at least one real friend. Maybe Miss Merriweather was telling her to let that be enough.

"And now," Miss Merriweather said, "I really do need to go."

Five minutes later, bundled into her winter clothes and clutching her backpack, Alice was back outside and on her way to the subway. She walked slowly, thinking

that she'd buy a hot chocolate and drink it before she got on the train, which would give her time to make notes while the conversation was still fresh in her mind. She hadn't planned on spying on Miss Merriweather. Millie probably would have thought to do it, and that boy, Jeremy the so-called Bigfoot hunter, would have too, but not Alice. It wasn't until she saw the educational consultant hurry past the coffee-shop window that she decided to follow her.

Quickly pulling her coat back on, Alice ran outside and trailed Miss Merriweather down into the subway and onto the platform for the uptown trains. She was careful to keep her distance and make sure there were people between them. When the train pulled into the station, she let Miss Merriweather get on first, and then Alice found a spot in the car behind hers and watched through the windows to see when Miss Merriweather got out.

That turned out to be the Columbus Circle stop, which made it easy for Alice to hide herself in a group of chattering, field-tripping Girl Scouts as they made their way up the stairs and into the light. Miss Merriweather was walking briskly, with her oversize purse, the one Alice knew she used to carry school information and a laptop, tucked tightly against her side.

Alice trailed her as she walked into an office building, said something to the security guard, signed a ledger, and got onto an elevator. Waiting until the elevator's doors slid shut, Alice approached the desk with her most pathetic look on her face.

"I'm supposed to meet my grandmother at her dentist, and I think just missed her. She just got onto the elevator, but I can't remember which floor she said."

"Sorry, miss," said one of the guards, and the other said, "Do you have a phone? Don't all kids have phones?" By then Alice had peeked at the register and seen "Cecelia Merriweather, 18th floor."

"Oh, never mind, I remembered!" she said, and gave the guards a twinkling smile and slipped onto the elevator just as the doors slid shut.

Inside, Alice was surrounded by a typical crowd of adults in the middle of a workday: men in suits, women in skirts and high heels, some carrying briefcases, others carrying Styrofoam containers that smelled of curry, almost all of them peering at their iPads or their phones. When the elevator reached the eighteenth floor, Alice tried to exit, but a man's hand came down on her shoulder, pushing her back inside.

"This floor is restricted," he said.

"I have to meet my grandmother," said Alice. She'd only caught a glimpse, but the eighteenth floor appeared to house a typical office: glass doors, sofas, and a coffee table in a waiting area, a woman with a headset sitting behind a desk.

The man was looking down at her. He wore a blue suit, and Alice saw that he had a laminated badge clipped to his lapel. She felt her skin go icy as she saw the initials DOI and, underneath it, a holograph of an eye. *Creepy*, she thought as she snuck another glimpse and saw the same eye etched into the glass on the office doors. It made her think of something, but she couldn't figure out what. Had she seen that eye before?

"I—I'm sorry," she stammered. "I don't think I'm in the right place."

The man's grip didn't loosen, and Alice thought frantically of the lie she'd told downstairs. "I'm supposed to meet her at the dentist's office," she finally blurted, praying that the building actually had a dentist's office somewhere inside of it.

For a few seconds that stretched out like taffy, nothing happened. Finally the man's grip loosened. "Try down on the fifth floor," he said gruffly, stepping out into the hallway. Alice watched him as the elevator doors slid shut.

Miss Merriweather was in there, behind those glass doors with their etching of that eerie, all-seeing eye.

Alice found a vending machine on the third floor and sat at a table in the corner of what must have been an office's break room, eating a bag of potato chips. When an hour had passed—long enough, she guessed, for a dentist appointment—she took the elevator back down to the lobby and stopped at the desk with the guards.

"Find your grandma?" one of the guards asked.

Alice nodded. "But I almost got off at the wrong floor. There were glass doors with an eye on them?"

The guards exchanged an uneasy look. "Government offices," one of them said.

"What part of the government?" Alice asked. She cast her mind back to all the field trips she'd taken when she'd gone to school in New York City. "My friend's mother is a district attorney. We got to go to her offices once. And I went to the International Spy Museum in Washington."

"Not that kind of government," the other guard said. He was shorter, younger, with thick black hair under his cap.

"Is it the CIA?" Alice lowered her voice.

"Government," said the second guard. "That's all we know. The people who work up there all have key cards to get in."

Alice thanked them and went outside. Her mouth felt dry and her knees felt wobbly. She knew what this meant. Miss Merriweather was not a good fairy like she'd imagined, watching over Alice, keeping her safe. She worked for, or with, the government. She was one of the bad guys. She might have been responsible for snatching Alice away from the Yare, away from her real parents, for dumping her with Mark and Felicia, for moving her from one terrible school to another, for ensuring that she'd never be happy.

Miss Merriweather worked for the government. And now she would tell them about Alice's suspicions that she wasn't human and that her parents weren't her real parents. The men with the eye on their badges would be watching. Alice would have to be very careful—oh so careful, she thought, as Millie would say—as she tried to figure out the truth.

Alice pulled out her phone, noticing that Millie still hadn't written, before opening a new email. "PLEASE WRITE AS SOON AS YOU CAN," she typed, in all capital letters. "I NEED TO TALK TO YOU." Then, hoping that Millie would get her message and find a way to write, she zipped up her coat and walked down to the subway.

# CHAPTER 5

*Millie*

"ANOTHER CUP OF TEA?" MILLIE ASKED SWEETLY.

Old Aunt Yetta was looking at her from behind her gold-rimmed reading glasses. They had spent the morning, at Millie's request, tromping through the snow, walking deep into the drifts in the forest for the roots and barks they'd need to replenish the Tribe's stocks. They'd filled their baskets with licorice root, sassafras, and aspen bark, and Old Aunt Yetta had quizzed Millie about tinctures for healing broken bones and teas for treating earaches. Millie, who had absolutely no desire to take on Old Aunt Yetta's role as Healer or her father's post as Leader of the Yare, tried her best to answer correctly, and just said "slippery elm bark," which seemed to be useful for everything, when she couldn't think of a different answer.

"You are a frustration," Old Aunt Yetta said with a sigh after Millie had guessed "slippery elm bark" for the third time in a row.

*You're a frustration,* Millie thought about saying. *You and the rest of the Elders, who don't understand that all I want to do is leave.*

Instead, she tried to look sorry, with her eyes downcast and her face-fur drooping, and she promised to do better. Back at Old Aunt Yetta's house, Millie settled her friend on the couch in front of the fire and offered to make Old Aunt Yetta her tea.

The cozy little kitchen had low ceilings and brightly colored hand-braided rugs on the floor. Millie put the kettle on the flame, and then pulled pinches from the bundles of dried herbs that hung in rows on the pegboard on the wall. Orange peel and cloves, elm bark for Old Aunt Yetta's bone-fret (what the No-Furs called Arthurltis), hawthorn for her heart, and a spoonful of the lavender honey that Millie and Frederee had collected that fall.

And then . . .

Millie's quick fingers touched the bottles of tincture

of valerian and one of magnolia bark. Those went into nighttime teas, the ones that brought on restful sleep. That was what Millie needed, just an hour of her friend dozing on the couch while Millie did what she had to do. She nibbled at her face-fur, and then it felt like she had fallen into a No-Fur television show and she was watching her small hands moving deftly, crumbling the sleeping-stuff into the boiling water, straining the tea into Old Aunt Yetta's favorite cup, and stirring in extra honey to disguise the taste.

"Thank you, dear," Old Aunt Yetta said, and Millie felt her muscles tense as her friend took her first sip, then swallowed.

"Interesting," she finally said. Millie tucked a blanket around her friend's legs. Then she pulled on her winter coat, a thick many-layered parka special-ordered on-the-line. Most Yare did not need a coat—their dense, wiry fur was quite enough to keep them warm—but Millie's fine, silky fur was more like a decoration than a pelt, and she'd spend the entire winter with the shivers if it wasn't for her store-bought coat, her on-the-line fur.

"I will be going now," she said, and Old Aunt Yetta looked at her closely.

"You are missing your friend," she guessed. Millie felt

a spasm of guilt, even as she nodded. Alice had written to her every day, sometimes more than once, but Millie had been so preoccupied with trying to submit her video that she hadn't found the time to write back. Every day that she could manage it, she'd have Frederee tape her—from up close, from far away, even from behind. Every day, the system would reject her application, displaying the same cheery message about how it was sorry that something had gone wrong. *I have gone wrong,* Millie thought. She'd even tried to shave her face with the sharp edge of a kitchen knife, but as soon as the fur was gone, it started growing back.

"A good friend is the most valuable thing you will ever have," Old Aunt Yetta was saying, which only made Millie feel worse. "And Alice is as good as gold. Brave, and with a loyal heart."

"Yes," said Millie, and she wondered about her own heart. Alice was so lonely—more lonely, even, than Millie was—without a single Yare to understand her. That night that Alice had grabbed Millie in the water, it felt like Alice, not Millie, had been the drowning one. Millie loved Alice, and she loved hearing about the No-Fur world. She recognized too that she envied her friend so much: her freedom, her gadgets, her subway pass card, her life in the city, all the places she'd been and the things she knew, and, most of all, the way she could move through the world as she wanted, because her parents didn't seem to care. (If Millie's parents decided to care any more, they'd just start carrying Millie around on their backs all the time, the way they had when she'd been a baby.)

Millie loved Alice . . . but sometimes she felt like Alice wanted to have Millie all to herself, that she didn't like it when Millie tried to talk to the other girl No-Furs at the Center, or when Millie described dreams that didn't perfectly line up with Alice's own ideas. Millie wanted to be famous, while Alice seemed to think that the No-Fur world was a terrible place and that the best thing you could do was hide from it, tuck yourself deep into the woods, in a Yare-style dugout carved into a hill, disguise your door with twigs and leaves, and hope that no one ever found you. She knew that if she made too much of a fuss about *The Next Stage*, Alice would ask her questions she didn't want to answer; questions about why she was in such a rush to leave her parents and her Tribe and a world where everyone loved her; questions about why she, Alice, wouldn't be allowed into the Yare village and why she should help Millie chase her dreams when Millie wouldn't help her find a place to call home.

Millie tugged the red knitted cozy over the teapot and pulled Old Aunt Yetta's afghan up to her chin. She built the fire up to a blaze and carried in a dozen more logs to keep it going through the afternoon.

"You're a good girl," Old Aunt Yetta said, sighing as she turned her body toward the fire.

As guilt pulsed through her, Millie shut the door and started walking the path toward her home. Only, instead of going left, she doubled back around to Old Aunt Yetta's house and ducked under the window, listening, until she heard the soft buzzing of Old Aunt Yetta's snores.

She made herself count to one hundred, taking a breath after each number, before she eased the back door open, snuck inside, and tiptoed into the kitchen, where she scrambled onto the counter, kneeling and peering onto the top shelf. The bottles, half a dozen of them, labeled "For Maximus" in Old Aunt Yetta's spidery handwriting, were all still there. The first time Millie had met Alice, she'd stolen one of the bottles, certain that it contained the potion to remove a Yare's fur. It was a special tincture that Old Aunt Yetta had made for the times when Millie's father, in his capacity as the Tribe's leader, had to venture to the posting office to do the Mailing, sending Yare goods to Etsy, which was a person, or maybe a person who ran a shop and who sold their scrubs and organic soaps. Millie had put the bottle in her pocket, intending to swim across the lake and swallow it when she arrived, but the lake was much larger than it appeared, and the bottle had been lost in the process of Millie's near drowning.

For weeks she'd been on edge, waiting for someone to notice that the bottle was missing. But, of course, in the weeks after she'd met Alice, the Tribe had been threatened by discovery, and it was only Alice's cunning that had kept them safe. Probably with all of that going on, Old Aunt Yetta hadn't had time to re-count her stores of potions. Which meant that Millie could take another one and hope, again, that no one would find her out.

She closed the cupboard, hopped to the ground, slipped back out of the cabin, and went through to Old Aunt Yetta's garden, where carrots and peppers and potatoes and squash would grow in the summer, and where her goat, Esmerelda, was penned. Millie wanted to be close, so that if something went wrong she'd be able to cry out and, she hoped, wake up her friend. But she also wanted to be hidden, so that none of the other Yare could see her if it worked.

Millie slipped behind the little lean-to where Esmerelda slept. The goat blinked at her, then bleated, then went back to snuffling through the snow. Millie uncapped the bottle and smelled its biting peppermint scent, so sharp that it made her eyes water.

*In for a penny, in for a pounding,* she thought, and tipped the flask to her mouth. The liquid burned as soon as it touched her tongue, and it traced a line of fire down her insides. Millie managed only the tiniest sip before she started shaking, and she crammed her hand against her mouth to stop herself from howling. Oh, it hurt, it hurt so much; it was pain she'd never imagined; it felt like her skin was being bitten by a thousand fire ants, like she was trying to turn herself inside out.

She opened her mouth, thinking that she would scream, that she couldn't not scream, when she felt herself shuddering. There was one final, terrible blaze of heat and pain, like her cells were trying to fold themselves in half. And then . . . Millie looked down. Her arm was bare. Her fur was gone!

She put the bottle in her pocket and used her hands to confirm. No fur on her face, none on her neck or her ears; no fur on her shoulders or her chest or her belly. No fur anywhere. She jumped in the air, joy surging through her, thinking about the mirror she'd hidden in the rafters in the loft in the Lookout Tree.

But then Millie heard a knock, followed by Old Aunt Yetta's snort. She heard the floorboards creak as Old Aunt Yetta walked to her front door. Frozen in place, unsure whether she should try to hide or whether leaving would make noise and attract attention, Millie heard her mother's voice.

"I can't stand it anymore," Septima said. She sounded miserable, her voice completely unlike the sunny, sing-songy, slightly screechy tone she typically used when addressing Millie (unless she was scared about something that Millie had done, some risk that Millie had taken, and then her voice would drop to a reedy whisper).

"Have a seat, dear," Old Aunt Yetta said. "We will talk."

Millie heard her mother sniffle, heard the squeak of the couch springs as she sat and the sounds of Old Aunt Yetta fussing in the kitchen, filling the kettle, adjusting the flame.

"Ever since that night, I keep thinking about it," Septima said, and now her voice was almost a moan. "Thinking about all of it. What I should have said, what I should have done."

"It's over," said Old Aunt Yetta. "Over and done with."

"It is not," said Septima in a sharper tone than Millie had ever heard her mother use. "It is not over. It will never be over. Not when I can't stop remembering and wishing I'd done different. Every day I see Millie grow up, and I know that I can never keep her safe, and I think . . ." Her mother was crying now, and Old Aunt Yetta was making cooing, comforting noises.

Millie couldn't move, couldn't blink, couldn't breathe. What was her mother talking about? What—or who— could she not stop thinking about? What did she wish was different?

"We did our best," Old Aunt Yetta was saying. "Our best is all that any of us can do."

"It wasn't enough," Septima said, her voice rising to what was almost a shout. (Septima, who never shouted!) "It wasn't enough, but it isn't too late. We should do something," Millie's mother said. "Tell her, at least. Maybe if she knew—"

Millie heard Old Aunt Yetta set the kettle down with a bang. "Never think it!" she said, and her voice was a low, angry growl. "Never for a minute. That would bring danger down on us, and danger down on her. And then what?" Her voice gentled. Millie heard footsteps, the sound of

Old Aunt Yetta settling down on the couch. "There is a thing that the No-Furs say. 'Burn the village in order to save it.'"

*But that makes none of the sense,* thought Millie, just as her mother said the exact same thing.

"Of course it doesn't." Old Aunt Yetta's voice was low and soothing. "If you think, 'I will do this thing, this big thing, and maybe it will cause disruption and sorrow and pain, but at least it will be the right thing to do, and at least I'll feel better having done it,' what do you get?"

Her mother's voice was tear-choked and tiny. "A b-b-burned village, I guess."

"A burned village is right. Think, Septima. Think of what would happen if she knew. Think what would happen to her. Think of what would happen to us."

"But it's not right," Septima moaned. "We kept ourselves safe. But what was the cost of it?" Millie could imagine her mother's eyes getting wide, could see her hand holding Aunt Yetta's tightly. "What does it matter if we're safe, if we left her to pay the price?"

"She is safe too." Old Aunt Yetta's tone indicated clearly that there was nothing more to say about this mysterious person—or was it a village?—that had her mother so worried.

Septima wasn't done. "There must be something," she said. Her voice was bleak. And then she was crying again, and Millie could only hear words and broken phrases here and there, Old Aunt Yetta murmuring, "There, there," and her mother repeating variations of "It's all my fault."

Millie didn't want to leave. She wanted to stay and listen, to try to puzzle out who the "she" might have been, and why it hurt her mother to see Millie growing up, and how saving a village could mean burning it. But she knew that if her mother caught her hanging around Old Aunt Yetta's house with a stolen flask of potion in her pocket— or, worse, if she saw Millie furless—that would be the end of any hope she had for *The Next Stage* or, really, of ever leaving her bedroom until the start of Planting Season, when every Yare's help, even little Florrie's, was required. She checked her pocket to make sure the little flask of potion was still there, as her mother's voice rose.

"If only I could tell her I was sorry," Septima said. Her voice was full of pain and guilt, and Millie wanted to run to her, to hug her and tell her that whatever she'd done couldn't be all that bad. Then, maybe, she could find out what on earth her mother meant. Sorry to whom? Sorry for what? What could her mother, who'd never done anything to hurt anyone, who was always the first with a pot of soup or stew or fresh-made bread when someone was hurt or sick, who moved through the world so fearfully that it was as if even the rustling of the wind in the trees frightened her, possibly be so sorry for? She had sounded miserable. More than miserable. She sounded haunted.

Millie pulled her hood up, then tightened its strings until only her eyes and the tip of her nose peeked out. Her bare hands were covered by thick woolen mittens (something else none of the other Yare required), her legs were thickened by two layers of leggings, plus her boots. Still, she could feel the sting as the wind worked its way through the wool and the cotton and blew against her bare skin. It was so strange. She felt bare, even though she was completely covered, exposed in a way she'd never been exposed before. Was this what it was like to be a No-Fur, to move through the world feeling naked and undefended? She shivered and wondered how long it would take for her fur to come back . . . and who her mother had been talking about.

*A mystery,* Millie thought as she walked to the Look-out Tree with her mittened hands in her coat pockets and her hood cinched tight. She'd hidden Alice's laptop under her bed, and she knew she should be taking advan-

tage of her furlessness to finally record her audition, but she'd never felt less like singing in her entire life.

Millie climbed the tree, the way she had a thousand times before. From her perch way up high, she could see the entire Yare village spread like a patchwork quilt beneath her, in squares of snowy white and dirt brown. There was her father at the edge of the forest, chopping wood, and there were Frederee and Tulip, gathering kindling, and there was little Florrie, building a snow fort. When the wind blew, it lifted the faint voices of the women who were quilting, loud enough for Millie to hear their chatter, or Esmerelda's bleats. She could smell simmering apples, cooking with maple syrup and cinnamon that the Yare ordered on-the-line; could feel the bite of the wind on her cheeks (once, she'd had a scarf, but the other littlies had made so much fun of it—*your borrowed beard,* they'd called it—that Millie had refused to wear it).

For the first time, she found herself thinking about Septima's life and what her mother might have been like as a girl. Was she always scared, always timid, always terrified of the No-Furs? Had she loved anyone before Maximus, maybe a boy in her old village, which, Millie vaguely remembered hearing, was somewhere south and west of their encampment? What was it like for her, watching her husband venture off into the No-Fur world when it came time to do the Mailing or even drive the littlies for their Halloweening? And what on earth had she been talking about with Old Aunt Yetta? What person had she failed or left behind?

*A mystery,* thought Millie again. A real, actual mystery, right here in the Yare's village, where, usually, the only mysteries were things like Who Stole Frederee's Pants off the Clothesline (answer: Millie) and Who Tried to Join the Standish Girl Scout Troop (answer: Millie) and Who Tried to Follow Maximus into the Forest When He Went to Do the Mailing (answer: Millie again).

Small as she was, Millie thought with satisfaction, she was an expert at sneaking, at overhearing things, at tucking herself in small spaces or feigning sleep while her parents talked. She would listen. She would hide. She'd ask careful questions. She would try to figure out what her mother had been talking about, what Septima had done that she so desperately, mournfully regretted. Maybe she could even try to fix whatever it was, to make it come round right.

# CHAPTER 6

*Jeremy*

NORMALLY, JEREMY BIGELOW CHERISHED each day of vacation, dreading the morning when school started up again. His brothers paid attention to their own activities. His parents paid attention to his brothers. None of the mean kids from school showed up to ask Jeremy if he was taking Sasquatch to the homecoming dance or if he'd seen a leprechaun underneath a four-leaf clover. Nobody cared if Jeremy wanted to watch TV all day long; or have popcorn for lunch; or spend all afternoon walking through the woods, looking for the Bigfoot he'd glimpsed when he was ten years old, the one who'd started him on his path.

But ever since his misadventure in the forest and his subsequent appearance in the newspaper, not to mention his mother having her identity stolen and his dad spending all of his free time locked in his home office, getting ready for the tax audit, Jeremy found himself counting the days, then the hours, then even the minutes, until he'd be able to escape his mother's reddened eyes and his father's pacing and muttering. He couldn't wait to get out of the house, to escape the way both of his brothers looked at him as if he were a quarterback who'd dropped the ball on his way to a game-winning touchdown, or he'd screwed up the last equation that would have solved the mystery of nuclear fusion.

"Bye, Mom!" he called, shouldering his backpack and climbing aboard his bike. It was still cold out, the sky a dull gray, the air damp. The snowbanks that edged the lawns had grown a dirty crust of car exhaust and salt and sand, but the roads were clear. He was pedaling along, his head full of thoughts of the girl named Alice and whether the Experimental Center was back in session yet, when a dented and dirty white van pulled up alongside him.

Jeremy had watched enough rated-R movies with his brothers to know that a beat-up-looking van cruising slowly beside a kid on a bike on an empty road never meant anything good.

"Good morning, Jeremy," the driver called. Jeremy gulped, thinking that, as bad as a van was, it was probably even worse when the driver knew your name.

Jeremy pedaled faster. The van sped up.

"I just want to talk to you," said the man. "A little friendly conversation." Jeremy's legs pumped frantically, his breath burning in his throat. The van sped up again, keeping pace with him easily. Jeremy raised his head. If he could make it to the top of the hill, he could pop a wheelie and get his bike up and over the metal guardrail, then ride through maybe fifty yards of forest before hooking onto the old railroad tracks that the Standish Town Council had been talking about converting to a bike path since Jeremy was in kindergarten.

"We have information," the man was saying. "We can help you, Jeremy. That's all we want."

*Yeah, right,* thought Jeremy. He was standing up now, slamming his feet down on the pedals, but he could tell that he was losing momentum. If these were the people who'd left that scary letter at Jo's house, the ones responsible for his parents' current misery, they weren't trying to help. If these were the good guys, his dad wouldn't keep getting pulled over by the police, and his mother's credit cards would still be working. He inched up the hill, the van's engine sounding like thunder in his ears, its motor taunting him while he blinked sweat out of his eyes, looking for the cutoff and the dull metal guardrail. He'd watched Ben jump over it a hundred times; had tried it a dozen times himself, each time raising his nerve and turning his front wheel away right before it was time to pull it up into the wheelie.

But that had just been for fun. This time it mattered. Jeremy tried to pedal harder, but he wasn't Ben, and he could already feel his bike slowing and wobbling. Gasping, his throat burning, the bike lurching from side to side while he pedaled as if there were a gun to his back, he cut his bike hard to the left, pumped his right leg, then his left, closing his eyes. When he felt his front tire kiss the guardrail, he shifted his weight backward, pulling up on the handlebars as hard as he could, praying for his bike to rise up high enough to clear the railing.

For a second he thought he'd done it. He felt the handlebars lift; he felt the front tire rising. Then it was as if the world remembered that he wasn't Ben or Noah; he was just Jeremy, plain old unremarkable, not-very-athletic Jeremy, and the rules of gravity still applied.

His tire hit the guardrail. The bike came crashing down. Jeremy was tossed over the railing and onto the ground, bouncing and rolling, branches jabbing him, crusty snow scraping him, dirt and pine needles streaking his hands and his back.

For a moment he just lay there panting, staring at the sky, and listening to the crash and clatter of his bike rolling down the hill. Probably the man in the van would kidnap him. That might actually come as a relief. He wouldn't have to go home, where his parents were preoccupied and miserable, or back to school, where everyone treated him like a joke.

Then the driver was standing above him, his wide body blotting out the sun. "That's gonna leave a mark," he said. He held out his hand. Jeremy ignored it.

"Come on, Jeremy," said the man, and pulled him to his feet. Jeremy hated the way his legs wobbled, hated the way his stupid eyes were filling with stupid tears, because the man sounded kind. His hand was big and warm and rough, and it gave Jeremy's hand a brief squeeze before letting go. Jeremy brushed his bruised palms off on his ripped pants, walked himself to the van, opened the door, and climbed inside.

From the outside, the van was nothing special, a

battered old thing with a bashed-in left front fender and a cracked taillight, the kind of vehicle a plumber or electrician might drive. Inside, though . . . Jeremy looked around. He'd once seen a video about a billionaire's private jet, and the interior had looked something like this. The floors were carpeted, the walls and even the ceiling were covered in swanky-looking padded leather, the color of coffee the way his mother drank it, with lots of cream. There were swiveling seats up front, and two more seats in the second row. Jeremy was in one seat, and the driver sat in the other. There was a small table between them, and polished wood desks that folded out of the backs of the front seats. Four screens hung from the ceiling, showing four different views of the town, including one of Jeremy's school and one of—he peered closely to be sure—Jo's house.

"You've been watching us," he said, feeling unease moving through his body and making his skin prickle. The man—tall, dark-haired, fit, and slender, with sunglasses over his eyes—nodded.

"The two of you have been able to make more progress in tracking down Bigfoots in a single year than our entire agency has in the last decade." The man made the gesture of doffing an invisible hat. "We're impressed."

Jeremy felt himself flushing, pride briefly overwhelming his anger and his shame and fear. Up close, he could see the shadow of stubble beneath the man's freshly shaved cheeks and a single scar, the kind chicken pox sometimes left behind, high on his left cheek. He smelled bracingly of aftershave and mouthwash, and he was chewing cinnamon-flavored gum. Jeremy could hear the snap, snap, snap of it and could see the man's heavy jaw rotate. He watched as the man, whose dark glasses were still in place, pressed his fingers against the top of a cabinet built into the wall. Its lid lifted, and he reached inside and handed Jeremy a clean, warm towel.

"Shower's in the back, and I think I can find you some clean clothes," he said.

Jeremy reached out, feeling his fingers close around the terry cloth. The morning had started to take on the feel of a dream. "Who are you?" Jeremy asked. "Where are you from?"

"I think you know that, son."

"The Department of Official Inquiry," Jeremy said. He could recall the feel of those words underneath his fingers, on the letterhead Jo had found in her house, that strange, staring eye above them. "You guys left a letter for Jo. Inside her house."

"This is urgent business. We needed to make contact."

"You scared us," said Jeremy, aware that he sounded like he was whining. "Why'd you do it that way? Why do you even care about—" He started to say "Bigfoots," then changed his mind and gestured toward the forest. "Them?"

He understood, of course, why *he* wanted to find a Bigfoot, but why was the government interested? Why did this man care enough to kidnap a kid? Because surely his parents would notice that he was gone. Maybe not right away, Jeremy thought, but at some point. Like maybe if one of his brothers got sick and needed a kidney.

The corners of the man's mouth gave the tiniest twitch. "Clean up," he said. "Then we can talk."

"What about school?" asked Jeremy. When the man looked puzzled, he said, "I'm going to be tardy."

The skin at the corners of the man's eyes crinkled. "I once defused a bomb wired to a car radio in under ninety seconds without the driver noticing. While the car was moving. I think I can get you out of seventh grade for the morning."

"Cool," Jeremy said, before he could remember that he was talking to one of the bad guys. He bent his head—although the van's ceilings were so high that he didn't have to duck too much—and made his way to the back of the van, which seemed much larger than the exterior suggested, pulling an accordion-style door closed behind him. There was a stall shower, a toilet and a sink, and a neatly made single bed that folded up into the wall. Most of the space was filled by a desk piled high with papers and books, some of the same ones that Jo kept: *A Bigfoot Hunter's Journal* and *The Truth about the Yetis* and *Finding Hidden Creatures* and *Bigfoot: Truth or Myth?* A topographical map of Standish, with colored pins dotting it, hung above the desk, along with other marked-up maps, one depicting the United States, the other the entire world. On top of that map was that eye logo and the words "*oculo videt in abscondito,*" the Latin words that Jo had told him meant "the hidden eye sees all." Jeremy stared, and when he turned he saw the man looming behind him.

"A lot of woods here." The man had snuck up behind him, somehow, without Jeremy hearing. Behind the dark glasses, his face was expressionless. His jaw worked. The gum snapped. "Deeper than you'd think." Not one single word sounded threatening by itself. The man could have just been making conversation, remarking on the size and depth of the woods that surrounded Standish, but Jeremy imagined he could hear what the man wasn't saying: A boy could get lost in those woods, could be lost and never found.

Jeremy gave a weak smile, and then hustled himself into the shower.

Ten minutes later, Jeremy, toweled dry and dressed in a pair of borrowed sweatpants and a plain blue collared shirt, sat in one of the captain's chairs, with the man in the other one. The man was sipping from a mug of coffee, and there was a mug of what smelled like hot chocolate on the table in front of the other chair. Jeremy picked it up, feeling the warmth through the heavy ceramic. He lifted it to his mouth. Then he stopped.

The man was watching him, and he must have guessed what Jeremy was thinking, because the skin around his eyes got crinkly again. It wasn't quite a smile, but it still managed to convey amusement.

"Here," he said, reaching out his hand. Jeremy handed over the beverage, watching closely as the man took a swallow.

"See?" he said. "No poison. I promise."

Jeremy thought that maybe the man could have calibrated the dosage, putting in enough poison to affect Jeremy without harming himself. Or he could have built

up an immunity, taking tiny doses of the poison over the years, until he could swallow a gallon of it without any ill effect. Then he told himself he was being paranoid. After all, he had already been run off the road by a man in a van who'd been lurking around Standish for weeks, a man who'd been spying on him and his friend and threatening his family and could possibly be planning to kidnap him or worse.

Except, ever since he'd pulled Jeremy up off the cold forest floor and walked him into the van, the man hadn't done anything to keep him there. The doors didn't seem to be locked, which meant that Jeremy could have snuck out the back door instead of taking a shower; he could have gone running down the road to school or to the police station and told everyone what had happened. And did kidnappers let you take showers and give you clean clothes and hot chocolate?

The man was still looking at him with that amused expression. "Think about it," he said. "If I wanted to hurt you, I could have done it about a dozen different ways by now."

Jeremy accepted his drink and took a deep swallow. It was warm and not too sweet, just the way he liked it.

"What do I call you?" Jeremy asked.

The man extended his hand. "Milford Carruthers the Third. My friends call me Skip."

Jeremy wondered if this man was related to Milford Carruthers, the "famed Bigfoot hunter," and his youngest daughter, Priscilla, but decided not to ask. The less this man knew about what he and Jo had learned, the better.

"And before we go any farther, I owe you an apology."

Jeremy tried to look tough. "Yes, you do."

The man nodded. "We didn't approach this the right way. But we didn't know we were dealing with kids. From everything you'd managed to find, and the sophistication with which you did it, we figured you and Jo had to be PhDs at a minimum."

Jeremy felt pride swell inside him, like he was full of helium.

"We worked hard at it," he said, trying to sound modest.

"And, like I told you, you guys have gotten further than our entire agency. And we've got some of the best minds in the country . . ." Skip Carruthers stopped talking and sipped from his mug. "Well, let's just say that I was told they were some of the best minds in the country." His chilly tone made Jeremy glad that he was not the owner of one of those minds. "But let me start with your first question: Why? You asked why this was so important.

The reason is . . . Well. Let me back up. How much do you know about Them?" Jeremy could hear the capital *T* when the man said "Them."

"I saw one," Jeremy said. Skip leaned forward so fast that his coffee lurched in its cup, almost spilling out onto the table.

"You saw one?"

Jeremy reached for his phone, glad that it hadn't been cracked in the fall. The man leaned close, lips pressed together, body still, like a hunting dog that's just smelled a pheasant or heard the faint rustle of a squirrel. Skip Carruthers gestured for the phone and watched the blurry footage of what Jeremy knew was an enormous, furry creature in overalls and a floppy hat running lightly through the woods.

Jeremy's classmates—the few he'd trusted enough to show—had given him endless grief about the tape. Even Jo, who'd sworn that she believed him, hadn't looked too impressed. But Carruthers seemed to be watching like he was trying to memorize every second, watching it through once, then twice, then holding up a hand for silence and playing it again. The third time through, he stopped the tape and zoomed in as tightly as he could on the shadowy blur of the creature's face.

"It looks like he's wearing glasses," Jeremy pointed out. "See where the sun's shining?"

The man just nodded and watched the video from start to finish again.

"We've seen that one before," he finally said.

Jeremy's skin prickled. The man touched the frozen image with one close-clipped fingernail, tapping the creature's face.

"I'm going to tell you everything. But first," Skip said, "before we go any further . . ." He pulled a piece of white cloth from his pocket and wiped Jeremy's phone, front and back.

"Are you making sure you don't leave any fingerprints?" Jeremy asked.

This time the man's lips quirked, as well as the skin around his eyes. "Your screen was a mess," he said, and handed it back. "And now," he said, "I'm going to tell you why it matters. Why it matters more than anything else you or I will ever do with our lives. Why it matters more than anything else in the world."

Three hours later Jeremy stood in the lunch line at the Standish Middle School cafeteria, being teased by his classmates. Business as usual . . . except he was still so busy trying to make sense of everything he'd heard that morning that he barely even noticed the abuse. All morning he kept his face still, kept his body moving from class to class, putting it behind a desk, walking it through the hallways, but inside, his brain was whirling, like his kitchen's garbage disposal when it was trying to break up onion skin or ice.

"Yo, Bigfoot boy," said Hayden Morganthal, using two fingers to flick Jeremy between the shoulder blades. "You're holding up the line."

Jeremy jumped, then shoved his tray along the metal railings, accepting a partitioned plate filled with mashed potatoes and cubed turkey and gravy, mushy peas boiled past green to gray, and a fluted paper cup of cranberry sauce. He felt like he'd spent three hours on another planet and had been dumped back down on Earth without the benefit of a parachute.

*The power to cure cancer,* Skip Carruthers had told him. *To cure diabetes and Alzheimer's disease. The power to cure anything. It's all in their blood.*

"You gonna gimme your two fifty or just stand there looking pretty?" asked Mrs. Martin, who wore a black hairnet over her dyed black hair. Jeremy reached for his pocket before remembering that he'd left his filthy, shredded jeans in the van, with his lunch money still inside of them.

"Sorry," he said. "I . . ."

But Mrs. Martin wasn't looking at him. She was, instead, frowning at the iPad that the school had started using for a cash register. "Huh. Sorry. It looks like you're all paid up for the rest of the year."

Feeling like he'd just fallen even more deeply into his strange dream, Jeremy nodded. He walked through the lunchroom, taking his usual seat at the end of a bench at a table full of other oddball kids, all of them ignoring each other. He opened his container of milk, remembering.

"Why don't you just tell them that?" he'd asked Mr. Carruthers. He'd accepted a second mug of hot chocolate and a corn muffin. "If the Bigfoots' blood really can do all these things, why wouldn't they, you know, just give you some blood?" An awful thought went scurrying through his mind as he imagined furry bodies hanging from hooks, attached to tubes, being drained, emptied out until there was nothing left. "You don't need, like, *all* of their blood, do you?"

Mr. Carruthers had shaken his head. "No, not all of it. Just a drop or two, really. Our labs could do the rest. But as to why we don't just ask them . . ." He turned toward the laptop that stood open on the desk. "It's not as if we can just send them a letter. We'd have to make our request in person. Which means getting close enough for us to ask and them to listen. And that," he concluded, "is where you and your friend Josette come in."

"Jo," Jeremy had corrected automatically, knowing how Jo hated it when people used her entire name.

"Jo," Jeremy whispered out loud at the lunch table, loud enough so that Sophie and Olivia, who were sitting at the next table with the rest of the popular girls, whispering and giggling, giggling and whispering, ceased both activities and stared at him. Jeremy ignored them. If Bigfoot blood could do what Mr. Carruthers said, if it could cure all those things, help all those people, then it could help Jo, too, prevent her from having to go through the other surgeries she'd told him that she'd need. And if he was the one who made it happen—who convinced a Bigfoot to donate a few drops of blood—then he would be the one who'd helped her. Not just her, either, but every sick person in the country. In the world. He'd be a hero.

That thought had him on the verge of telling Skip Carruthers absolutely everything that he and Jo had learned, about the little furry girl he'd spotted paddling across the lake, and the big, red-haired girl at the

Experimental Center, and how Jo had sent their hair off to a lab and learned that neither one of them was human. He'd been leaning forward, mouth open, ready to spill, when something made him stop.

He thought about all the times he'd ever been lied to by a grown-up and about how badly the Department of Official Inquiry had scared him; how it had felt to see his name typed on a letter that promised consequences for him and for his parents if he and Jo didn't give up their search. He'd pictured his father's timid smile when the police cars were at their house, and thought about how his mother had been practically crying on the phone with the bank as she'd begged them to let her talk to an actual person. Finally, he remembered how he'd felt when his parents told him he hadn't gotten into the young artists program at Juilliard, how his last chance to be special and important in their eyes was gone. The Bigfoot had given him hope, new hope that he could do something big, be someone who mattered, and he wasn't sure if he trusted Skip Carruthers not to use him, the way grown-ups always seemed to use kids, taking their ideas and their work, then taking the credit.

Mr. Carruthers was looking at him, moving his jaw from side to side. "Everything all right, son?" he asked, and when he put his hand on Jeremy's shoulder, Jeremy had nodded and said that everything was fine.

In the end, he'd been careful, playing it safe. He hadn't told Skip Carruthers everything, or even most of it, even after Mr. Carruthers had apologized for scaring him and Jo, had told him, again, that his agency believed it was dealing with not just adults but possible "covert agents," people from another country, or even just "homegrown radicals" trying to poach American Bigfoots for their own purposes. "There are people like that. Poachers. People who don't care that the Bigfoot blood can solve global health crises. People who just want the fame and fortune of being the one who proved that Bigfoots were real."

Jeremy, who'd had many elaborate daydreams of precisely that fame and fortune, kept quiet. When Skip Carruthers said, again, "Tell me what you know," Jeremy tried to keep his voice steady when he said, "Why don't you go first?"

Carruthers had opened a manila folder with the word "Classified" typed on the tab and that eye on the front. Jeremy saw his school picture paper-clipped to a document that Mr. Carruthers flipped over too quickly for Jeremy to see more than his name and his parents' names typed at the top. Mr. Carruthers moved rapidly through the stack, but Jeremy saw what he thought were photocopies of the same newspaper stories he'd read; the *Standish Times* reports from the ill-fated rally; and then—he dug his teeth into his lip again, to keep from gasping—a close-up of the gray-furred girl he'd seen at the Experimental Center. The one who'd first said she was dressed up as an Ewok for Halloween; the one who'd then said she had a skin condition. The one Jeremy and Jo knew wasn't human.

Carruthers turned another page, and this time Jeremy couldn't keep from gasping. "That's him!" he shouted, reaching for the picture, knocking his elbow against his mug, which would have spilled all over everything had the man's hand not darted out with an almost uncanny speed and grabbed it. Jeremy barely noticed. "That's him! That's the one I saw in the woods!" He looked up at Mr. Carruthers, eyes wide, cheeks burning. "He's real," he said. His voice seemed to echo off the walls of the van. *"Real."*

Mr. Carruthers put his big, warm hand on top of Jeremy's for just a minute. "Of course he is," Carruthers replied, as if Jeremy had said something totally obvious, and Jeremy felt his whole body relaxing, something deep inside of him unclenching, like he'd finally released a breath he didn't know he was holding. When he smiled, his teeth were so white and so even that Jeremy didn't think they could be real. And when he asked, "Want to help us find him?" it was impossible to keep from nodding and grinning and saying, "Yes, sir, I do."

Mr. Carruthers—"Call me Skip," he'd said, more than once, but Jeremy, who'd been taught to call grown-ups Mr. and Ms. and Mrs., was having a hard time doing it, maybe because Mr. Carruthers kept his dark glasses on and chewed his gum like he wanted to hurt it and because of the little scar he had (maybe chicken pox, Jeremy thought, but maybe a bullet wound)—was the most terrifying grown-up he'd ever met. He knew everything; he knew things before Jeremy even had a chance to tell him. He too suspected that the little girl with the skin condition wasn't actually a human girl and didn't actually have a skin condition. He believed that the large male Bigfoot, the one Jeremy had seen, was related to the smaller one, and the two of them lived in the forest on the other side of the lake, the direction from which the gray-furred girl had arrived in her canoe, and that there might be others there, including an old female called either Yetta or Lucille, one they'd been hunting for years.

"Lucille," said Jeremy. "She was the one . . ." He'd wanted to say, *the one Priscilla Carruthers told us about,*

135

before he remembered that that was a piece of information he'd decided to keep private. "The one in the paper,"
he finally said. "Wouldn't she be, like, super-old now?"

"That's the thing about Bigfoots," Carruthers said.
"We think that they live a very long time. Much longer
than we do."

"My dad says he read that humans are living longer
than they used to," Jeremy said. "He said that when he
was a boy, seventy or eighty was old, but now there's
people that old all the time. And I've got a grandfather
who's ninety-one, and he's still, like, totally with it."

Something moved across Skip Carruthers's face,
something that made him look the opposite of how he'd
looked when Jeremy had amused him. His lips tightened;
the skin around his eyes furrowed. But all he said was,
"Yup, lots of old people."

After that, Jeremy was careful not to interrupt. He
listened as Carruthers explained how a Bigfoot tribe had
been rumored to live in Standish for years and how back
in the 1960s the government had sent agents to scour
the woods but had found nothing. He waited for Mr.
Carruthers to mention Alice, the red-haired girl from
the Experimental Center, the one whose hair Jeremy had
found and Jo had tested, the one who wasn't human. But

if Mr. Carruthers knew about Alice, and how she was friends with the gray-furred one, how they'd even claimed to be cousins, he didn't say anything, and Jeremy elected not to mention her or Priscilla Landsman and what she'd said about looking inside the biggest heart.

In the end, he and Mr. Carruthers had agreed to share information. Jeremy and Jo would continue their hunt, and they would tell Mr. Carruthers what they learned. In return, Carruthers would let him be the "public face" of the Bigfoot discovery. When Jeremy asked why, knowing that if their positions were reversed he'd never let anyone dream of taking credit, Carruthers had given him a tight-lipped smirk and said, "You're a smart kid. You tell me. Which story do you think John and Jane Q. Public would like better: kid finds Bigfoot in the woods, or government agent from Washington tracks one down?"

It made sense, Jeremy thought, but he still couldn't help feeling that there was something sneaky about it, something insincere about the man's promises, not to mention the way he never took his glasses off, which meant that Jeremy never saw his eyes.

They'd exchanged telephone numbers and email addresses, even though Jeremy was positive the Department knew where he lived, knew how to reach him, and was already monitoring all of his devices. They'd shaken hands. "Keep me posted," Skip Carruthers had said. When Jeremy had asked if there was anything specific he should do or anyplace special he should be investigating, the man had shaken his head and said, "Just keep doing what you're doing. It's worked out well so far." He'd dropped Jeremy off at school at ten fifteen, and when Jeremy had gone to the office, the receptionist had greeted him with a wave and asked him how the dentist had gone. "Fine," Jeremy said, feeling dizzy and overwhelmed. The wheels had started to turn.

When the fifth-period bell rang, Jeremy threw his uneaten lunch in the trash. He moved his body through the hallways, into his chair and out of it again, back to his locker, and then, after the final bell rang, out the front door. He was halfway to the bike rack before he remembered his trashed bike, which he'd last seen in the forest, five miles away, too far for him to walk before it got dark. He was reaching for his phone, hoping his mom would be around to give him a ride, and not busy on the phone with the credit card people, when he heard Austin Riley say, "Whoa, Bigelow, sweet wheels!"

Jeremy trotted to the bike rack, surprised and yet not surprised to see his bike, no dents or scrapes, the bent wheel straightened out, the crooked handlebars restored. New knobby tires had replaced his regular old ones. There were gleaming new spokes and rims, a new leather seat, new handlebar grips, new shock absorbers.

"Christmas present?" Austin asked, and Jeremy nodded, reaching for the envelope that had been taped between the handlebars, and was unsurprised to see the Department of Official Inquiry's by-now-familiar stationery, that strange, all-seeing eye. Only now, instead of typed-out threats, the note had a handwritten promise: "This is only the beginning."

At home Jeremy knew, even before he heard his father's delighted shout, even before his mom high-fived him, even before he and his brothers were packed into the station wagon to go celebrate with a big steak dinner, that the audit had been canceled and his mom's identity had been restored. Better yet, his father had been sent an unexpected ten-thousand-dollar refund, along with the tax agent's most sincere apologies. Nor was he surprised when, at the end of the meal, his dad asked for the check and the waiter came back to the table to tell them that it had already been paid: "Sorry, sir, I've been requested not to tell you by whom."

His mother celebrated the reactivation of her credit

cards and the restoration of her good name by drinking two glasses of champagne and giggling as she leaned against Jeremy's dad, resting her head on his shoulder and even—Jeremy had to look away—kissing his neck. Jeremy's dad had dabbed a blob of whipped cream on her nose, and she'd laughed, saying, "Shoo, fly," and waving her hands at him to go away while Jeremy looked around the restaurant, praying there wasn't anyone he knew eating there that night.

When they finally made it home, Jeremy went up to his room to start on his homework and logged in to the school's system. He was unsurprised to find that, according to the school's records, he'd completed every assignment for the rest of the semester . . . and had gotten As on every one.

*You should have given me a few Bs,* he thought. The steak and baked potato felt like concrete in his belly, as he heard Skip Carruthers's voice, calm and kind and trustworthy, telling him how important the Bigfoots were; explaining that this was only about help ("We'll help them, and they'll help us!"); telling him, again, that this was only the beginning.

# CHAPTER 7

## Alice

"A-LICE," CALLED JESSICA WITHOUT LOOKING away from her lighted makeup mirror. "Your freak friend is here!"

Alice felt her hands clench. She'd finally made it back to the Center after a week in Hawaii with her parents, where her father had spent every day hunched on a lounge chair next to the pool with a towel draped over his neck, yelling at people on his phone, and her mother had vanished into the spa. Walking on the beach, swimming in the clear water, even running in her first race had all been fun, but she'd been desperate to be with her friends . . . and, of course, her not-friend Jessica Jarvis.

"Freak" was not a word that was approved of at the Experimental Center for Love and Learning. At least it hadn't been, until last fall, when Alice and Millie and then every kid in the place had stepped forward, into the glaring lights of the local TV stations, and announced, "I'm a freak." After a long conversation that included the entire school community, Phil and Lori had called for a vote and agreed to "reclaim" the word "freak," turning it into a compliment instead of an insult.

Still, Alice detected a certain tone in Jessica's voice. Jessica and her friends had tricked Alice last fall, luring her into the water for skinny-dipping, then stealing her clothes, taking her picture, and posting it, alongside various monsters, including Bigfoots, all over campus for everyone to see. It had been awful—except, Alice knew, if it had never happened, then she wouldn't have carried a plate of brownies down to the lake in the middle of the night. She wouldn't have heard Millie splashing, and she wouldn't have saved her, and she wouldn't have started on the path that would, she knew, lead to the truth about her life.

"Merry New Year's!" said Millie, stomping snow off her boots as she stepped into the seventh-grade girls' cabin. She wore a pair of blue snow pants, laced-up boots, and a parka with a fur-trimmed hood. Except, Alice saw, the hood wasn't fur-trimmed. That was just Millie's silvery fur, which stood out around her face in a bristle when she was excited or upset or cold.

"Alice!" Millie said, and stood on her tiptoes to fling her arms around her friend. Alice hugged her hard, breathing in Millie's scent of wood smoke and maple syrup, feeling Millie's fur brush her face. It felt like coming into a warm house on a cold night, like that first sip of water when you've been thirsty for hours. *My friend,* Alice thought as Millie pulled away.

"Look at you!" said Millie. "You are toasty gold! And you have the spotty bits on your nose!"

"I'm tan. And those are freckles," said Alice, smiling, the way she always did, at the funny way that Millie spoke. Once, she'd asked whether all humans looked naked to the Yare, and Millie had said no, but she'd answered so quickly, and she'd looked away when she'd said it, so that Alice thought that she was just being polite. "And I have so much to tell you!"

"I have so much to tell you!" Millie echoed. She'd written Alice back, finally, but just a few sentences that talked about "technical difficulties" and made vague reference to a "secret" that she'd learned.

"Can you two continue this joyous reunion some-where else?" asked Jessica, who was doing something to her hair with a curling iron.

"Leavedb thembd alone." Taley sniffled. She was flopped on her bunk bed, reading a book and sounding as congested as ever. Alice guessed that the allergy clinic where she'd spent her break hadn't been much help.

Millie grabbed Alice's hands. Alice picked up her jacket, her hat and scarf and mittens, and the two of them walked outside, heading into the woods, their breath pre-ceding them in frosty, cloud-shaped puffs.

"Tell me your telling!" Millie urged.

"Okay. Do you remember that boy? The one who was in the paper? The one who organized that rally?"

"The one who chased you," Millie said immediately. "The bad, no-good No-Fur."

"Is that what you call him?" Alice asked. When Millie nodded, Alice said, "Before I left, when I was waiting for Lee, the boy came and found me and told me something."

Millie's eyes narrowed. "Did he hurt your feeling?"

Alice smiled a little. "Not exactly. He told me that he'd found some of my hair and sent it to a lab for analysis and that they found out . . ." She looked at Millie, who was holding very still and watching her carefully. "He said I wasn't human," she finished.

"Oh, Alice," said Millie. Her little hands were curled into fists, and her silvery eyes were narrowed, like she was ready for a fight. "Of course you are human! No matter what that bad boy tells you!"

"No, no," said Alice. "He wasn't trying to be mean. He was saying—at least, I think he was saying—that I'm . . ." She pulled the icy air into her lungs until her eyes watered. "That I'm Yare."

Instead of being overjoyed, Millie looked sad, even sympathetic. She stood on her tiptoes and patted Alice's shoulder. "The bad boy was teasling you. That can never be."

"I don't think he was teasing," said Alice, pronouncing the word carefully, so that Millie would hear. "And why would he want to be mean to me?"

"Because," said Millie, "you made him look foolish."

"True," said Alice. They both smiled, remembering how Alice, with her hair down, dressed in a furry vest, had run, leading the boy and his band of followers on a merry chase through the woods, all the way to the gates of the Experimental Center.

"He sounded like he meant it," Alice said.

"He would want to sound that way, I am thinking. So that you'd believe him," Millie said.

Alice wanted to stomp her foot in frustration. When she'd imagined this talk, she'd thought that Millie would be delighted. She'd imagined Millie hugging her, dancing in glee, promising to help her "get on the bottom of things." She hadn't thought that Millie would be skeptical and dismissive, and she wasn't sure quite what to do.

Millie was shaking her head again. "What you are saying . . . it is a thing that has never happened."

"You're saying that, for hundreds and hundreds of years, no Bigfoot ever had a baby with a human?"

"No Yare that I am ever hearing of," said Millie, saying the word "Yare" a little more loudly than the rest of the sentence. Alice realized that she'd said the *B*-word— Bigfoot—which the Yare considered a very rude slur. She felt her face get hot.

"Okay, but there's other Yare, right? Other Tribes? Yare that you don't know, that maybe do things differently?"

Millie was shaking her head. "Maybe this is a thing that has happened, long-and-long ago, but as long as I've been alive, I am knowing that the Yare keep away from the No-Furs. We hide from your kind."

"What about your uncle? Your father's brother? Didn't he run away?" Alice knew that he had. Millie had told her the story of her father, Maximus, and how his brother had "had the curiosity," just like Millie, and how one dark night he'd left a note and taken a canoe and gone paddling away, off into the No-Fur world, never to be seen again. His name had been taken back by the Tribe and was never meant to be spoken out loud.

"But that was long-and-long ago," said Millie. "Before I am born."

"How long ago?" Alice asked.

"Before the war," Millie replied.

"Which war?" Alice asked. Millie waved one silver-furred paw in the air in a dismissive gesture.

"We do not call the wars the same as you. This was the one before the Great Depressing."

Alice stopped. "Before World War One?" she asked.

Millie reached up to swat a handful of snow from a low-hanging pine bough. "The Big War, yes. This is what my parents are telling me. That before this Big War, and the Great Depressing, is when my father's brother, whose name is not to be spoken, ran away."

"Millie," said Alice. She felt out of breath and slightly wobbly on her feet. "How old is your father?"

Millie made a pushing-away motion with both of her hands, a Yare gesture Alice had come to learn meant embarrassment or confusion, or a desire to change the subject. "Oh, I'm bad at reckoning No-Fur time."

"Okay," said Alice. She was thinking of one of the rare compliments her mother had ever paid her, after she'd pestered her for some treat or permission to stay up late to watch a show. *Alice, you are nothing if not persistent.* "How old are you?" she asked Millie.

"I will be having thirteen summers this year," Millie said. Then she frowned, and her fur seemed to droop. "But I am smallish for my age. Even Florrie, who has only six summers, is bigger than me." When she raised her head, her fur seemed to perk up and quiver with indignation. "It is not fair." She looked at Alice and touched Alice's curls and sighed. "I would be giving anything to be tall and strong like you."

Alice flushed at the compliment but pressed ahead, determined to stay on topic. "Okay, so you and I are basically the same age. How many summers have your parents had?"

"Many and many," Millie said in a voice that was still maddeningly calm.

"How many," Alice asked, "is many and many?"

148

Millie made her flicking gesture again.

"Millie, this is important," Alice said.

Alice heard Millie muttering under her breath as she nibbled her face-fur and, Alice hoped, tried to count. "I am thinking one hundred and some," Millie finally said. "Old Aunt Yetta's had two hundred summers. There was a party for her Name-Night." Millie's expression became dreamy. "There were mince pies and squash pies and Mallomars for me, from on-the-line. Mallomars are my favorites."

Alice stopped walking. She felt the same dizziness she remembered from a classmate's eighth birthday party, which had been held at an indoor trampoline park, where she'd bounced and flipped and bounced and flipped so many times that the world had started spinning and she'd had to be helped off the trampoline so that she could lie down.

"Old Aunt Yetta is two hundred years old," she said.

Millie nodded. "Are you ever having the Mallomar?" she asked, trying, again, to change the subject. "My papa says they are a seasonal item. Stores can't sell them in the summer because the chocolate and the marshmallow will melt."

"Your parents are more than one hundred years old."

Millie nodded again.

"Do all Yare live that long?" Alice asked.

"As far as I am knowing," Millie replied.

"Will you live that long?" Alice asked.

Millie shrugged. "My parents worry, because of my smallness, that maybe I am different, somehow. So I do not know." She bent, scooped up snow to form a snowball, then tossed it in the air. "I think that bad boy was teasling on you." She turned so that she was looking Alice in the face, her gaze on Alice's eyes. "I know that you are lonely with your parents and wishing for things to be different." When Alice nodded, Millie reached out and took Alice's mittened hands in her own. "I wish they could be different too."

Alice felt her eyes filling with tears. Maybe that boy, Jeremy, had been teasing her, getting her hopes up, getting her to believe that somewhere, out in the world, she had parents who loved her. Probably Millie was right. Alice would just have to be content knowing that she had a friend, even if she could never truly be part of Millie's Tribe. The Yare had reluctantly let themselves be seen when their lives were in danger, but Alice knew she wouldn't be invited back for sleepovers or Name-Night parties, wouldn't be spending time in Millie's cozy underground lair or joining the Yare in their feastings, not even if she showed up with Mallomars. As long as they saw her as one of the No-Furs, she could never truly belong.

"May I tell you my news?" Millie asked politely, and Alice made herself nod, even though it felt like her belly was full of rocks, like each of her limbs weighed a thousand pounds, and even nodding was an effort. She tried to look excited as Millie's face broke into a big grin.

"Well," said Millie, and started talking very fast. "I filled out the application on *The Next Stage*'s site-web—"

"Website," said Alice.

"As you say. I have to record an audition. I tried and tried, with the camera pointing . . ." She gestured down toward her chest. "So they wouldn't know about my . . ." She gestured up at her face-fur. "But every time it wouldn't let me upload my song, because it said a face must be showing. And so I thought"—Millie paused, then said—"it could be you!"

"What do you mean?" Alice asked.

"Only this," said Millie. "I will stand behind you. You will be looking into the camera. You will move your lips and I will do the singing, and nobody will be the wiser!" She stopped, looking expectantly at her friend.

Alice plucked at the edges of her mittens and readjusted

her hat. She could feel the Mane escape its elastics, curls and tendrils pushing at the bright pink fleece. "But what happens if they pick you?" she asked. "Don't you have to go and sing for them in person?"

Millie stood on her tiptoes and whispered in Alice's ear. "I have a potion," she said. "From Old Aunt Yetta. For making fur go away. If I get picked, I will use it."

Alice considered. "So why don't you use it to do the audition?"

Millie frowned and nibbled at the fur around her lips. "It hurts. It hurts a lot. Maybe it is because it was meant for my father, not for me, and he is big, and I am small. And I only have the one vial of it!"

"But what happens if I pretend to sing, and then you get picked, and you're you, not me?"

Millie raised her hands to her ears and shook them, like she was shooing away smoke. Alice knew that gesture too, and it meant, *I'm excited, and don't bother me about details.* "We will burn that bridge when we come to it. But for now, can you be me? Please?"

Alice would have liked nothing better than to pretend to be Millie and help her friend, but the thought of being on camera, with her stocky body and her wild hair, left her feeling sick. People made fun of the way she looked.

It had happened all her life. People who saw the audition that Millie wanted to record would probably laugh too, like everyone else did. "It's not that I don't want to help you—"

"Please," said Millie, and grabbed Alice's hands, holding them tight in her own furry paws. "Please help. This is all I've ever wanted. Please say you will."

Alice's stomach did a slow flip, thinking that no one would believe it. Millie was small and sweet and charming, and sounded that way. Alice was none of those things.

"Let's think this through," she said, which was something her own father (if he really was her father) would say . . . except Alice knew that it sounded reasonable, but it always meant no, and from Millie's frustrated expression, she could tell that her friend had come to the same conclusion. "There has to be another way," she said, and led Millie back toward the seventh-grade cabin. "I'll help you brainstorm."

Millie shook her head.

"There is no other way," she said. "I have done thinking through. I have thought of everything! I can't do the potion yet—if I steal more, Old Aunt Yetta will be knowing—and there's only five days left for me to send in a video!"

"I'll do it," came the voice of Jessica Jarvis, floating through the frosty air.

Both girls turned. Jessica wore a black cape trimmed with white fur, instead of a bulky down parka or a wool coat. Her gloves were black leather, also trimmed with white, and she wore knee-high winter boots with white laces.

Millie glared at her. "Were you leaves-dropping?"

"Eavesdropping," Alice and Jessica both said.

"And I was not," said Jessica. "You two weren't exactly whispering."

Alice gave Jessica a hard look. She and Jessica had been enemies after the skinny-dipping incident, and things had not improved when Millie had forced Jessica to tell the whole world—or, at least, most of the town of Standish—that Jessica had a tail, a fact that Millie had only guessed at that had turned out to be true. They'd made a temporary and tentative truce after that revelation, but that didn't mean Alice liked her or trusted her. "Why would you want to help?" Alice asked.

"Because," said Jessica, in the lecturing tone she used when explaining something she found completely obvious, like the importance of curling one's eyelashes or always using hair conditioner, "they don't just pick singers and dancers on *The Next Stage*. They pick spokesmodels."

Alice looked to her friend for confirmation. Millie was nodding wildly. "Yes, yes, this is a true thing!"

"That still doesn't explain what's going to happen if she gets picked to audition in person," Alice said.

Jessica gave a small and charming shrug. "We'll just say that Millie was shy. Because of her skin condition. When they look at her"—she paused, giving Millie's fur a condescending smirk—"I'm sure they'll understand. And then I'll tell them that they're getting two for the price of one."

"You'd do it?" Millie was practically dancing in excitement, her feet, in their clumpy snow boots, making hash marks in the snow. "You will do this thing for me?"

"As long as you promise to do something for me," said Jessica. "A favor to be specified at a future date."

Alice felt like she'd been punched. Millie knew what Jessica had done to Alice, how Jessica had gotten her snobby friends to put Alice's picture up all around campus, how they'd all laughed at her. She'd been certain that Millie would say, *Never think it,* in the haughty voice she used sometimes, the one that reminded Alice that she would be the leader of her Tribe someday. *I will not be doing any of the favors for you. I will be figuring this out with Alice, my friend.*

Except Millie didn't say that. Millie was, instead,

agreeing eagerly to do whatever Jessica wanted. "Any-thing," Millie was saying. "Anything!"

And then, as Alice watched in disbelief, Millie slipped her arm through Jessica's, and the two of them were walking ahead of Alice, back to the cabin, talking about songs and dresses and hairstyles and how Millie would hide. Alice trailed behind them, telling herself not to be jealous, trying not to notice how well the two of them matched, both the same height and shape, with Millie's silvery fur a pretty complement to Jessica's shiny, darker locks.

*Millie is still my friend,* Alice thought, but her body told a different truth. Her eyes were stinging, full of unshed tears, and the hands that she kept crammed in her pockets out of habit and embarrassment had curled them-selves into fists. She realized, as she trudged through the cold, that Millie hadn't told her the secret she'd hinted at in her email . . . and now, of course, it was too late to ask.

With her head down, her hat pulled low over her ears, and her shoulders hunched, Alice didn't notice that someone had followed them into the woods. She didn't hear the faint crunch of boots on the snow. She didn't see the shadow that fell across her own or hear a sighed exhalation or feel the fingertips that brushed the back of her winter jacket, as soft as a mother's kiss.

# CHAPTER 8

## Jeremy

JEREMY HAD READ A LOT OF BOOKS ABOUT SPIES and detectives, so he knew how to prepare for a stakeout. He dressed in his warmest clothes, his thickest wool socks, and the insulated ski gloves he'd inherited from his brother Ben. He packed a thermos full of hot chocolate, four energy bars, and, after some consideration, an empty plastic bottle in case he had to pee, even though he figured that if he got desperate he could just run into in the woods.

He and Jo had tried for days to figure out what Mrs. Landsman's words "the biggest heart" could possibly mean. They'd each thought of the kindest, most generous

157

people they knew: Mrs. Koenig, who'd led three decades' worth of Brownie troops on camping trips; Ms. Miller, who'd won Teacher of the Year ten times at the high school and was known for buying prom dresses for girls who couldn't afford them, and even taking in kids who had difficult home situations and letting them live in her guest bedroom. Sadly, neither of those estimable ladies recognized Priscilla Landsman's name. Neither did their parents or the town's priests, rabbis, or Sunday-school teachers. Jeremy had an idea—"wild but plausible," said Jo—that Warren, Mrs. Landsman's companion, might have been the possessor of the biggest heart, but when they called him to ask, he said he didn't know what they were talking about, and when they asked to meet with Mrs. Landsman again, Warren said that she'd "taken a turn for the worse."

"Please give her our best wishes," Jo had said, sounding unusually formal. She ended the call, sighed, and stared at her map of Standish.

"I could go look in the woods," Jeremy said. "Maybe there's a cave with an opening shaped like a heart."

"Or a tree," said Jo, and gave another sigh. That was when Jeremy decided that, in addition to investigating the forest, he would try to make contact with Alice at the

Center, to see if she'd learned anything about herself or her so-called cousin that she might be willing to share. His plan was to hang around the Experimental Center, probably behind the big falling-down pile of a building at the top of the hill that held the dining hall and offices and classroom space. When he saw Alice, he'd figure out a way to approach her. He would ask if she remembered what he'd told her about not being human. He'd figure out whether she believed it, and he would ask if she wanted to learn the truth about herself. He'd even practiced saying that phrase in the mirror, in a deep and mysterious voice, just to increase the chance that she would say yes, instead of calling for help or running away.

He was not expecting to leave Standish Middle School at the end of the day and find Alice waiting for him, just outside the chain-link fence that separated the athletic fields from the street.

She was dressed in a puffy dark-blue winter jacket, boots, and snow pants. Her hair was mostly tucked up under a gray hat, but he could see reddish-blond pieces of it blowing around her face. He jogged toward her, and she raised a hand in greeting.

"I need you to help me," she said.

"Um, okay. With what?" Jeremy asked. He was aware

159

that some of the other kids—Hayden and Austin and Sophie—were staring at him, noticing him talking to a girl, a strange girl. He took Alice's elbow, steering her onto the sidewalk, and started to walk.

"Where's your cousin?" he asked. "The one with the skin condition?" He'd almost said "the furry one" but, luckily, had thought better of it.

Alice shut her eyes. She looked so sad that Jeremy felt like he should do something, except, of course, he had no idea, ever, about what to do with girls.

"She's busy," Alice said.

"Busy with what?" Jeremy asked, even though it was obvious, even to a boy, that Alice didn't want to talk about it.

"Busy trying to be famous," Alice said. "All she cares about is . . ." She shut her mouth, pressing her lips together hard. Her cheeks were pink, and she was walking so quickly that Jeremy had to almost jog to keep up. "She's just busy. Too busy to help me. And I need help. I need to figure some things out."

"I can help," he offered. "I've got a lot of free time." Alice looked at him sideways. "My friend and I . . . my friend Jo," he said. The tips of his ears felt hot, and he couldn't seem to make himself stop talking. "Jo with no *e*. She's a girl. A girl Jo. You saw her . . ." He was going to say "the night we chased you" but went with "the one in the wheelchair" instead.

"You're not supposed to say that," said Alice. "You're supposed to say that someone *uses* a wheelchair, not that they're *in* it."

"Why?"

"Because if you say that they're in a wheelchair, you make the wheelchair their defining characteristic, but if you say that they use a wheelchair, then they're still a person first," Alice said. Her tone hinted that she was reciting something she'd been made to memorize.

Jeremy thought about this, while Alice speeded up. He trotted to catch up with her again. "What do you need help with?" Jeremy asked.

Alice didn't slow her pace, but the pink in her cheeks faded, making her look slightly less like she'd been slapped. "I have to find out who I am. Where I belong. I thought Millie would help me, but Millie's obsessed with *The Next Stage*. You know, that TV show where people do stuff to try and win money."

"Don't they sing?"

"Some of them. Some of them tell jokes or do magic tricks or dance or make human pyramids." Alice's voice was trembling. "Millie wants to audition for it. That's the

161

only thing she cares about anymore." Alice walked on in silence with her hands deep in her pockets and her eyes on the ground. "I thought she was my friend," she said, so quietly that Jeremy wasn't sure he was meant to hear. "But she was just using me. To get my laptop, and so I could tell her things about the world, so she could *win*," said Alice. The last word came out almost like a sob, bristling with pain and scorn. Jeremy snuck a glance to his left and, sure enough, Alice was swiping at her face with one mittened hand.

"I'm sorry," said Jeremy, because that seemed like the only thing you were supposed to say when a girl started crying in front of you.

Alice sniffled and shrugged. Then she said, "I want to ask you a question."

"Go ahead," Jeremy said.

"When you told me I'm not human, what did you mean?"

Jeremy thought of his dad, sitting him down in the dining room to tell him that the coach had called and that Jeremy hadn't made the travel soccer team. He remembered his mother when the letter had come from Juilliard to say that he hadn't been accepted into their Pre-College Division young musicians program. There was the teacher who'd told him that he hadn't been picked to participate in the Science Olympiad and the director of the sixth-grade play telling him that he had not been cast as Captain Hook or Mr. Smee or even as one of the pirates. "We need trees!" the lady had said. "You could be a tree! I bet you'd have just as much fun as anyone else!"

Grown-ups always tried to be nice, they tried to remind you about all of your good qualities and tell you how special you were and wish you "better luck next time," but it never really mattered. In the end, no matter how nicely you said it, bad news was bad news.

"I think that you're a Bigfoot," he said. "You and your cousin. Or maybe you're just part. Like a half or a quarter."

"I know," said Alice, "what 'part' means. But why do you think *that*? Why don't you think I'm, like, a hobbit or a vampire? Something like that?"

Jeremy told her. He explained that the DNA analysis of her hair had come back as inconclusive. He told her about the histories of Bigfoots in the forests of Standish and how for years the government had been trying to find them.

"But I'm not from here," Alice pointed out.

"Where are you from?"

"New York City." Her face looked thoughtful, and her

words were coming slowly, like she was thinking them over before she spoke. "I was born in Vermont."

"Well, there you go. Forests." Jeremy was trying to sneak a peek at her feet, which, in their snow boots, looked big but not necessarily abnormally large. He wondered if there was a polite way to ask her if she had hair anyplace that girls weren't normally hairy, then quickly decided against it. "I don't know . . . do you feel like a vampire?"

This earned him a short laugh.

"Or a hobbit?"

"I like breakfast," Alice said. Jeremy realized that she was making a joke, and he smiled and didn't mention that there was a government agency searching for Bigfoots, that one of its agents was currently cruising the streets of Standish, piloting a deceptively crummy-looking van around, looking for her and her friend.

"So if I'm not human," said Alice, "if I'm a Bigfoot, then how did I end up"—she gestured back toward the school—"you know, in the human world?"

Jeremy decided that honesty was his best bet. "I don't know," he said. "There's a lot I don't know. What are your parents like?"

"My dad works in finance," Alice said. "My mom . . ."

She looked unhappy as she began tucking strands of hair back up underneath her hat. "My mom is thin. That's her job. She does other volunteer stuff, but mostly she exercises, and she doesn't eat." Alice made an unhappy sound that only slightly resembled laughter. "I don't really look much like either one of them."

"Were you adopted?"

Alice shook her head. "I checked. Or I tried to check. They both say I wasn't, though, and there's pictures of me in the hospital with my mom, right after I was born."

"People can fake pictures," Jeremy suggested.

Alice shrugged. "I guess they could. But why?" Her gaze was still on the road. More hair had escaped from her hat again, obscuring her face. "Why would they adopt me and then pretend that I was theirs? Especially when . . ." She turned her face away, so that she was looking toward the woods, and Jeremy had to strain to hear what she was saying. "Especially when they don't even really like me."

Jeremy didn't know what to say to that. "I guess there's lots of reasons people would lie."

"What kinds of reasons?" asked Alice.

"Well, money," Jeremy said. "Maybe they got paid to take care of you and pretend that you were"—he almost said "human" but chose, instead, to say—"theirs."

"Okay," said Alice. "So pretend I'm half-Bigfoot, half-human. Why would someone give me to my parents and pay them to pretend that I'm their kid? What's the point?"

The answer was right there, swelling in his mouth like a toad that wanted to hop out. He wanted to tell her what Mr. Carruthers had told him. *Because your blood can cure things. Because Bigfoots are practically immortal. Because maybe they were growing you, like a plant in a greenhouse, until your blood was ready.* But what would Alice do if she found that out? Jeremy wasn't sure. He wasn't even sure what *he'd* do if he learned that his blood had magical healing powers. Run, probably. Assume that there were people hunting him and that he had to hide.

"I don't know," he told her. "Maybe they just . . . I don't know . . . wanted to see how you'd grow up. Maybe they're waiting to see."

"See if I turn into a Bigfoot?" Alice looked at him, right in the face, for the first time. Her eyes were wide and clear, her hair a tangle around her cheeks, and her expression was frightened. "You can't tell anyone," she said. "You have to promise."

"I won't," said Jeremy. He liked Alice. She was honest and straightforward, not trying to hide that she was scared. Of course, Jeremy acknowledged, she was also talking to him. Most girls didn't.

"Promise?" Alice asked.

"Promise," Jeremy said, even though the word felt slimy in his mouth. He was already thinking about the next time he'd see Mr. Carruthers, who might be in his van, somewhere nearby, watching them right now. He decided that he wouldn't tell Mr. Carruthers he'd made contact with Alice. Even though Carruthers had apologized—very convincingly—for the bad stuff he'd done, even though he'd repaired Jeremy's bike and paid for his school lunches and fixed his grades somehow, even though he'd told Jeremy how smart he was, Jeremy didn't trust him. His good deeds didn't erase the bad ones. He worked for the government—for that creepy agency, with its weird eye logo.

Most of all, though, Mr. Carruthers was a grown-up, and Jeremy knew that you could never really trust that tribe. They'd lie to you and tell you it was for your own good; they'd say "you're going to feel a little pinch" before they gave you a shot that would make your arm burn for the rest of the day; they'd say "this hurts me more than it hurts you" when they grounded you or told you that you couldn't watch the scary movie you'd been waiting to see for months or took your phone away. They'd even say "You'll have a great time being a tree in the school play," when it wasn't true at all. The pirates and the Lost Boys got all the big laughs, plus a standing ovation. The trees got nothing.

"What are you thinking?" Alice asked.

Jeremy shook his head. "My friend Jo and I are trying to find out more about Bigfoots in Standish. We found someone who knew one—"

"Who?"

Jeremy told her about their visit to Priscilla Carruthers. "She told us to look in the biggest heart, and we don't know what it means."

Alice looked at him sharply. "What'd she say?"

"Look inside the biggest heart," Jeremy repeated. "We've already talked to, like, the Teacher of the Year and this lady who was in the paper for being a Brownie troop leader, and I've gone through all the topographical maps to see if there's, like, a cave or a rock formation somewhere up in the hills."

Alice was smiling. "The biggest heart," she said.

"What, is that someone at your school?" Jeremy asked. He should have thought along those lines before. A place called the Experimental Center for Love and Learning might have named its dining hall the Biggest Heart, or given a Biggest Heart award to a guidance counselor or something like that. But Alice, still smiling, was shaking her head.

"I know where it is," she said. "And I'll bet you do too."

Jeremy stared at her. There was something teasing at the edge of his memory, something he could almost, but not quite, call to the front of his mind.

"Did you ever go to the Standish Children's Museum?" Alice asked, and, just like that, it clicked into place. "They took us there on a field trip last fall, and I remember that there's a—"

"Giant model of the human heart," Jeremy finished. "Oh my God." He grabbed her by the hands and whirled her into a brief dance that was as enthusiastic as it was clumsy. "You're a genius!"

Alice gave a modest shrug. "We don't even know if I'm right yet. But if there was someone who knew something about Bigfoots in Standish—some kind of expert—doesn't it make sense that whoever it was would work near the forest?"

"The museum makes sense," said Jeremy, who'd been sent there on field trips at least once a year since kindergarten. "There's that whole History of Standish Valley display . . ."

"And the exhibit about native wildlife . . ."

"And if you were trying to find things out . . . ," said Alice.

"You could say, 'I'm from the children's museum,'" said Jeremy. "And everyone would want to help you, because who'd tell a children's museum no?" He grabbed Alice's mittened hand with his gloved one. "Let's go. Right now. Can you go? Do you have to go back to school?"

Alice stopped. Her shoulders slumped. Even the pom-pom on top of her hat looked droopy.

"What?" Jeremy asked.

"Nothing," said Alice. "Only . . . what if it turns out that I am a Bigfoot? Then what? I always thought I was different and that if I found out what I was, then I'd know where to go. I'd have people. But now . . ." She closed her mouth.

"There's other ones out there," he promised. "I saw one once." He showed Alice his film, which she watched with apparent interest, but when it was over, she sighed, and still looked droopy. Jeremy wondered if she was thinking about her cousin, the one who'd suddenly gotten so interested in *The Next Stage*.

"Knowledge is power," he said, which was something his science teacher liked to say.

"I guess," Alice said. Even though she didn't look convinced, she followed him to Jo's house.

"Of course," said Jo, when they told her about their museum theory. "The heart. That has to be it."

Ten minutes later, with Jo and Jeremy on the tandem bike, Jo's walker strapped to the carrier, and Alice on Jeremy's bike, the three of them set out for the Standish Children's Museum, where, luckily, admission was free to anyone with a student ID on school days.

"We close in half an hour," said the lady behind the front desk. Jo assured them that they just needed a quick minute. They got their hands stamped and walked through the quiet, echoing halls, which smelled like dust and school lunches and were filled with glass display cases full of Standish's native flora and fauna.

It was a small museum, nothing like the ones Jeremy had visited in Boston and Philadelphia. Instead of inter-active displays with sound and lights and video and things that kids could do, there were dusty glass cases contain-ing taxidermied birds and squirrels and dioramas about Standish's first settlers. The dioramas, Jeremy noted, hadn't even been updated to show that there had been people liv-ing in the so-called New World long before Columbus and, later, the pilgrims showed up.

He went to the largest diorama, which he remembered from previous visits. It depicted a man in black knee breeches and a black brimmed hat with a musket over his shoulder, standing on top of a hill. Jeremy remembered the cocky tilt of his head, the way his booted foot seemed not to be resting on the ground so much as stomping on it, the presumptiveness of his posture. His attitude was one of ownership, as if he were the king of all he surveyed. Jeremy looked down at the plaque. "Grayson Standish, who settled this town in 1671 and gave Standish its name," he read. He wondered if the Bigfoots had been there when Grayson Standish showed up, if the Bigfoots had helped the new arrivals clear the land and cut the trees, plant and dig and build houses, before the humans decided that the Bigfoots were freaks and drove them into hiding.

"Come on," said Jo, who leaned on her walker and led them down a hallway lined with flickering fluorescent lights, past a display of the native birds of New York—all of them brown or gray or brown and gray, as far as Jeremy could tell—and into the room that held the museum's one decent attraction, the gigantic model of the human heart. The deal was, kids were supposed to pretend that they were red blood cells, and follow the course of the blood through the chambers of the heart, up and down and, finally, out. The last time Jeremy had been in there, he'd felt uncomfortably squashed, and that had been years ago. He looked at Jo dubiously.

"Do you trust me?" she asked. He could see excitement in the crinkled-up corners of her eyes, the way her mouth was lifted in a smile. Alice, meanwhile, was looking doubtfully at the narrow entrance, maybe wondering if she'd get stuck.

Jeremy scrubbed his hands through his brown hair—too long, he could tell, and his mother, again, hadn't remembered to give him money for a haircut—then shrugged and followed Jo up the staircase, with Alice behind him. He could hear the sound of a heartbeat booming in his ears. There were hidden speakers built into the walls of the model, to make it realistic, he remembered, but had it always been this dark? At least it didn't smell like blood, Jeremy thought, although it did have the unpleasant tang of the inside of an overripe sneaker.

They climbed up into a ventricle—at least, Jeremy thought it was a ventricle—and then Jo whispered for light. Jeremy and Alice pulled their phones out of their pockets, using their flashlight apps to cast bright beams of illumination, and Jo ran her hands carefully against the wall.

"There's people coming," Alice whispered.

Jeremy could hear two chattering toddlers and a mother, telling them to be good. Then Jo pressed something on the wall, and suddenly Jeremy could see seams in the wall of the heart—the outline of a door.

"Push," whispered Jo . . . and, when they did, the door swung open. Jo slipped through it. Jeremy followed her, and Alice followed him, and then there was sudden silence as Alice closed the door, and the noise of the heartbeat ceased.

"Well, hello!" called a man's booming voice.

Jeremy blinked. They'd entered what looked like a storage area, a high-ceilinged room filled with the museum's castoffs. He saw a skeleton missing a femur, rows of trilobite fossils on a wheeled cart, glass cases filled with insects and dusty butterflies on pins . . . and then, ambling toward them, a large, smiling man with hands the size of loaves of bread and a white lab coat as big as a ship's sail.

Jo was staring at him with her mouth hanging slightly open. "You're Marcus Johansson," she said.

The man nodded, giving them all a friendly smile and spreading those big hands wide. "Guilty as charged."

Jo looked at Jeremy and Alice. "Marcus Johansson," she repeated, like she'd said the name of a president or

a pop star. Alice looked at Jeremy, who shrugged. "Dr. Johansson—he's an anthropologist? The most famous paranormal scientist in the country? He used to work at Harvard, and then he started his own research center in Washington—"

"And then I fell out of favor with the government," Dr. Johansson said with a smile that sat easily on his big face. "New administration. They decided they'd rather spend their money on tracking the size of the crowds at the president's speeches, than on little green men from outer space."

Now Alice was nodding. "I heard about this. There were hearings in front of Congress, right?"

Jeremy remembered: the same man, maybe the tiniest bit smaller, in a suit and a tie instead of the lab coat, his tightly curled hair cut shorter and his voice rising as he leaned into the microphone and said, "If we are committed to exploring the outer reaches of space, why not be just as brave about understanding the wonders inhabiting our own world, hiding in plain sight?" He wondered if Skip Carruthers and the Department of Official Inquiry knew about this man. He'd have to be careful, the next time he saw Mr. Carruthers, not to tell him about the secret behind the museum's heart.

"There were indeed," said Dr. Johansson.

He held out his hand, first to Alice, and then Jeremy felt his own palms and fingers swallowed up in what felt like an ocean of warm flesh, with a grip that was surprisingly gentle.

Marcus Johansson was at least six inches taller than Jeremy's oldest brother, who was already six foot two, and he was big everywhere, broad-shouldered and blocky, with a big, round belly and thighs the size of Jeremy's entire torso. His skin was warm brown. A curly black beard curved from one earlobe to the other, and his little round glasses almost disappeared into his cheeks when he smiled. A gold wedding band looked like it was sinking into the flesh of his left hand's ring finger, like a doughnut disappearing into a vat of frosting. Jeremy wondered how big that band would have been if Marcus could have taken it off and whether he'd had to have someone make it up special for him.

He greeted Jo last, bowing slightly over her hand.

"We emailed," she said, still sounding starstruck. "You probably don't remember."

"Of course I do," he said. "You asked some very perceptive questions about migratory patterns of Wahkiakum tribes."

Jo looked like she was going to faint as Dr. Johansson led them across the long room. "Time is short," he said, "and our enemies are all around us."

Jeremy felt a quiver of unease, like a feather brushing against his back. *He knows,* he thought as he followed Dr. Johansson past a model of a Neanderthal, one of a velociraptor, a long table with ten seats pushed up around it, and a vending machine in the corner. It was dark, with all the high windows covered by shades, and a little spooky. Jeremy told himself that there was no way Dr. Johansson could know about Skip Carruthers. Nobody knew. Jeremy hadn't told anyone anything. He'd kept his mouth shut.

"Have a seat," said Dr. Johansson. They'd come to a fireplace, with a fire smoking inside of it, and a fancy-looking carpet and armchairs and a couch. Everyone found a seat, and Dr. Johansson passed around a cookie tin, then stood and started flicking switches.

When the lights were on, the room looked a lot less scary. A long wooden table stood against the wall. It held two laptops and a desktop computer, an old-fashioned-looking microscope, and an open family-size bag of pretzels. There were photographs on the wall, one of an incrementally smaller Marcus, in cap and gown, standing between two beaming people who were probably his parents, then another of a Marcus with no beard and bushier hair, in a different-colored cap and gown, with the same two people, only the man was less bald and the woman wasn't wearing glasses. The third picture showed someone—Marcus, probably—in a football helmet and a green-and-silver uniform, his body airborne and apparently floating over the field, with one muscly, tattooed arm outstretched and one big hand cradling the ball against his body.

"College," he said, tapping the young-Marcus cap-and-gown picture. "Lo these many years ago."

"So this is where you've been," said Jo, who still looked starry-eyed.

"Do you live here?" Alice blurted. Jeremy looked at her, feeling grateful, because he'd been wondering the same thing himself.

"Sometimes I do. Bedroom and kitchen are back there," he said, pointing toward a door beside the fireplace. "When my friends and I saw which way the wind was blowing—when we realized that our new president not only wasn't going to invest in the paranormal but he might even try to persuade me to use what I knew for . . . well, let's just say the wrong causes—I thought it would be prudent to keep myself"—he gestured at the room around them—"out of the public eye. I have some friends who still believe in the cause, and I had a long-standing relationship with the museum. When they built their addition, I was able to talk them into putting up a false front. On paper, on the blueprints, this"—he waved his hand around the expansive rooms—"is just marked 'storage.' And so here I am."

"But doesn't the government know that Standish is one of the places where people say they've seen Bigfoots?" Jo asked. "Wouldn't they look for you here?"

"I'm sure they've looked, but they haven't found me yet," said the doctor. He took a seat in the immense leather chair and picked up his pretzels. The seat was shiny with use, and the wood creaked gently as he sat. Jeremy watched as he examined all three of them, his gaze shifting slowly from Jo to Jeremy, and then to Alice. "I guess I should ask how you found me," he said.

Jo was the one who told the story of their meeting with Priscilla Carruthers, how she'd told them to look in the biggest heart, and how Alice had been the one to figure out what her directions had meant.

"Ah, Pris," Dr. Johansson said, his smile widening. "She's always been a friend to the cause. Gave us free access to all those woods her family owns. Donated enough money to the museum to make all of this possible." He stretched his arms over his head, then tilted the pretzel bag toward Alice. "Nice going," he said.

Jeremy and Jo and Alice exchanged a glance. *Do we tell him?* Jeremy wondered, before deciding that it was up to Alice to tell him—or not—that she was possibly part Bigfoot.

Alice took a pretzel. Dr. Johansson dipped his hand into the pretzel bag. There was barely room for it to fit. "Anyone?" he said, offering the bag to Jo, then Jeremy, who each took a pretzel to be polite. "Sorry," he said. "I was just finishing a second snack." He crunched a pretzel into nothingness in two big bites, then looked at Jo.

"Let's get caught up. Tell me what you guys know about Bigfoots," he said. He still sounded friendly, but his gaze had sharpened.

Jo and Jeremy took turns talking. Jeremy described the Bigfoot he'd glimpsed in the woods when he was ten. Jo talked about how she'd spent a lot of time in hospitals, and how her online wanderings had led her to websites that claimed that Standish had once been a hotbed of Bigfoots.

"And you?" asked the doctor, looking at Alice, who

shifted in her seat. She hadn't taken her coat off, Jeremy saw, and her hat was still snugged down tight over her ears. "What's your interest in our large-footed friends?"

"Science project," Alice mumbled, with her eyes on her boots. Even if Jeremy hadn't known that she was lying, her flat voice and expressionless face would have been a giveaway.

Dr. Johansson crossed the room. Knees creaking, he knelt down in front of her and took her hands. "Hey," he said. His voice was quiet, pitched for Alice's ears alone. "I get it. I know."

"You know what?" Alice said, in a voice that wobbled a little.

"I know what it's like to feel like you don't fit in anywhere. Like you're not like other kids. Like nobody understands you." He gestured down at himself. "I was six feet tall when I was ten years old, and I was so heavy that they had to bring in a special scale to the nurse's office when they weighed us. Whatever you've got going on, I bet I've got a story just like it."

Alice lifted her head, and Jeremy could see that her eyes were glittery with tears. "I thought I found a friend," she whispered. "And then these guys said . . . they said I wasn't human, so I thought . . ." She reached into her coat pocket, pulled out an envelope, and slipped a picture out from inside of it. Jeremy peered over the doctor's shoulder, but all he could see was a lady in a hospital bed with a baby in her arms. "It's from my baby book," said Alice.

"Uh-huh," said Dr. Johansson, getting to his feet. "Mm-hmm."

He held out his hand for the picture. When Alice turned it over, he carried it to a scanner on the long wooden table, then sat down. A few keystrokes, and the picture was on his screen. Jeremy could make out details: the lady's sweaty hair, the tubes running from both of her arms, the crowd of white-coated figures gathered around her. With surprising delicacy, the doctor raised his large fingers to the screen, pinching at the image, then spreading his fingers apart. The picture bloomed in close-up. Jeremy could see flowers in a vase on the bedside table, a plastic pitcher of water, a stack of papers . . . and a familiar letterhead.

He heard Jo's indrawn breath, heard the doctor grunt, then say, "Uh-huh," as he felt his own mouth go dry. The top page on the bedside pile said Upland Community Hospital and appeared to have information about the new baby, her length and her weight and something called her Apgar score. It was the page underneath it that had caught everyone's attention, the page topped by the words "Department of Official Inquiry" and the unmistakable logo of a staring, all-seeing eye.

"Our friends in Washington seem to have attended your arrival," said Marcus, sounding grim. Alice opened her mouth, like she was about to say something, but then she just shook her head.

"And looky here," said Marcus. His expression was eager, eyes wide behind the glasses, looking like Jo when she'd just pounced on some new tidbit of information on the Internet. His chair squeaked as his fingers rattled at the keyboard. Jeremy watched the screen as the doctor did something with his mouse, zooming in tighter and tighter on the single swath of Alice's skin that the blanket left exposed.

"You see that?" he asked.

"Oh, wow," Jo breathed. "Is that . . . ?"

"Fur," said Alice. Her voice was barely a whisper. "I had fur." She sat down, yanked up the leg of her pants, and examined her (completely hairless, to Jeremy's eyes) ankle, first the left one, then the right. "Where'd it go?"

"We can add that to our list of questions." Marcus stood up and gave Alice's shoulder a squeeze. "You all right?"

"Fine," Alice said, with her eyes still on her legs. "Except that those people—these government people—they know about me." Her voice was tiny, almost inaudible. She took her picture off the scanner, put it in her pocket, and huddled in her armchair, with her arms around her knees and her chin resting on top of them. "A lady in the picture, I met her when I was six. She said she was an educational consultant. She was supposed to help my parents figure out where to send me to school. But then I saw her in the picture, and I went to see her, followed her, when I was home for break. She went to an office." She pointed at the screen. "Their office. The Department of Official Inquiry."

"Are you sure?" asked Dr. Johansson, and Alice nodded. "I saw the name and the eye. It was on the door. And you couldn't even get off the elevator on their floor. There were guards by the door, and you needed a special ID card to get in." She stopped, swallowed, and rubbed her eyes. "They've known about me since I was born."

For a minute, they all stood in a circle around her, Marcus with his hand on one shoulder, Jo with her hand on the other, and Jeremy with his hands in his pockets because he didn't know where to put them.

"It's okay," said Marcus. "We're the good guys, and it's a good thing you found us. We'll keep you safe. I promise."

Alice was shivering, shaking her head. She'd pulled

off her hat and unfastened her hair so that big chunks of it were hanging like curtains in front of her face. Jeremy thought that she was crying. He didn't blame her. If he was the one who'd walked into a giant heart, found a hidden office, and learned that a shadowy government organization had been keeping track of him since birth, he'd probably be running around screaming or begging his parents to get him a new identity and a new place to live.

Marcus got up and made them all hot chocolate, and Jo murmured softly to Alice, saying things that Jeremy couldn't quite hear while he sat feeling useless and uncomfortable and more like a boy than he ever had in his life. He imagined that his betrayal was somehow visible on his face, like Jo or Marcus or even Alice herself would be able to look at him and know that he'd been talking (*not just talking*, his mind whispered, *but conspiring*) with one of the government agents who'd been trying to find Alice.

Finally, Marcus came back with three paper cups and another bag of pretzels.

"Okay," he said, settling his bulk back into his enormous chair. "Story time." He leaned back, staring up at the ceiling. "Once upon a time, round about nineteen fifty-two, the government got very interested in the possibility of other life-forms. Not in outer space, where most of our previous efforts had been focused, but right here on good old mother earth. They formed the Department of Official Inquiry, which began as a branch of the CIA. First director was a guy named Milford Carruthers from right here in Standish. He was a Bigfoot believer from way back. A very charismatic, very persuasive, very wealthy guy. He had a sighting of his own." He waited for Jo and Jeremy to nod, and said, "After that, he went from being a believer to something more along the lines of a fanatic. He spent the last years of his life in the forest, looking, and when he died . . . when he died, he left almost all of his money to the government, to fund the agency that was tasked with finding Bigfoots."

Marcus told them how, under Carruthers's direction, the Department hired the smartest historians and anthropologists to research what they were calling Hidden Creatures. "Your vampires, your zombies, your leprechauns and what-have-you," he said. "They zeroed in on what we know as Bigfoots as being the most plausible. Most of the others, they had nothing but stories and rumors and so-and-so's great-great-great-grandfather who once swore he saw a Yeti in a snowstorm, or somebody's grandma who said a leprechaun stole her dancing slippers from next to the lake. With the Bigfoots, not only did they have Carruthers's firsthand account, but the same elements to the stories kept coming up. Same settings, same descriptions of the creatures. Whether it was the Pacific Northwest or upstate New York, you'd get reports of tall, hairy creatures who lived in the woods but who were intelligent, who had language, who seemed curious about our world, and who—and here's the important part—were exceptionally long-lived."

Jeremy, who'd read some of these stories and who'd heard about this from Skip Carruthers, nodded along.

"So the search went on for years. Decades with nothing to show but footprints and bent branches, and weird footprints on Snickers wrappers." He smiled. "It seems like they really like Snickers bars. Eventually the people who wrote the Department's checks got tired of waiting. Instead of anthropologists and ethnobiologists, they hired ex-military people. Trackers. Hunters." He paused, his eyes back on the ceiling. "Soldiers."

Alice shivered. Jeremy drummed his fingers on the knees of his jeans.

"How'd they get from wanting to find a Bigfoot to wanting to hunt one down?" Jo asked. "Why was it such a big deal?"

Marcus pointed at her with one of those enormous,

deft fingers. "Officially—as far as there was an official record—they thought that these creatures might be a threat, and they were investigating to keep America safe. Less officially . . ." He looked up at the ceiling again. "There was some talk that their physical attributes— their strength, their longevity—might somehow translate to humans, and if we studied their biology, if we could get a sample of their blood, it might give us some insight into our own diseases. But if you were running a government, what would you do with a creature that was intelligent, with incredible size and speed and strength? Creatures that could heal themselves quickly, lived so long that they were close to immortal, and were almost impossible to kill?"

As the veteran of half a hundred movies about aliens and mutants and superheroes, Jeremy had a guess, but it was Alice who answered, in a small, bleak voice.

"You'd want them for the army," she said. "You would want them to fight our wars."

"Give the lady a prize," said Marcus.

For a minute there was silence so complete that Jeremy imagined he could hear the dust settle on the old exhibits. Alice rocked forward, still with her hands wrapped around her knees. "But I don't have any powers," she said.

"Unless breaking everything you touch is a power. Or getting kicked out of seven different schools. Or not having any friends."

The chair gave its loudest squeal yet as Marcus shifted, then reached over to his desk to pick up a notebook and a pen.

"Ever broken a bone?" Marcus asked her.

Alice shook her head.

"Needed stitches?" he asked.

Another head shake.

"Concussion?" he asked. "Any childhood illnesses? Measles, mumps, chicken pox?"

"I'm totally normal," she said, her voice small and bleak. "I'm not . . . I can't do anything special."

Alice thumped her heels against the floor, again and again, beating out a furious tattoo.

"You know what? I bet I'm a dud. Or a squib, or whatever you call a Bigfoot who isn't really a Bigfoot."

"Hey," said Jo, and Dr. Johansson moved to pat her shoulder. Jeremy remembered Alice running through the forest, ducking under branches, leaping over streams, lifting and tossing logs out of her way like they were nothing. "You're a good runner," he said.

Alice gave him a small, sad smile. "I'm a giant klutz,"

she said, and Jeremy felt like someone had tied a thread around the center of his heart and cinched it tight.

Alice pulled at her hair again and then, with a deliberate gesture, she pushed it away from her face, tucking it behind her ears so that they could see her eyes and mouth again, and sat up straight, with her feet on the floor. "Whatever Bigfoots can do, whatever powers they have, I don't have them. I'm just a regular kid." She looked at the doctor, hands out, palms up. "Or else they'd have taken me away, right? This Department? If they know where I am, and they know what I am, they could just take me any time they wanted."

"Maybe, maybe not," Marcus said. "Did you move around a lot?"

Alice shook her head. "I've gone to eight different schools, but I've lived in the same place my whole life."

"Never changed your name?" Marcus asked. Alice shook her head. "How about a makeover? Did your parents ever, I don't know, give you a haircut for no good reason?"

Alice touched her unruly pile of hair and gave a snort of not-laughter. She was sitting up straight, and her expression was resolute. She looked, Jeremy thought, like the figure on the bow of a ship, bravely facing the elements, with her hair flying out behind her.

"Could be you've got powers you don't even know about," Marcus said. "I've got some people who could do a full work-up, but they're in New York City."

"Tell me where to go," Alice said. "Ask them how soon they can see me. I want to know where I came from," she said, in a voice that was ringing and clear. "I want to know the truth."

# CHAPTER 9

*Millie*

WHEN THE NO-FUR NAMED JESSICA JARVIS had proposed her plan, Millie had agreed only because she couldn't think of another way of getting a video submitted before her time ran out. She'd wanted Alice to help her, but Alice hadn't wanted to do it. Even if she had, Millie imagined that it would be frustrating, having, every day, to convince Alice that she looked a-okay, that Millie could film her and no one would think she looked weird.

Jessica had no such doubts about herself, which was good. Still, Millie hadn't actually been convinced that it could work. Maybe Jessica wouldn't be able to sync-lip convincingly. Maybe Millie wouldn't figure out a way to stay hidden while singing loudly enough for people to believe that her voice was coming from Jessica's mouth. Or maybe—the most likely possibility—the judges at *The Next Stage* were used to people trying to fool them in precisely this way and would immediately recognize that the girl who was moving her lips was not the girl who was actually singing.

The deadline for submitting audition videos was five p.m. on Friday, and it was after three by the time Jessica had decided on an outfit (a short gray skirt, a gray-and-pink striped sweater, pale gray tights, and soft suede boots). Luckily, Jessica knew the words to "Defying Gravity" from *Wicked*. "My parents take me to see all the shows," she'd said, and Millie had almost swooned with jealousy, imagining what it would be like to sit in a Broadway theater and watch actors perform the shows.

They ran through the song twice. Then Jessica stood in the corner of the seventh-grade learners' cabin, Millie crouched down beneath her, with her fur smoothed down and her arms held tight against her sides. Alice held her phone, filming Jessica mouthing the words as Millie sang them. They did it three times, then uploaded the first attempt, which they all agreed was the best one. Millie noticed that Alice sounded less than enthusiastic as she said, "Yeah, it's great!" Millie promised herself that, as soon as the video had been accepted, she'd ask Alice what was wrong and reassure her that they were still friends, that it was the two of them who were a team, and that Jessica was just a convenience, a means to an end. She would tell Alice about everything she'd seen and heard—that she'd heard her mother crying, saying that they hadn't done enough about something or someone, and together they would figure out what. Millie dreamed that she could even spend the night in the cabin, tucked up tight in one of the bags-of-sleep, and they could whisper together all night long, even though she knew her mother would never ever allow it.

Except, somehow, as soon as *The Next Stage* emailed to say "Congratulations! Your audition has been ACCEPTED!" Millie had been so busy dancing around the room with Jessica, the two of them shouting with delight, that she hadn't even noticed that Alice had slipped away. Then Millie had had to hurry back home before anyone noticed she was gone, so she didn't get to say good-bye.

And then, the very next morning, she snuck Alice's laptop into her bed to check her email, and there was an actual message from an actual producer at the show, writing to say that she had made the first cut and that her audition tape would go live on the website at noon eastern standard time and would be up on the show's website for the next forty-eight hours. "If YOUR SONG is one of our TOP SIX VOTE GETTERS, you'll be MOVING ON to the NEXT ROUND . . . and, just maybe, to THE NEXT STAGE!" the email read.

So of course there was nothing else to do but make an excuse to her parents about feeling too unwell to go to her lessons, and then lie in bed in a frenzy of impatience as her mother dosed her with goldenrod tea, waiting until she could finally sneak out of her bedroom window and go racing through the woods as fast as she could. She then waited underneath the windowsill of the Lodge until the learners filed in for lunch, so that she could report this unbelievably exciting new development to Alice and Jessica. Jessica's delight touched off another round of shrieking and dancing around. When Jessica left, to make the rounds of the dining hall and ask the other learners to vote for her ("Yes," Millie heard her saying, in a voice full of false modesty, "I do have a lovely voice!"), Alice just gave her a quiet "Congratulations."

"Alice," Millie said. "Are you all right?"

"Fine," said Alice, without meeting Millie's eyes. "I'm just busy."

"Are you wanting your laptop back?"

"Keep it," said Alice. "My parents get me a new one every Christmas."

Millie reached into her knapsack, meaning to give her friend the dried plum hand-pies she'd packed, but Jessica grabbed her arm and pulled her into a book-lined room with a fireplace—*a liberry,* Millie thought.

"We have to start strategizing," Jessica announced. "Alice, we need you!" she singsonged through the open door, and Alice came slouching in, with her eyes on the floor, like she was carrying something heavy on her back.

"What do you mean about stratergizing?" Millie inquired.

"Look," said Jessica, as she loaded *The Next Stage*'s home page on her iPad. At noon, just as the email had promised, twelve new videos had appeared beneath a banner that read "Hot New Talent!"

Jessica clicked, and Benjamin Burton's deep and terrifying voice filled the room. "Welcome to *The Next Stage.* Take a look at today's twelve competitors. Once you've seen their audition tapes, we invite you to step into our virtual voting booth and cast your ballot for your favorite. The top six will advance to the next round."

Jessica clicked the link to their audition, and Millie

heard her own voice, high and sweet, fill the room. Her singing sounded fine as ever, but when it was paired with the image of a beautiful girl moving her mouth along with the words, somehow it sounded even better. It didn't make any sense, but it was true.

Then she looked underneath Jessica's image, at the vote totals. She—they—had thirty-seven votes. The competitor next to them, a hula dancer named Leilani, already had over a thousand votes. The accordion player next to her had twice as many as that, and the six-year-old magician right above him had somehow amassed more than five thousand.

"How has this happened?" Millie asked as she felt her heart plummet and her hands go cold with disappointment and fury. "How can people be voting with such a quickness! They haven't even had time to watch all of the auditions!"

"People get their friends to vote for them," Jessica explained.

Millie peered at the totals, then shook her head. "I am not believing that this person has"—she looked at the number underneath the singer in the top left-hand corner—"seven hundred and eighty-two friends."

"Not *friend* friends," said Jessica. "Social media friends."

"What," Millie asked, "is social media?"

Jessica rolled her eyes and muttered something about homeschooled losers. "Okay. Social media is, like, where people go online to talk about things."

"Like a vbirtual waterdb coolerdb," snuffled Taley, who was curled up in an armchair in front of the fireplace.

Millie didn't know what a water cooler was and wasn't entirely sure what "virtual" meant in this context. So she sat, listening closely, as Jessica explained.

"This is Facebook," Jessica began, showing Millie a website that appeared to be videos of cooking and pictures of weddings or vacations at the beach or No-Furs doing skiing. "It's mostly for old people. Your mom's probably on Facebook."

*My mom definitely is not,* thought Millie. She looked over at Alice, hoping to exchange a knowing glance with the one No-Fur who knew the truth about who she was, but Alice was staring at the fire, and Millie couldn't tell if she was listening.

"Twitter," said Jessica, drawing Millie's attention back to the screen, which was now full of mostly words, with far fewer pictures and videos. "Also for old people, but at least some of them are old people who watch TV." She showed Millie *The Next Stage*'s accounts on the websites, pointing out how many thousands of friends or fans or followers the show had amassed.

Finally, Jessica opened up InstaChat, which she claimed was by far the most popular social-media website, especially with kids and teenagers and, most important, with *The Next Stage* viewers. "See, look at the Amazing Marvin," she said. She hit a few buttons, and there was the magician, a little boy in a black silk top hat, the same one he wore on *The Next Stage* page. "He's already got seventeen thousand fans."

"But how?" Millie asked. This did not strike her as fair at all, if the people she was competing against could simply call on the reserves of admirers they'd already collected.

"He joined the site two years ago, and he's been posting a new video every week," said Jessica.

Millie moaned out loud. "We'll never catch up," she said.

"Maybe not," said Jessica. "But we have to try."

They spent the next few hours online, building an InstaChat page, posting their audition video, and then recording another song.

"Now," Jessica said, "we have to start liking people."

Millie was starting to feel faintish from hunger. It had been almost three hours since she'd eaten the last of the jelly rollies and hand-pies she'd put in her knapsack. As she watched, Jessica went back to the Amazing Marvin's page and clicked "like."

"Why are we liking him if we want people to vote for us?" Millie asked.

"Watch," said Jessica. Sure enough, within a minute, the Amazing Marvin had "liked" them back, and then a slow trickle of his friends and fans and followers made their way first to Millie's InstaChat page, and then over to *The Next Stage*'s virtual voting booth.

"Now we just have to like everyone we can find who's auditioning or who's a fan of the show with more than five thousand—"

"I am sorry," said Millie, whose head was whirling, "but I am now requiring some foods." When Jessica stared, Millie touched her face-fur and said, "It is one of the symptoms of the medical condition I have. I need to eat."

"I'll go find something," said Alice, and left the liberry without a look back. *She is angry,* Millie thought . . . but then she somehow accidentally deleted a link that she'd posted on another competitor's Facebook page, and got so involved in trying to fix it that she forgot to ask Alice what was wrong and barely remembered to thank her for the lentil salad and bread and cheese that she brought

back from the dining hall. By the time the sun was setting, she and Jessica had 9,311 votes, the fifth-highest tally
on the page.

It wasn't enough.

"We need to post new videos and photos every day,"
Jessica said, without looking up from the screen. "At least
once a day. That's important. And we have to friend and
fan as many people as we can."

Millie nodded, knowing that if her parents discovered that she had Alice's computer and learned that, in
spite of their warnings, she had been consorting with the
No-Furs, that she was visiting the school every day, that
she'd let herself be recorded and put on-the-line—even
if it was only her voice, and no one could see her—and
that she had sent the audition in to a national No-Fur
contest and was ardently, actively trying to get people to
vote for it, it would be enough for them to set her feet on
the road, to excommunicate her from the Yare Tribe and
make sure she had no place in the world.

"Start packing," Jessica said. "And start figuring out
some kind of story to tell these people when we get
picked."

"If we get picked," Millie corrected. She was surprised to realize that a part of her did not want to get

picked at all, did not want to have to figure out a story to explain her fur and her claws, did not want to have to venture into the No-Furs' biggest city. Already, everything seemed so much harder than she'd imagined, when she'd thought that all you needed was a pretty singing voice. Now it was clear that a good voice was only the first part of it. You needed a pretty face to go with the pretty voice. You needed lots of clothes and lots of songs and lots of friends you'd never met to vote for you. And what if, at the end, she stood alone on the stage, with confetti raining down and Benjamin Burton himself presenting her with a check for a million dollars, only there was no one to celebrate with her? What if winning the competition meant losing her friend, her Tribe, her family?

*This is what I wanted,* Millie thought as she trudged back around the lake, feeling the cold seep through the soles of her boots and the wind bite through her face-fur. *This was my dream,* she thought as the howling wind disguised the sound of the footsteps padding along after her, and the deepening shadows hid the tall, cloaked figure that had followed Millie all the way around the lake and stayed behind her almost until she slipped through her front door.

# CHAPTER 10

## Alice

ALICE HAD THOUGHT THAT MILLIE WAS preoccupied about getting her audition video sent in. Once she and Jessica made it through the first elimination round, though, she longed for the days when Millie had merely been preoccupied, instead of obsessed.

Every time she could steal across the lake, Millie was in their cabin, sitting with Jessica, the two of them huddling over some screen, clicking and liking, fanning and friending. Or they were standing in front of Jessica's closet, trying to select her next outfit, or they were scrolling through Riya's and Taley's iPods, trying to figure out their next song. Alice, who'd felt invisible her entire life, had never felt more ignored or less important. It had always hurt, but it hurt so much worse when the person making you feel like nothing had once made you feel like the most special and interesting person in the world.

*Some friend,* Alice thought as she heard Millie and Jessica laughing at something amusing they'd found online. Possibly some joke of the Amazing Marvin's. Millie hadn't noticed Alice's absence the day she'd gone to the Standish Children's Museum with Jeremy and Jo, and she'd never asked whether Alice had figured out what Jeremy had meant when he'd said she wasn't human.

*It doesn't matter,* Alice told herself, pulling the scrap of paper out of her pocket, where she'd kept it ever since Dr. Johansson had given it to her. He'd written "Wayne Clinic" on top, and then the ten digits of its Manhattan telephone number. "No address," Dr. Johansson had said. "They're underground."

"Like you?" Alice asked. She was thinking of his hidden office and the Yare's sod houses, tucked beneath the hills, but the doctor explained that, in their case, "underground" didn't mean a basement or behind a giant heart. "They don't exactly have a fixed location. You call, and you tell them your name and that I sent you, and they'll tell you where to go."

She'd wanted to talk to Millie about Dr. Johansson and his secret office and the clinic, but Millie was too busy to do more than nod at her before she and Jessica hurried off to do some *Next Stage*–related task. Millie wasn't a real friend. Millie hadn't believed her, or even wanted to admit the possibility, when Alice had told her that she might be Yare. Probably all she'd wanted was Alice's laptop and a way to get closer to pretty, popular Jessica Jarvis.

But once Alice had proof, Millie wouldn't be able to deny it. She would have to take Alice to her village, to the place where Alice really belonged. Maybe they'd be friends again, once Millie knew that Alice, deep down, was like her, not like one of the No-Furs who hunted and tormented her people. Or maybe Alice would find other friends in other Yare villages. Millie had told her that there were more of them, all over the country. Maybe Alice could travel around, from Vermont to West Virginia, meeting the different Yare, finally finding a real home.

But to get there, she had to make the call. Her hand was shaking only a little bit as she punched in the numbers, then pressed the phone tight against her ear.

"Hello?"

Alice had been expecting a more formal salutation, a

"This is the Wayne Clinic," a "Good afternoon," or a "How can I help you?" Not this whispery, somehow greedy old man's voice. She imagined a bald head and age-spotted hands, a bony, slumped body leaning over the receiver behind an otherwise-bare desk. She pictured him sitting there, alone, day after day, just waiting for that phone to ring . . . maybe in an office in a New York City skyscraper with an all-seeing eye etched on the glass door.

"Hello?" he said again, and now he sounded both greedy and annoyed. "Who is this?"

*You're being silly,* Alice told herself. "My name is Alice Mayfair."

"Alice," the man said, except "hissed" would more accurately reflect the way he spoke. He sounded pleased. Alice felt terrified. "Al-isssss."

Without thinking, Alice shifted her thumb to hover above the button that would end the call. Something was wrong with this man, something was weird about the way he sounded, and even though Jeremy and Jo had been friendly, and Dr. Johansson had been nothing but reassuring and kind, this didn't feel right.

But Alice didn't hang up. She no longer trusted her instincts. She'd believed that Millie was her friend, and that had been wrong. She'd thought Miss Merriweather was just an educational consultant who wanted to help her, and that had been wrong too. She'd thought Jeremy and Jo were the bad guys, but they'd ended up being more help to her than Millie had. And so she told the voice in her head that was insisting *Hang up now* to shut up and let her go about her business.

"Dr. Marcus Johansson gave me this number," she said. "I would like to come in to be tested."

"Of course, my dear, of course," said the man. His endearment sounded the way a dead snakeskin that Alice had once touched felt, somehow dry and slippery at the same time; scaly and strange and entirely repellent. Also, the man hadn't asked what Alice wanted to be tested for. *Maybe this clinic only tests for one thing,* thought Alice. "How soon would be convenient?"

Alice named the date of *The Next Stage* auditions, thinking that she and Jessica could team up with a lie and ask Phil and Lori for permission to leave campus. She could even volunteer her apartment as a place to sleep. Her parents wouldn't be home—during their call last week, her mother had mentioned a business trip to Japan that her father would be taking and how she herself would be at a retreat in the Berkshires.

"No sooner?" asked the man, and now Alice was positive

that she was hearing disappointment. Disappointment and greed. *Hang up,* said the voice in her head, which was getting even louder.

"Who are you?" she blurted, even though she hadn't planned on asking. "Are you one of the doctors?"

The old man chuckled. "I'm nobody special. No one who need concern you. A lowly receptionist." It sounded like some kind of inside joke, the kind Alice hated, where the person talking knew why it was funny and the person listening had no clue. "Are you certain you can't come sooner?"

"Sorry," Alice said. "I'm in school."

"Of course, my dear, of course. So we'll see you in three weeks. The day of your appointment, we'll text you our location."

"Okay," said Alice. "Do you need my number?"

"We have it," said the man. "Take care of yourself," he added. Normally, that was just a polite way to end a conversation, only somehow it didn't sound like a pleasantry. It sounded like a demand, like this man would hunt her down and hurt her if he found out that Alice hadn't been flossing her teeth or sleeping eight hours a night.

*He wants me,* Alice thought. Only that wasn't quite it. He wanted something from her, but what? She was just a kid, and even if she was half-Yare, she didn't have any of the Yare's special strengths or abilities. Doctors had been measuring her, testing her abilities, taking her blood, for as long as she could remember, and nothing had ever come of it. Still, she was reminded of the Graeae from the Greek mythology that the learners had studied in the fall, the three old women who only had one eye and one tooth between them and had to pass them back and forth. *He wants my eyes,* was what she thought. But that was crazy. Her eyes were as ordinary as the rest of her.

"I will," Alice promised, and then the line was dead.

Instead of going back to her cabin, Alice walked into the woods, moving automatically along the path that she'd run dozens of times, as fall had slipped into winter, as the dirt had been covered with leaves, and then the leaves had been covered with snow. Those runs always soothed her, the way her feet would pound out a rhythm, the way she'd pant, her breath catching like a fishhook in her side, and how she'd push through the pain, her muscles swelling with blood, hair sweaty, cheeks flushed, mind clear, thinking of nothing but the next step she'd take, the next breath she'd pull into her lungs. *The truth will set you free* was something that Lori and Phil told them all the time, when they were urging the learners to be honest about who had stolen Phil's blue hair dye or who had posted a comment reading "PLEASE SEND REAL FOOD" on the Center's InstaChat page underneath a picture of vegan shepherd's pie.

Once Alice knew the truth about herself, she would be free. She could thank her parents for taking care of her, and she could even thank her former friend Millie for inadvertently, accidentally helping her to learn who she really was. Then she'd march herself off into the woods like that guy Thoreau whose book they'd read in English class, only, unlike Thoreau, she would find her people instead of solitude. When she went into the woods she would never, ever come back.

# CHAPTER 11

*Jeremy*

"WELL?" ASKED MR. CARRUTHERS.

Jeremy was still trying to catch his breath. He held up one finger, feeling Mr. Carruthers's impatience filling up the van like a bad smell. Every week for the last three weeks, at least once, maybe twice, Jeremy would be riding his bike home from school when he would hear the throaty hum of the van behind him. His first instinct was always to pedal away as fast as he could . . . but what good would that do him? He'd tried that once, and all he'd gotten were ripped pants and a smashed bike and the familiar humiliation that had accompanied him for his entire life. It was easier, he'd learned, to lean his bike against a tree or a telephone pole, climb into the van, and give Mr. Carruthers a few tidbits of information, some little tastes of truth.

That had worked the first few times, when he'd seemed content to hear that Jeremy was watching the Experimental Center, that he'd seen the little gray one crossing the lake, or that he'd caught a glimpse of the big one in the forest. Jeremy would even toss in a little misdirection: how he was almost certain that the big one had been heading to Mount Standish, or how he'd started leaving Snickers bars under the trees and how they'd always be gone the next day.

"Good work," Carruthers would say, making notes of what Jeremy had told him, or "Keep trying!" But as the days had turned into weeks, Mr. Carruthers's patience had evaporated. He wanted Jeremy to make contact, or at least find out where the little gray one was going when she crossed the lake. So far, Jeremy had said that he'd tried, and failed, and Mr. Carruthers hadn't complained . . . only now, it seemed, Jeremy had come to the end of the man's patience.

When he climbed into the van, there weren't pleasantries, or even a "hello," let alone an offer of hot chocolate like Jeremy had gotten on his first visit.

"I need some information," Carruthers said, leaning so close that Jeremy could see the strands of gray in his hair and could smell stale coffee and cinnamon gum on his breath. Mr. Carruthers made his lips move into the semblance of a smile, but the wrinkly skin around his eyes didn't wrinkle. "You understand, it's not me, it's my bosses," he said. "They're paying to keep me in this crappy—" He caught himself. "In this *little* town for months. You know there are Bigfoots out there. I know there are Bigfoots out there. But if I can't give them something, some kind of substantive proof, a photograph or a footprint, I'm going to find myself in Alaska for the rest of the winter because some kid thought he saw the abominable snowman on a ski slope." He gave Jeremy a serious, man-to-man look. "They know where you live," he said.

Jeremy swallowed hard and thought that "they" meant "him," because Mr. Carruthers, for all his kindness, was part of the Department too.

"They know who your parents are. They're going to start leaning on your family again, and this time, I'm not going to be able to stop them." He tried another smile. "Unless you give me something I can work with."

"The little gray one is going to New York this weekend," Jeremy blurted. It was like the words fell out of his mouth before he had time to plan them. But as soon as he'd spoken them, he realized that he'd stumbled into the perfect solution. He knew that Alice had made her appointment with the Wayne Clinic that weekend. He also knew that New York was enormous, and if the Department was off hunting for gray-furred Millie, then Alice would be able to make contact with the clinic and have her testing done and not worry that people were looking for her.

Jeremy also knew—because Alice had told him—that Millie was going to audition for *The Next Stage* at Carnegie Hall, and if there was a place less likely for the agents to go in search of a creature who hated and feared the human world than a world-famous performance space, Jeremy couldn't think of what it might be. Alice would be safe, and Millie would be safe, and Mr. Carruthers couldn't be mad at him, because Jeremy had told him the truth.

"New York," Mr. Carruthers said, leaning close. "Are you sure? And do you know where she's going?"

Jeremy nodded, unspooling his lies the way he'd reeled out the thread attached to his kite, one windy day on the beach when a sudden gust had lofted it high into the sky. "I heard her talking with the red-haired girl. She's going to a science-fiction convention at the Javits Center," he said.

Now Mr. Carruthers looked both angry and incredulous. "Really?"

"Yup. The red-haired girl told her that nobody would stare at her at a place like that. They'd just think she was a cosplayer. It would be like Halloween."

Mr. Carruthers didn't appear to be buying this, but so far he wasn't saying that Jeremy was lying. "And it's this weekend?" he finally asked.

"Yup," Jeremy said, feeling grateful that he'd overheard a couple of kids at his lunch table talking about an upcoming convention.

"But they're not going together."

Jeremy felt the tips of his ears get hot. "Nope. The red-haired girl said she's got a big test to study for."

Mr. Carruthers made notes, and Jeremy took a deep breath. This was good. It was better than good. It was perfect. Carruthers would go to New York, chasing after Millie, not Alice. Jeremy would escort Alice to the clinic, if she'd let him, and if it turned out that she was a Bigfoot, he'd convince her to go public. He, not Mr. Carruthers, not the Department of Official Inquiry, would have the glory of proving that Bigfoots were real, and he'd make sure Alice was safe.

Mr. Carruthers pulled off his sunglasses. He leaned

close, so that his eyes, with the tiny ribbons of red in the whites, were looking right into Jeremy's. "Tell me everything," he said. "Everything you heard the two of them say."

Jeremy nodded and spun a tale that was, as always, a blend, bits of the truth seasoned with stuff he'd made up. He said that Millie would be wearing a trench coat and taking a bus and telling people that she was a Tribble. She'd meet friends she'd made online, friends who thought she was a human girl in disguise.

Carruthers nodded, scribbling notes. "And you're sure she's not going with the other girl?" he asked.

Jeremy's ears got hotter. "I'm sure." His mind churned as he tried desperately to think of something that could throw Mr. Carruthers even further off the scent. Maybe more truth, he thought, and tried for a man-to-man kind of smile. "You know. Junior-high girls. Maybe they're having a fight or something."

"Huh." Mr. Carruthers's face was expressionless. Jeremy could smell his own sweat, could even feel a bead of it sliding down his spine. Finally, Carruthers smiled. "Well, that's even more than I'd hoped for." He clapped Jeremy on the back. Jeremy tried not to flinch, or to move, even though the slap hadn't exactly been gentle. "Good work, son." He leaned across Jeremy, grabbed the door handle, and slid the van's door open, letting in a blast of cold air. That was Jeremy's cue to jump out, collect his bike, and pedal home. Instead, he sat still, trying not to shiver as he met Mr. Carruther's gaze.

"What will you do?" he asked. "What will you do if you catch her?"

"Nothing that concerns you." Carruthers was already reaching for the phone he kept clipped to his belt, probably in a big hurry to call his bosses and tell them what he'd learned. "Of course we'll keep you in the loop."

"You can't hurt her," Jeremy said. "And you can't . . . you know . . . if there's some big announcement, you have to say that I was a part of it. Me and Jo." He was furious at the notion of Carruthers and his Department capturing Millie and taking all the credit, even though it wouldn't happen—not next weekend, or any weekend—because Millie wasn't going anywhere near the Javits Center and was actually going to a place where they'd never think to look for her. "I'm the one who found her. I'm the one who's been keeping track of her. I'm the one who told you where she'd be!"

"Easy, big guy." Mr. Carruthers, who was smiling now, put his hand on Jeremy's forearm. "We always give credit where credit is due. But trust me, you don't want to be part of the, um, acquisition." His smile widened, his lips thinning until Jeremy imagined he could see every one of his teeth. "It's the kind of thing that could get . . . messy."

When Jeremy finally climbed out of the van, his legs were so wobbly that he knew better than to even try pedaling. Instead, he walked his bike all the way home. He and Jo would have to figure out how to stay with Alice and keep her safe and how to get word to Millie, just so she could be extra careful. He and Jo would have to be certain that nothing messy happened to either one of them. Because, he thought, as a car sped by, sending a plume of icy puddle water to soak Jeremy from his knees to his shoes, if anything did happen, it would be 100 percent his fault.

# CHAPTER 12

## Millie

FOR AS LONG AS SHE COULD REMEMBER, MILLIE had woken up the same way. First, her mother would part the thick curtains that covered the single, narrow window in her room, letting in as much light as the window would allow. The house would be warm, smelling of toast and tea, as the first faint sunlight crept across the quilt on Millie's bed. "Wake up, my Millietta," Septima would sing in her high and cracking voice. "Wake up to greet the day."

Millie would stretch and wiggle her feet into her soft leather moccasins that her mother had sewn. She would go to the privy, tucked under a neighboring hill, to do the necessary, and when she came back to her bedroom her mother would have set a basin of warm water on the little table next to Millie's bed, with a bar of sweet-smelling soap. Millie would wash her hands and face, comb her fur, and clip in one of the little flower-shaped bows that her parents ordered on-the-line.

There would be a fire burning in the kitchen, and bowls of thick porridge with cream and butter and brown sugar and raisins, or warm slices of fresh-baked bread. Millie would sit at the table with a steaming cup of what Old Aunt Yetta called "growing tea" in front of her, a tea made with special ingredients to keep her healthy and strong and, hopefully, to help her grow to a normal Yare size. Her mother would urge her to eat, and her father would look at her with affection, sometimes squeezing her shoulders with both of his big hands. When she'd finished clearing the table and helping Septima wash and dry the dishes, one of her parents would walk her to school and hand her a small snackle, along with her lunch sack, before she walked through the door.

Ever since her audition video had been accepted, her days began differently. At five in the morning, when the sky was still dark, the alarm on Alice's laptop would chime. Millie would turn it off before her parents could hear, and then sit up in bed, with the room lit by the eerie blue glow of the screen.

First, she would go to *The Next Stage*'s home page to check the comments on their audition video and type in her own comments underneath the most popular positive remarks. This would boost those comments to the top of the string and encourage more people to write. She'd check on the number of votes that had come in during the night, and feel happy if she and Jessica were still in the lead, and feel a leaden misery, like she'd swallowed a bellyful of stones, if they weren't.

Next, she would go to the InstaChat page that Jessica had set up, the place where they'd been posting new content. Again, she would check the number of thumbs-ups, the number of "likes" and "loves" and "favorites," and she would like and love and favorite the favorable comments, and write the same things underneath them: "So glad you enjoyed!" and "Thanks for the love," along with "Please please PLEEEEEEEEEASE don't forget to MAKE US NUMBER ONE on *The Next Stage*," along with a link directing people to the correct page. It made Millie feel uncomfortable, asking so baldly for strangers to do her a kindness, like they owed her anything more than just their time, but Jessica had said that this was the way things worked, on-the-line, and had even shown her the Facebook pages of famous singers and bestselling authors, all pleading for people to purchase their books or their albums, to watch their videos and play their songs, to make them Number One.

By the time she heard her mother's light footsteps in the hall, Millie would have been awake for close to two hours. Her back would feel achy, and her eyes would burn, and she'd feel sick and stuffed and a little dizzy, like she'd eaten something too cold or too sweet much too quickly. Her mind would be crammed with words, good and bad:

*Beautiful singing*

*I've heard better*

*Such a pretty little girl*

*She's maybe a six, needs to lose 10 lbs*

*She must be related to one of the judges if she's actually in the finals*

"Just ignore it," Jessica had told her, when Millie would fret over the mean stuff. "People are angry. They're just looking for a dog to kick." Millie couldn't understand why the No-Furs were so mad and why saying something unkind to a stranger on a screen would make them feel better, but she just added it to her list of No-Fur behaviors that made no sense. In a single motion, she would slip the laptop underneath her mattress, pull the covers up to her chin, then lie back with her eyes shut as her mother bustled around the room, opening the curtains, giving Millie a kiss, singing her good-morning song.

That day was a Friday, the day she and Jessica—and Alice, she reminded herself—would be leaving for the city. Millie had packed her best dress and her not-best dress, the snow boots that she wore outside, and the moccasins for indoors. She'd packed her toothbrush and a bar of the sweet soap that her mother made and slipped Old Aunt Yetta's potion into her pocket, and she'd rolled and folded everything until it fit into a plaid flannel pillowcase that she'd knotted and tied to a stick. (She had an old canvas knapsack with leather straps that had once been her father's, but it smelled slightly like mildew, and Millie thought the idea of a bundle on a stick much more charming than simply cramming her things into a backpack.) The stick was propped in the snow beside the Lookout Tree, and the bundle was waiting on the platform in the tree's top branches.

After breakfast, Millie would leave for lessons, but after going into the dugout where Teacher Greenleaf and the rest of the littlies were waiting, she would ask to be excused. She would climb the Lookout Tree and sneak the bundle down the tree's trunk. She'd attach it to the stick. And then, while the class studied fractions and reviewed the Ten Common Techniques for Evading the No-Furs or did their run-and-hide drills, she would trot away from the Yare encampment, around the lake, to the Experimental Center, where, Jessica had told her, a van would be waiting to take them to New York City.

The thought of it made her stomach do a flip and made her fur feel bristly. *Break it down*, was what Old Aunt Yetta told her to do when something scared her. *Think of each piece on its own and how you will get through it.* Millie had been on a school bus, trick-or-treating with the rest of the Yare littlies, then Alice, and so a van would be mostly the same. At least, that was what she tried to tell herself, even though she knew that the van would go on the highways, not just little town roads, and even through a tunnel, under a river, where Millie was sure she'd be able to feel the weight of all the water pressing down. Alice's part-ment, she told herself, would be much like the learners' cabin, only fancier, and in a tall building, with its rooms perched high in the sky—which, Millie thought, would be like the Lookout Tree. She wasn't even letting herself think about the audition itself, or about actually being in the city. Whenever she did, her heart started beating so

fast that the world got wobbly, and she'd have to sit with her head between her legs, taking big deep breaths until her pulse settled.

Millie told herself that this—a stage, an audience, the possibility of fame—was her dream, the only thing she'd ever wanted, but as she'd gotten closer to the audition date, she found herself missing the way things had been. She missed waking up slowly in the warmth of her blankets. She missed singing just for pleasure, not always thinking about whether Jessica would be able to mouth the words convincingly as Millie sang them, or whether favorite songs would turn out to be the kind of thing voters liked. She missed her time with Alice, their nights by the lake, in the darkness, with Millie hidden in the bushes and Alice sitting on the ground next to her while they traded secrets and stories and talked about what they wanted from the world.

But now Alice was angry and sad. Whenever Millie tried to talk to her—about the vote getting or about how Millie was becoming increasingly convinced that someone was following her through the forest—Alice would answer in single words and find an excuse to be somewhere else. That was her fault, Millie knew. She'd never meant to abandon her friend. It was almost as if it had happened without her even noticing, like they'd slipped apart so quickly and completely that she wouldn't have been able to stop it, even if she'd tried.

She must have sighed, because Septima was looking at her sharply. "Millie, what is troubling you?"

"Not a thing," said Millie, helping herself to a dried-apple pancake. She was thinking how much better it would have been if she'd been born a No-Fur and Alice had been a Yare. Then Millie would have been able to sing with no one stopping her, and Alice would never have to wonder where she belonged, and would have been happy in the woods.

She folded up three more pancakes in a cloth napkin and took a last swallow of goat's milk. "Happy day," she told her parents, and both of them kissed her good-bye. Millie tried not to think of how they would fret when it was three-of-the-clock, then four, then five, and she hadn't come home. She had left them a note underneath her pillow, telling them not to worry, that she was safe and with friends and would be home Sunday night, but telling her mother not to worry was like telling the sun not to rise in the morning, like telling the birds not to sing.

Outside, in the winter morning, it was still more dark than light. Millie's breath formed frosty white clouds in

front of her. The moon hung low in the sky, reflected in the lake. She could hear her feet crunching through the ice-crusted snow and feel the sharp, cold air stinging her cheeks as she walked. It was a beautiful morning, lovely and still, but Millie didn't notice. She was thinking about the audition and whether an upbeat, happy song would get more votes than a sad kind of love song and which would be easier for Jessica to pretend to sing. Millie was so deep in thought that at first she didn't hear the steps— slow and cautious, then quicker and louder—of someone coming up behind her.

She glanced over her shoulder and saw a tall, hooded figure, all in black, coming toward her fast, on feet that seemed to skim the snow.

Millie quickened her pace. The figure followed along, faster and faster. Millie began to trot, then run. Whoever was behind her was gaining, getting closer with every step. Millie could hear the rasp of her pursuer's breath in her ears. She was too afraid to turn around, too scared to scream. All she could do was squeeze her eyes shut as a big hand grabbed the collar of her coat and hoisted her into the air.

Millie screeched, her legs flailing and her feet paddling helplessly above the snow-covered ground, wondering who

227

had gotten her. One of the No-Furs, she thought, as she wriggled and screeched, and now it would be just like she'd always been told. She'd be put in a cage, displayed in a zoo, treated like a freak, something more like an animal than a person. She would never see her parents or friends. Or her Tribe. She would never sing again. That thought made her howl more loudly than ever, until she heard a woman's voice in her ear.

"Millie," it said.

Millie instantly went still. She felt her mouth drop open as she tumbled to the snowy ground.

"Millie," Septima repeated, and held out her hands, pulling her daughter to her feet. "I know where you are going."

Millie's heart lurched. She felt her neck-fur and face-fur quiver with fear, even as she made herself look up, trying to make her expression innocent and a little pathetic. "I'm just going to my lessons."

"I know," Septima sighed. "I know." For a minute she was quiet, looking out at Lake Standish. Across the miles of water, the kids and the teachers at the Experimental Center were probably all still sleeping, snug in their beds . . . and, all over the world, people with computers might be looking at Millie's audition or at the Amazing

Marvin's magic tricks or at Trisha Doyle, who was the grown-up singer who'd had the most votes the last time Millie had checked.

Millie felt like she was going to burst with anxiety and disappointment. To come so close to her dream—to have it right there in her hand, right there for the taking—and then, on the day before her audition, to be foiled by her own mother.

"It's not f—" she started to say, when her mother interrupted.

"Go on," Septima said.

Millie blinked. "What?"

"Go," Septima repeated, and handed Millie a basket. "Go on and see your friend."

Millie just stared. She couldn't think of a single word to say. Her mother—who'd kept Millie so close, who'd carried her everywhere until Millie was three, who'd been known to lurk around the schoolhouse and even hide herself in bushes so that she could watch Millie during lesson time—giving her permission to go out among the No-Furs?

"You have a friend," her mother was saying. Millie nodded uncertainly, still not believing that her mother intended to let her go. "I understand that a friend is an

229

important thing. I know you have been lonely."

Millie nodded again, feeling a timid flicker of hope that maybe this wasn't a trick or a trap. Then a thought seized her. "Have you been following me?" she whispered. "All this time?"

Her mother looked at her with fond exasperation, an expression Millie had seen on her familiar face at least a thousand times.

"I had to keep you safe," she said. "That is what mothers do."

Millie remembered hearing her mother cry to Old Aunt Yetta, remembered her saying that she should have tried harder. Taking a guess—a wild one—she said, "Did you ever go out there? Out with the No-Furs?"

Septima gave her daughter a faint smile. "Do you have time to listen?"

Millie nodded, thinking of the last time she'd been in the learners' cabin, how Jessica had piles of clothes and shoes heaped up on her bed and how she was meticulously constructing outfits for the audition. She had a few hours before Jessica would be ready, and she knew they wouldn't leave without her.

"Then come," said her mother, and Millie followed her to the school yard, then up the thick trunk of the Lookout

Tree. Millie's little treehouse was warm enough, with piles of blankets and even a battery-operated heater that her father had purchased on-the-line. Millie snuggled in one corner. Septima stood on her tiptoes, reaching and pulling something out of a crack between the roof and the wall. As Millie watched, her mother carefully unwrapped the layers of tape and plastic.

"Was this your place?" Millie asked.

"Long-and-long ago," said her mother, using her sharp nails to rip through the tape. Finally, she finished her unwrapping. The plastic had concealed two things: a wooden box with the words "My Keepsakes" on the top and a big book with the word "Scrapbook" on the cover. She smoothed her hands over the box's surface, sat down on her own nest of blankets, and looked at her daughter. "This is my faulting," she said. Her voice sounded miserable, and her eyes were on the floor. "All my faulting. The why of it. How you are the way you are. All my faulting."

"What do you mean?" Millie asked. She was looking at her mother and thinking, the way she normally did, that the two of them could not be less alike—Septima, with her soft voice and downcast eyes, her neat, simple dress, and her dark, dense fur that looked like everyone else's, and Millie, who was loud and bold, whose fur was silvery, who was not like any of the other Yare at all.

"Because, long-and-long ago, I wanted to go out into the world. I wanted . . ." She made a choked noise, then gestured toward the high, narrow slit of the window, a movement that took in the snowy, silent world beyond. "And now you are just like me. And I can't keep you safe, no more than my parents could keep me from running away."

"You ran away?" Millie stared as Septima gave a shame-faced nod. "Did you want to be famous?" Millie asked.

Septima's mouth lifted in an unhappy kind of smirk. "Something like that. But not the same as you. I wanted to be a track star." She looked at her daughter. "Are you knowing what that is?"

"I think so," said Millie. "Running? On a track?"

"Not running," said Septima. "Not for me. Throwing." Her hand curved, like she was cradling a giant egg. "You know I am from . . ." She lifted her hand toward the sky, bringing her fingers toward her palm, then spreading them out again, a Yare gesture that meant "far away."

Millie nodded.

"And you know I was runtish."

Millie nodded again. She'd heard stories of how Septima was small and sickly, so tiny that her village had despaired of her survival. Her Healer had dosed her with tonics, rare meat, and fresh air, and her folks had tried to feed her up, the same way Septima now did with Millie, but Millie knew her mother had always been small and weak as a littlie until she'd grown to be a normal size, the way Millie hoped that she herself would grow.

"We lived in the forest, a'course, but there was a town, and the town had a school, and the school had a track team. One day I was gathering berries, and I'd wandered far-and-far, and I saw them. No-Fur boys and girls, racing around in a circle or jumping or throwing." A ghost of a smile lifted Septima's lips. "One of the girls got angry at the coach, and instead of putting the shot where she was supposed to, she threw it into the woods, as a joke. It landed almost at my feet. I thought it was a sign. So I picked it up"—Septima's hand curved again—"and I threw it back . . ." She lifted her hand behind her shoulder, then made a throwing motion, then smiled in earnest. "I have never heard No-Furs be screaming so loud or be running so fast. All of them ran but the coach. He stood at the very edge of the woods and shouted, 'Whoever did that, come to practice tomorrow, and let's see if you can do it again.'"

Millie listened, still not quite believing what she

heard as her mother described doing exactly what Millie had long dreamed of: finding a way to make her fur disappear, then venturing into the world.

"Do not ask me the how of it," Septima said, her voice so stern and her face so fearsome that Millie nodded immediately, secretly thinking that it had to be the potion, the same one she'd stolen from Old Aunt Yetta. Then her mother told a story that was like Millie's own singing story, a story of wanting not only to go out into the No-Fur world but to find the thing that you were best at, a story of wanting to shine.

"That first day, the coach watched me throw and said I had much of the talent. He showed me the right way to do it, and I practiced and practiced, at home, with rocks. And I was good." Her face took on a wistful expression. "I was very good. I could throw it farther than any of the No-Fur girls could, and farther, even, than most of the boys. That should have been enough, just to know that I was the best of them."

"But it wasn't," Millie said.

Septima shook her head. "The coach said he was needing a note from my parents and a copy of my birth certificate so I could be in the tournaments." Septima pronounced "birth certificate" with great care, the way

Yare typically did with unfamiliar No-Fur terms. "I could write a note, but I had no certificate. I told him that it was lost. He said for my parents to go to City Hall and ask for another. He gave me a unifrom."

"Uniform," Millie corrected. Her mother gave a rueful smile.

"It is so long I am forgetting." Septima flipped the scrapbook open. "Shot Putter Leads Track Team to Victory," read the headline of the first story, and there was a picture of Millie's mother, her fur gone, and her skin a golden, coppery color, in a sleeveless shirt, white with stripes across the chest, and baggy shorts and knee socks pulled up high. She had a great mass of black hair atop her head, pulled back into intricate braids. Instead of smiling at the camera, she was looking shyly off to the side, like she wanted to be invisible, like she wanted to disappear . . . except not entirely. There was something about the defiant tilt of her chin, the corded muscles of her forearms, and the coiled strength of her body that suggested a kind of stubbornness, a will to make herself known and seen. It was strange and yet familiar—familiar, Millie realized, from her own reflection in the looking glass that hung above the chest of drawers in her bedroom. She too longed to be where she wasn't. She too dreamed of a life she could never have. She too would use whatever power she had to get herself where she wanted to be, to make a place for herself in a different world.

Millie stared, tracing the picture with her fingertips, struggling to line up this version—this regular, No-Fur girl version—of her mother with the tremulous, fur-covered Septima she'd always known. She looked like a completely different person, like she was barely Yare at all.

Septima sighed and looked down at her hands.

"It wasn't fair, really," she said. "The Yare are much stronger than the No-Furs. Of course I'd be a good thrower. But it wasn't that I wanted to beat them . . ."

Her voice trailed off, and Millie, who thought that maybe she understood, said, "You just wanted to know."

"Yes." Septima nodded. "Just to be there, and to know, that was all. Not to win, but just to know how I did, compared to the others. Just to know . . ." She ran her fingers over the scrapbook's cover and gave Millie a shy smile. "Although I always was liking the bus rides to the meets." Her smile widened. "We'd sing songs on the bus. I had a cheeseburger once when we went for lunch."

"So what happened?" Millie asked as she filed away the image of her mother on a bus, in a restaurant, ordering, paying for, and eating a cheeseburger, for future consideration.

It was quiet for a moment, so still in the little treehouse that Millie could hear the wind outside. Then Septima started flipping the pages. "Track Team Sweeps to Victory," "Overbrook Standout: Homeschooled Septima Yare Is a Shot-Put Prodigy," "Yare Takes Gold at West Virginia State Championships."

Millie bent her head, reading one of the stories. "'Watching Septima Yare drop into her crouch, then explode into a balletic whirl, hurling the shot put feet—sometimes yards—farther than her competitors, it is hard to believe that she learned the sport just this year, on her own. "She's a natural," said Donal Gregg, the Overbrook High School track coach. "She's the best I've seen in twenty years of coaching, and that includes boys and girls." While the shy seventeen-year-old, who has been homeschooled for her entire life, declined to speak to this reporter, her performance on the field speaks for itself. Asked about Yare's future, Gregg said, "She can take this as far as she wants to. I don't think the Olympics are outside the realm of possibility."'

"The Olympics," Millie breathed. Septima's hands were twisting in her lap. Millie turned another page. "Yare Named to All-State Squad. Next Stop: Junior Nationals." There was another picture, this one of Septima lined up with four other girls, each one in the uniform of a different high school. In this shot Septima met the camera's gaze with a bold, pleased smile. Her braids were arranged differently, twined around her head. She cradled the shot behind her ear, and her eyes were narrowed as she peered past the photographer.

"So what happened?" Millie asked again.

Septima pressed her lips together. "One of the other girls made a complaining . . ." She paused, then corrected herself in a quiet voice. "A complaint. We were training together once a week at a school in Wheeling. I took a bus to get there. The first two practices were fine, but at the third one, the coach took me aside. There was another No-Fur man with him, a man I'd never seen before. First the coach said I'd never been submitting my physical. Of course, I'd never had one. I did not know what to say. Then he told me"—she ducked her head, and her voice was so quiet that Millie could hardly hear her—"that some of the girls did not think that I was . . ."

"Human?" Millie whispered, with her heart in her throat.

Her mother shook her head. "They did not think that I was a girl. I was too big and too strong, and I didn't look like the rest of them." Even over the distance of all the years, Millie could hear the hurt and bewilderment and shame in her mother's voice. "The other man was a doctor. He said that they would do an examining, to check, and then all would be well."

Millie felt her skin go cold. If they'd done an examination—if a coach or a doctor had ever learned her mother's truth—it would have been a disaster. Not just for her but for her entire Tribe, maybe even for all the Yare in the world.

"What did you do?" she whispered.

"I said I needed to talk to my parents. They told me they could do the examining right now, right in the nurse's office at the school. I didn't know . . ." Septima was shaking all over, her fur quivering. "I didn't know if they'd look and be able to tell what I really was. So I excused myself—to call my parents, I said—and I ran. I ran, and I ran, and I thought of what would happen if they found our village, if they ever learned the truth of it. All through the night, I ran, and walked, and I promised, never again. The No-Fur world was no place for me. Best to stay hidden. Best to stay where I was safe."

Septima pressed her lips together tightly, and then gave Millie her familiar crooked half smile.

"And then what?" Millie whispered. She imagined that she was walking alongside her mother, through the dark night, shivering in her shorts and her track team sweatshirt, terrified and alone.

"I could not go back," her mother said. Her voice was soft, full of old pain and regret. "I thought maybe they'd come looking for me—the coaches, or even a reporter— and they'd find the Tribe, and I could not bring the No-Furs to the Tribe's door." She ducked her head, mumbling into her chest-fur. "And I could not tell my parents what I'd done. They would not have understood. They would have set my feet on the road." She gave a great shudder. "So I just kept walking. I knew there was a Tribe up here, from the Gatherings. I walked at night and I slept in the daytime. I followed the light of the moon."

Millie's fur was prickling and her mouth was dry. "You just left? You never said good-bye to your ma and pa?"

Septima shook her head. "Not for long-and-long," she said. "I wrote them letters. And then, later, with the on-the-line, I could write to them that way. But then, I was young and frightened, and I wanted only to hide from what I had done." She pressed her lips together. "I was ashamed."

Millie wrapped her arms around her mother's neck, burying her face in Septima's shoulder. Her mother held her, rocking her gently, patting her back and smoothing

240

her fur, the way she had when Millie was very small.

"But here is the truth of it," Septima said. "I know what it feels like to want." Again, she gestured toward the window and the sky and the world beyond it. "I know what it is to want more than what your own people can give you. To want something from the world."

Septima reached into the box, pulled out a dull metal ball, and tucked it underneath her chin, cradling it for an instant before setting it gently back in the box. Millie thought she caught the gleam of a medal or two in there, tied with lengths of faded ribbon, but she couldn't be sure. Her mother removed a sealed envelope and held it in her hand.

"I think also," she said, "that the No-Fur Alice needs you."

Millie felt herself blushing underneath her fur as a wave of guilt swept through her.

"I have been watching," her mother said. "Watching and hearing you singing your songs, making your recordings. This No-Fur Jessica has many friends, right?"

Millie nodded, thinking that was at least what Jessica wanted everyone to think. Boys liked her; other girls did too, with her beautiful clothes and her funny, cutting remarks.

"But Alice is different," her mother continued. "Alice is not much like the rest of them, is she?"

Millie shook her head. Her face was still hot with guilt. She knew that she hadn't been a good friend to Alice. She'd gotten too busy with all the liking and clicking and fanning and friending, too full of thoughts about which song and which outfit and how to make her fur disappear.

Her mother was looking at her steadily. "Will you be a good friend to Alice?"

"I will try," Millie promised.

Her mother lifted the small bundle Millie had packed. "You were going to stay the night at the No-Fur school?" she asked.

Millie nodded, still blushing. "Two nights," she said. "I will stay in their cabin." She felt sick with guilt at having to lie, and dizzy with relief that her mother just thought she'd found friends to sing with and hadn't discovered the truth of *The Next Stage*. She didn't know where Millie was going and what she intended to do. "I put a note under my pillow. So you wouldn't worry."

"I will always worry," said her mother. "Worry is what mothers do." She handed Millie the envelope, which held five twenty-dollar bills, as soft as the old clothes she kept to polish her good silver.

"My prize money," Septima said with a shy, proud

smile on her face. "For the meet that I won. In case you are having the emergency. Or your friends take you for a cheeseburger." She reached out and folded Millie's fingers around the envelope. "Have a care, my Millietta," she said.

Millie hugged her mother as hard as she could, and then, without looking back, she ran off to the path by the lake, carrying her clothes bundle and the basket of food. She could feel her mother's gaze still on her and she could feel the lie she'd told sticking in her throat like a malevolent toad. *I am having the sleep-over,* she thought. *Just not at the Center.* And whether she was sleeping in Alice's cabin or in Alice's parents' partment, Millie knew that Septima would worry just the same.

But that wasn't true. If her mother knew she was going to New York City, she would never let her out of the forest. And what if Millie actually won the contest? What if she was invited back to perform for the judges on TV?

*I will burn that bridge when I come to it,* Millie thought, she tightened the strings of her hood, fluffed her face-fur, and trotted lightly over the snow.

# CHAPTER 13

*Alice*

ALICE HAD SPENT HOURS PREPARING A SPEECH for Lori and Phil about how she and Jessica needed to visit the Museum of Natural History in New York City to complete their project on endangered whales. She had her lies lined up: Yes, her parents would be in the city (not true). Absolutely, she and Jessica would be supervised the entire time (they wouldn't). And of course Lori and Phil were welcome to call her folks to check in at any time (the calls would go right to voice mail, and urgent messages would be returned by Marcus Johansson, who'd been more than willing to give Alice his cell-phone number so that he could serve as a pretend parent).

When Alice had gone to the Center's office, Phil had been staring at his computer screen and tugging at his beard, and Lori had been fiddling with the Guatemalan worry dolls she kept in a basket on her desk. A few days before, the state's health department had done a surprise inspection of the school's kitchen and had fined them because Kate had left a water glass on the otherwise-spotless stainless-steel counter. The week before that, someone claiming to be from the Equal Employment Opportunity Commission had shown up to ask questions about the school's hiring practices. Lori's indignant cries of "No one is more inclusive than we are!" were loud enough that every learner in the entire school could hear them. A representative from the Environmental Protection Agency had inspected their septic tank and told them they'd need a bigger one, and the school had been fined for failing to have enough accessible bathroom stalls for the school to comply with the Americans with Disabilities Act.

"I'm starting to think this might be personal," said Phil, gazing mournfully at the latest citation, and Lori, with a handful of worry dolls, had started to sing "We Shall Overcome." All Alice had to do was mumble her request about needing to spend the night in New York

City, and Lori gave an absent nod and said she'd arrange for a van.

None of it had felt completely real. But now it was Friday morning, the air so cold that it hurt to breathe, the sky a brilliant, vivid blue. Jessica had packed an enormous wheeled suitcase and two duffel bags, one with shoes, the other with makeup and accessories. Millie arrived with her things bundled up and tied to a stick, like a hobo from Alice's history book. She also had a basket of snackles. "From my mother," she said shyly as Alice accepted a maple muffin, and Jessica said she wasn't eating carbs.

"Seat belts, ladies," said Chip, the driver, an amiable twenty-three-year-old and a cousin of Phil's who was in his sixth year of college.

Millie sat in the middle, with Alice and Jessica on either side of her. Alice had to show Millie how to pull her belt across her chest and latch it closed. She leaned her head against the window, letting her eyes slip shut, thinking that if she could will herself to fall asleep, it wouldn't hurt as much to be sitting beside the girl she'd once called her friend, with Millie's new friend—an upgrade, Alice thought—sitting on the other side.

When she felt Millie's furry paw brush her hand she kept her eyes shut. When she heard Millie whisper,

"Alice?" in a small and frightened voice, she pretended to be sleeping. Alice didn't open her eyes, not even when she felt Millie flinch as Chip merged onto the highway, not even when she heard Millie gasp and felt her cringe when someone honked. She didn't let herself think about how terrifying it must be to someone who'd only ever seen her little village and the Center and, for a few hours every year, the town where they went trick-or-treating, someone who'd never driven on a road with more than one lane or seen a place bigger than Standish or more than a few dozen people at a time.

Alice reminded herself of how it felt to hear Millie laugh and sing and plot with Jessica while Alice lay on her bed, seething, and the two of them ignored her. She remembered a dozen times when she'd been pushed to the edge of a room, outside of their circle. She wouldn't be won over with a kind word or a muffin. She wouldn't let Millie get close to her again, knowing how quickly Millie had abandoned her when a better opportunity arrived. She would ignore the fear she heard in Millie's voice and the slight tremble of her fingers. She'd get to New York and find out the truth of who she was and where she belonged, and then she'd go to that place and make some real friends.

# CHAPTER 14

## Jeremy

A FIELD TRIP TO WHERE?" ASKED HIS FATHER, squinting at the permission slip Jeremy had made on his computer and printed out so recently that the paper was still warm.

"New York City," Jeremy said patiently.

His father picked up a pen, then put it down, frowning. "Wasn't your class just there?"

Jeremy stifled a sigh. He'd been hoping his dad wouldn't remember last year's excursion to some big art museum, where a mothball-scented old lady with a whispery voice had led them around, talking about perspective and impasto and the painters' use of light.

"That was for art class. This is for music."

His father looked at the form, which asked for his permission for Jeremy to attend *The Next Stage* auditions at Carnegie Hall, then at Jeremy. Maybe, Jeremy thought, he was remembering the sad excursion the family had made to the Juilliard music school, back when they believed Jeremy was some kind of musical prodigy, instead of a slightly better-than-average singer and player of the oboe. "So you're not auditioning?"

"No. We're just watching the people who are."

His father's forehead furrowed as he frowned. Jeremy thought that he'd have more to say, but finally he just signed the paper, handed it back, and then pulled out his wallet and gave Jeremy two twenty-dollar bills and told him to have a good time.

"Thanks," Jeremy said, even as he was wondering why he bothered. The truth was, he could have just told his parents he was sleeping at a friend's house, or even left without saying anything at all, and they probably wouldn't have even noticed he was gone.

Back in his room, he reviewed the plan. He and Jo and Alice had met at the Standish Diner the previous Sunday to talk through the details. Jeremy and Jo had offered to accompany Alice to the city, but she'd turned them down. "I need to do this alone," she'd said.

"But you have to call us," Jo said. "As soon as they tell you where you're going. You have to call us, so we know where to find you, in case—"

"In case something happens to me," said Alice. "I'll tell you where they tell me to go, and I'll send you a picture when I get there, and I'll make sure my phone's on. That way . . ." She didn't finish the sentence, just tried to retuck the curls that had come out of her braid. Her face looked paler than it had the first time they'd met, with freckles standing out on her nose and her cheeks.

Jeremy nodded and made sure she had his number and told her good luck.

Outside, she'd turned left, walking back toward the school, and he and Jo had climbed onto the tandem bike to make their plans in the open air, where no one could listen in.

"We should follow her," Jeremy said.

"*You* should follow her," said Jo. "I'm fine on a bike, but on foot, not so speedy."

They agreed that Jeremy would be the man on the ground, trailing Alice through New York City, keeping watch and keeping her safe. Jo would stay in Standish, in her Batcave, with all of her computers up and running

and her network of experts—the ones they'd trusted enough to tell about Millie and Alice—standing by.

Dr. Johansson hadn't looked happy when Jeremy and Jo had told him that Alice had decided to go to the city alone. "I'd feel better if she had the two of you with her."

"That's what we thought too, but we couldn't change her mind, so we decided . . ." Jeremy shuffled his feet, until Jo jumped in.

"We're going to follow her," Jo said.

"It's for her own good," said Jeremy.

"Of course," said the doctor.

Jeremy wasn't surprised to find out that Dr. Johansson had all kinds of gadgets in the drawers of his gigantic desk, including a tiny camera to stick somewhere in the lobby of Alice's building that would broadcast an image of everyone entering and leaving to the screen of Jeremy's phone. The three of them consulted a map and online images of Alice's street, plotting out hiding spots and subway routes.

"I don't like doing this," Dr. Johansson said, typing rapidly, toggling between screens so fast that Jeremy couldn't keep up. "But it's the only way to keep her safe. Can you tell me her phone number again?"

Jeremy recited the digits. Then he saw an Apple logo

come up, then the words "override protocol." "What are you doing?" he asked.

"Sneaking in through the back door," Dr. Johansson said. "And turning on Alice's telephone's GPS locator. You know how most phones have a 'find my phone' feature?"

Jeremy did, having used that feature himself.

"Parents use it too, only instead of 'find my phone,' it's 'track my kid.' There's a lawsuit before the circuit court of appeals right now as to whether that's legal or if it constitutes an invasion of privacy, but until the judges make up their minds . . ."

He typed, then looked at the screen. Jeremy saw a map of Standish and a glowing red dot. "Alice," said Dr. Johansson. "She's at school. Or, at least, her phone is."

He showed Jeremy how to use the app to track Alice. They discussed which maps would be most useful in New York and what Jeremy should say if anyone asked why he was sitting outside of Alice's apartment building. Finally, Dr. Johansson gave him what he promised would be the most useful thing of all. That turned out to be a yellow MetroCard, a pass for the city's buses and subways.

"Good luck," he said, and Jo said, "Be careful," and Jeremy promised her he would.

In his bedroom, Jeremy packed a bag and checked

the maps he'd downloaded, tracing his route from Port
Authority Bus Terminal to Alice's apartment on the
Upper East Side, making sure he'd looked up every diner
and all-night coffee shop where he could stop in to use a
bathroom or get warm. A snatch of an old song began to
play in his head. "Every step you take / I'll be watching
you." It sounded creepy, like he was a stalker, not a pro-
tector, but as long as he was clear about his intentions, it
would all come out right.

"I'm one of the good guys," he said, just to remind
himself, and put a spare phone charger in his backpack
and zipped it shut.

# CHAPTER 15

## Millie

MILLIE SHUDDERED AS THE VAN EMERGED from the whooshing, terrifying darkness of the tunnel. "Are we there yet?" she asked, pressing her body into the seat, clutching the seat belt with both hands with her eyes squeezed shut.

"Stop doing that!" Jessica hissed.

"Doing what?" Millie asked.

"Making that noise," Jessica said. "You sound like a teakettle. And you need to stop doing that thing with your nose. Can you please at least try to look normal?"

Millie pressed her lips together and forced her face to relax. She could try to stop flaring her nostrils but she

knew she wouldn't be able to stop shaking. The city stank.
The air was thick, almost furry with the smell of exhaust
and burning rubber, of horse urine and half-rotted trash.
Her ears were being assaulted by the cacophony of what
sounded like a hundred car horns, a thousand voices
chattering and singing and shouting and sighing and
swearing in three dozen different languages. There were
people, people everywhere, more people than Millie had
ever seen or even imagined, people walking shoulder to
shoulder down the sidewalks, people standing in impatient clusters, waiting for the traffic lights to change,
people pushing their way into stores and offices, people
shoving their way out. The trip into the city had been terrible, but Millie could already tell that the city itself was
going to be much, much worse.

She'd been hopeful, at first, that the day would go
well. Millie had arrived at the Center and waited by the
seventh-grade learners' cabin until Alice and Jessica came
back from breakfast.

"That's all you've got?" asked Jessica, staring at Millie's
bundle. "Is that a pillowcase? And why'd you tie it to a
branch?"

"I saw it in a picture," said Millie, who was beginning
to think that Teacher Greenleaf's books on American

history might need some updating. "Is this not proper?"

"Most people," said Jessica, "would use a suitcase."

Millie considered. "I do not have suits," she said.

"What about your backpack?"

"That," Millie said, "is not being special."

Jessica made an unpleasant noise, told Millie to wait, and trotted back through the gates, leaving Alice and Millie alone.

"Hello," Millie ventured.

"Hi," Alice said. She was looking at her feet. Her back was stiff, her hands were in her pockets, and her hair, bundled underneath a red knitted hat, looked like it was pulsing against the yarn, desperate for escape. Millie offered her a muffin. Alice picked one and muttered, "Thanks."

When Alice didn't say anything else, Millie said, "It is nice of you to let us stay in your partment."

"A-partment," said Alice.

"Yes, a partment," Millie said. "I am not ever having seen one. Is it up very high?"

"We're on the thirty-eighth floor." Alice was still looking at her feet.

Millie wanted to tell her what she'd found out about her mother, how she'd once been a No-Fur track star and thrown a ball of metal farther than any other girl or boy, but Alice's stormy expression made her keep quiet.

When Jessica came back with the kind of bag called a duffel, Millie untied her bundle from the stick and tucked it inside. They met the driver, a big, amiable No-Fur boy named Chip with a beard and a funny, sweetish smell, a little bit like burning leaves. Millie liked him right away. *This will be fine,* she thought, as she climbed inside the van and buckled her belt.

Driving through the town of Standish was distressing but tolerable. But the endless hours they spent on the highway were a nightmare. Millie spent the first hour of the ride trying to get used to being in a car surrounded by other cars, trying to make herself stop yelping and grabbling on to the back of the driver's chair whenever they shifted into another lane, or when another car went whizzing by. Chip had called her a "backseat driver," and at first he'd just laughed when she'd cringed and whimpered, but the third time she'd grabbed at his seat, shrieking, "Stop!" he'd lost his temper a little bit and said that it wasn't safe and that if she couldn't sit still he would have to bring her back to Standish.

For a while Millie tried to watch the outside, as the forest thinned out and the traffic got heavier. She saw abandoned train tracks, the backs of shabby houses with trash bags piled up on half-rotted wooden porches, and sagging lengths of power lines, sometimes with plastic bags or sneakers hanging from them. She saw cars sitting on concrete cubes and shops with "For Sale" signs and broken windows. Once, she saw a dead deer, one that had probably been hit by a car as it tried to run across six lanes of highway. Its eyes were still open, and there was blood on its nose and its mouth, and Millie had turned away, feeling sick and sad and sorry.

Millie had tried to get Alice to talk to her, to tell her how to act and what to do, but Alice was pretending to be asleep. Millie knew she was pretending—a No-Fur's wake-smell and sleep-smell were different—but she also knew Alice didn't want to talk to her. Millie had been unkind. It didn't even matter that she hadn't meant to be unkind, that she'd just been busy and distracted, that she'd thrown in with Alice's enemy because that was the easiest path to success, not because she'd meant to hurt Alice. It didn't matter that she hadn't meant to hurt Alice. What mattered was that she had.

Now they were rolling slowly along Broadway, the actual street of Broadway, which was far less grand than Millie had imagined. The smell had changed to include the scent of roasting chestnuts in vendors' carts, and horses from horse-drawn carriages. She heard the whirr of bicycle wheels, the churning of motors, a hundred conversations. Everywhere she looked there were people, seething over the sidewalk like ants on a juicy piece of fruit. The buildings so high that they crowded out the sun.

"Millie!" Jessica hissed. Millie looked at her friend, and Alice gestured at Millie's face.

"You're staring," she said. "And your nose . . ."

Millie realized that she had been flaring her nostrils and tipping her head toward the window, the better to catch every gust of scent.

"I am sorry," she apologized, and then caught sight of a sign. "Eyebrow Threading. What is that meaning?"

"They take a thread," said Jessica, "and they use it to clean up your arches."

"Ah," said Millie, who knew what "thread" was but not how an arch might have anything to do with an eyebrow.

"And here's the famous Times Square," said Chip as they inched along through the traffic. Feeling dizzy, Millie stared at the signs, electronic billboards or advertisements for Broadway shows that had somehow been projected directly onto the buildings. There was a triangle-shaped concrete island that separated the streets into strands, and on the island was a booth labeled "TKTS," with a line snaking toward its windows, and red metal bleachers, and No-Furs standing in front of the bleachers, singing.

Millie found that she couldn't breathe. She'd try, but her breath would catch before she could pull it down into her lungs. What if she somehow got separated from her fellow travelers and lost in the thronging No-Furs, carried away like a twig in a storm-swollen stream?

Millie leaned forward, hearing herself wheeze, thinking that she might throw up. It was all too much—too much noise, too much light, too many voices, too many bodies too close together, too many things to see. She could feel the entire new world was pressing down against her: the looming buildings, the crowded streets, the smell of horse and hot dogs and dirty gray snow, and all of those people, thousands of people, filling the buses and the taxis, charging across the streets when the traffic lights changed.

She felt sick and small and, suddenly, desperate to be home, to tell Chip that she couldn't stay here and to please take her back to the Center.

Then she thought, *I have to try. If I don't try, I'll always wonder. For the rest of my life, I'll wonder.* And she remembered something she'd overheard Taley saying, a quote from a No-Fur lady named Eleanor Roosevelt, about how every day you had to do a thing that scared you.

"Why?" she'd asked, thinking about her mother, who hated to be scared.

"Becausedb," said Taley, "it helbs you grow."

Millie did not think she wanted to grow. Millie wanted to leave. Back home, she was the Leader's beloved daughter, brave, curious Millie, who'd parleyed with a No-Fur and saved the Tribe. She wanted her bed, she wanted her blankets, she wanted the smell of pastry and clean sheets and clean snow melting into a noisy stream, she wanted the sound of her father chopping wood outside her bedroom window and the feel of her mother's kiss on her head. It was ridiculous and pathetic for a Yare her age, and one who would be Leader besides, but Millie missed her mother and father. She wanted to go home.

*This must be homesickness*, she thought. She'd heard the term before and had some vague sense that it had to do with one's home actually being sick, full of coughing in the winter or poison ivy in the summertime. Now she knew. Homesick was when you felt sick because you weren't at home, sick with desire to go back to where you belonged.

She sat in the backseat, trembling all over, with her

breakfast rolling around in her belly and tears dripping down her cheeks and soaking her face-fur. She waited for Alice or Jessica to notice that she was crying and ask her what was wrong. Neither of them did. *I will be brave,* Millie told herself, and she managed five minutes of bravery, until a man on a bicycle, with a giant square-shaped parcel wrapped in red plastic with the words "GRUBHUB" written across it sticking out from his back like a tumor, caromed down the street, so close to their car that she was sure that his shoulder had brushed the window. He zipped in front of them, sped through a tiny gap between two cars, and shot across the street the instant before the light changed to red. Cars honked and people shouted as a taxi went crashing into a fire hydrant. Water sprayed up into the chilly air, and the man, without missing a stroke on the pedals, took one hand off the handlebars and raised his fist, waving it tauntingly behind his back as his bike coasted down the street. Millie decided that she could never live in New York City. She wasn't even sure that she could stand to be there for the night.

*I will be brave,* she thought again, except she didn't feel a bit brave, and she had never felt less like singing in her life. She was sure that if she tried, the only noise that would come out of her mouth would be a terrified croak.

They would laugh at her—the audience, the other competitors, the judges. They'd stare at her fur and ask what was wrong with her and if she had a disease. They would point and take pictures and post them on all the sites she'd become familiar with over the past few weeks—Mutter and InstaChat and Facebook and Only Connect and the rest of them—and then someone would trap her and put her in a cage, in a zoo, on display, never to ever see her loved ones ever again.

She opened her mouth to tell Alice and Jessica that she wanted to go home, but then the light changed again, and the car lurched forward, then jolted to a stop with its front about six inches from the back of a taxi.

"Sorry, guys," said Chip as all three girls shrieked, and Jessica's luggage came tumbling over the back of the seat. Chip, sounding jovial, said, "Welcome to New York," and Millie knew that she wouldn't be able to say anything, she would only be able to cry.

*I will wait,* she decided. This terrible ride had to end at some point. She would wait until dark, and she'd make some excuse to go outside for a bit of fresh air, and then, like her mother had all those years ago, she would follow the moon back to her Tribe, her bed, her home.

# CHAPTER 16

## Alice

ALICE CLIMBED OUT OF THE CAR, WALKED through her apartment building's door, waved at Stavros, the doorman, and uttered four words she had never before said out loud: "These are my friends." Even if it wasn't exactly true, it felt good to say.

Stavros tipped his cap and smiled, nodding as Jessica introduced herself and then tipped her chin toward Millie, over in the corner. Millie had wrapped her arms around herself and pulled the hood of her coat over her head and cinched it so tight that all you could see of her were her eyes and the tip of her nose.

"This is Millie," Jessica said. "She's got a rash."

Millie muttered a greeting.

Stavros turned to Alice. "I thought your mama was going for a few days," he said. "Lots of luggage. Lots of bags."

"Oh, you know my mom. She packs everything but the kitchen sink," Alice said. "She knows we're coming. She's on her way back right now."

Stavros nodded, and then, before Alice could look at his face to see if he believed her, she hurried the other two girls around the corner to the elevators. Millie kept her head down, with the oversize coat disguising her body and her borrowed duffel looking small and shabby in her arms.

Alice pushed the button, and when the elevator's doors slid open, she and Jessica stepped inside. Millie did not. Millie stood just outside the doors, and Alice saw that she was trembling and heard her breathing hard. Inside the hood, all of her face-fur was standing up straight, like a cartoon of a furry creature that had stuck its paw in an electrical outlet.

"Millie, come on!" Alice said, and tried to smile in case anyone was watching.

Millie shook her head. "It eats people!" she whispered. "I was watching! I saw!"

"Oh, for the love of God," Jessica muttered, and grabbed Millie's wrist, trying to tug her forward. Millie didn't budge.

"I saw," she repeated. Her eyes were enormous, so wide that Alice could see the whites under her irises, and her voice was whispery when she turned to Alice. "Two old people got into that one." She pointed at the elevator across the hall. "And when it opened its mouth again, they were gone."

"It's not a mouth, it's a door. It's an elevator. Like on *Friends*," Alice said, hoping desperately that Millie's favorite No-Fur sitcom actually contained footage of an elevator. "It goes up and down. It didn't eat them," Alice whispered. "It just carried them upstairs."

Millie squeezed her eyes shut and allowed Alice to lead her onto the elevator, giving a terrified squeak when an arm, clad in pink-and-ivory tweed, shoved itself between the sliding doors as they closed.

"Hold the door, please," came the distinguished tones of Mrs. Philpott, who lived on the seventeenth floor. Alice gave Millie a stern look as the older woman, clutching her teacup poodle, Pearl, climbed slowly into the elevator.

"Hello, dear," Mrs. Philpott said to Alice, and Pearl—who was tiny and white and went to the groomer's twice a week to have all her fur shaved off except for ball-shaped bundles around each of her paws and a topknot that Mrs. Philpott ornamented with a rhinestone bow—gave a little yip of recognition. The elevator began its ascent. Millie gasped and flattened herself against the wall.

"It's okay!" Alice said, and smiled at Mrs. Philpott. "My cousin," she said. "She's afraid of heights." Meanwhile, Pearl seemed to have noticed the strangers and began to growl low in her throat. Alice nudged Millie as soon as she realized that Millie was growling back.

"Pearl! Behave yourself!" Mrs. Philpott said, looking alarmed. "I must apologize. She's never done that before."

"She doesn't like her smell," said Millie.

"What was that?" asked Mrs. Philpott, who was hard of hearing and was, according to Alice's mother, too vain to wear hearing aids.

"She doesn't like her smell," said Millie, pointing her chin toward Jessica. "Because she has a—"

Jessica glared at Millie before she could say the word "tail," which was Jessica's big secret and which, according to Millie, was a thing that other species could smell. Pearl barked, squirmed out of Mrs. Philpott's arms, and stood on the floor snarling at Jessica, her teeth showing and what little fur she had bristling. "Nice doggy," said

Jessica, extending her hand. Millie moaned and tried to flatten herself against the elevator's back wall.

"Oh dear," Mrs. Philpott said as Alice bent down, snatched the little poodle, and handed her back. "Oh dear." She tucked her pet underneath her arm and practically ran through the doors when they slid open. Millie tried to follow her. Alice pulled her back in.

"Don't touch those!" Jessica said as Millie stared at the rows of buttons. "If you press them, we'll stop at every floor!"

"I want to stop!" said Millie, stabbing randomly at buttons. "I am not liking this ellervator!"

The doors opened again at the nineteenth floor, then again at the twentieth. On the twenty-second, Alice said, "We'll take the stairs," and pulled Millie out into the hallway, leaving a miffed-looking Jessica on the elevator alone. "Come on," said Alice, and sighed, dreading the climb. Millie hung her head.

"I am sorry," she said in a very small voice. "But I am never before being in a room that moved. And that lady had a bad smell."

"She wears a lot of perfume," Alice acknowledged, but Millie was shaking her head and shivering.

"Not a perfume smell, a sick smell." Millie looked at

Alice, her eyes still too wide, her nostrils flaring. "You couldn't smell it?"

Alice shook her head, even though, the truth was, she thought that she had noticed something funny about the air in the elevator. Millie was looking at her gravely.

"It is not just her," Millie said. "This whole building has a sickish smell." She shuddered. Her eyes were still enormous, and her fur, instead of bristling, seemed to have acquired a dispirited droop. "There's something wrong with this place. How can you live here with it smelling this way?"

"I don't smell anything. And be that as it may," Alice said, using one of her father's favorite expressions, "you can't just go around growling at people or talking about how they smell. It's rude." She began walking down the hall, toward the staircase, feeling Millie scurrying miserably behind her. "People are going to think there's something wrong with you. They'll know you don't belong here."

When she turned around, Millie's head was hanging even lower. "Sorry," she whispered. "I am being sorry."

"Come on," Alice said. She grabbed Millie's hand, leading her toward the door at the end of the hallway. The building's halls and public rooms were wallpapered and lit and carpeted, but the stairs, which hardly ever got used, were concrete, and the stairwells smelled faintly like the cigarettes the residents weren't allowed to smoke in their apartments. She could feel Millie's hand trembling. "Come on," she said again. *Good,* she thought as she felt Millie flinch. *Let her be sorry. Let her be scared.*

They climbed the stairs in silence, Alice taking them two at a time, Millie lagging behind her. "Come on," said Alice. "We can have a snack. A snackle."

Millie shook her head. "I don't think I can eat. I feel so . . ." She set one hand on her belly. "Nyebbeh."

"What does that mean?" asked Alice. "In this context."

This earned her a brief and quivery smile. "It means that I am very scared."

Alice thought. "When I get scared, my mother makes me tell her what's the worst thing that can happen. Usually the worst thing isn't even that bad." Even as Alice was speaking, she was realizing that this particular case could be the exception to Felicia's oft-cited rule. The plan was for Millie to wait for her name to be called, then step onto the stage with Jessica beside her, and explain that Jessica had lip-synced because Millie was shy. Jessica would wear one of her most stylish outfits. Millie would have swallowed her potion, but in case it didn't work or her fur came back, she would wear layers—socks and leggings and a long skirt, a high-necked blouse and a long-sleeved sweater and a knitted wool hat with flaps to cover her ears.

"The worst thing," said Millie, "is that someone could see me and know what I am. I could be trappled and put away in a zoo, never again to see my home."

Alice remembered how much she had always enjoyed her friend's poetic way of putting things. "If anyone tries," she said, "just tell them what you guys are supposed to say. About your glandular condition."

"I know we are supposed to be saying that," Millie whispered. "Will they believe it?"

"I think so," said Alice. "People believe what you tell them if you say it like you believe it." She climbed another half flight. "It also helps if you're a grown-up. What else?"

Millie listed her fears, one for each step. The judges at *The Next Stage* could refuse to let her sing because she'd gotten this far by lying and pretending to be Jessica Jarvis. Or they'd let her sing and she'd get so nervous that she'd faint or forget the words. "Or disgrace myself in some other way," Millie added. Or she'd sing but sound horrible. Or she'd sing and do fine, and they'd like her, but she wouldn't be able to figure out how to get herself to wherever they wanted her for her actual performance. Or her fur would come back, and they'd call the news crews and the tabloid photographers, and she'd be trapped and sent to a zoo.

For each fear, Alice had an answer. Of course there was a chance that the judges would decide that she and Jessica had broken the rules, but it was just as likely that they'd let them both compete. She was sure that the judges had seen nervous kids before and would let Millie start again if she got nervous. She pointed out that Millie had sung the song so many times that it would probably just pour out of her mouth, no thought required. Her fur could reappear, but she'd be covered from head to toe.

"And why buy trouble?" Alice asked. "My mom says you shouldn't worry about something unless you actually know it's going to happen."

Millie did not look especially comforted. "And what if they like me?" she asked. "What if I have to do it again?"

"Just worry about getting through this round first. My mom says it's like running a race. You just put one foot in front of the other." She was remembering all of her Septembers, every first day at every new school. *I know it's a lot,* her mother would say—which, maybe, was how Alice had known to say those words to Millie—*but you*

*just put one foot in front of the other. Just keep going. Don't look down.*

After what felt like an hour of climbing, Alice opened the door to the penthouse floor. The girls stepped out of the stairwell and found Jessica waiting, hands on her hips and one foot tapping impatiently, with her suitcase leaning against the wall and her duffel bags beside it.

"Your mother has much wisdom," Millie said. It surprised Alice, who wasn't used to thinking of her mother as wise or kind or patient. It was easier to think of Felicia as a thin and frowning presence, a woman who'd float in and out of Alice's bedroom—and her life—on a cloud of hairspray and perfume, a woman who could make Alice feel bad simply by being so lovely. But maybe that was . . . well, not wrong, exactly, but uncharitable. Just lately it seemed like whenever she reached for some bit of adult wisdom or piece of strategy or advice, it was Felicia's voice she was hearing in her head.

*Strange,* she thought, then she unlocked the door and heard Millie gasp. Even Jessica sounded impressed when she said, "Nice place."

Millie stepped forward tentatively on the glossy white marble floor—probably a material she'd never seen, Alice thought—and, with her fingertip, touched a petal of one of the lilies in the flower arrangement that stood in the Chinese ginger jar on the table in the center of the entry hall.

"That's not real, is it?" Jessica was staring at the little oil painting in its gold frame on the wall, where it had stood since Alice could remember.

"It's a real painting," said Alice, which was what her father said when anyone commented on the Monet.

Jessica pursed her lips and gave a soundless whistle. "What's your dad do?" she asked.

"Finance," said Alice.

Feeling shy, she led the other girls into the kitchen, one of the few places in the house where she'd ever felt even slightly at home. Millie was taking tiny, tentative steps, as if the shiny floor were ice that could collapse underneath her. She stared at the ovens and the towering stainless-steel refrigerator, which, Alice knew from experience, generally contained little more than champagne and fancy mustards, capers, and olives, garnishes for foods, not food itself. Millie touched the marble countertop, specially installed for rolling out pastry (her mother never cooked, but when they had parties, they'd bring in caterers who did), then ran one fingertip over the polished granite and oiled wood that made up the rest of the counters.

Alice bustled around, locating the peanut butter and honey she'd bought when she was home for break; pulling sprouted-wheat bread and butter from the freezer; emailing the grocery store for a delivery of fruits and vegetables, crackers and cheese, and oatmeal to make the next morning; and, finally, ordering pizza for their lunch.

Jessica had set herself up in one of the guest rooms, where she was unpacking her bags, pulling out the outfits she'd brought with her and holding them up to the light before arranging them on hangers to snap a picture. "Do you have a steamer? I'm going to have our followers vote," she told Alice.

"You're going to let them decide what you're going to wear?"

Jessica nodded. "People like to feel involved. And if they see me wearing the outfit they wanted, they'll be even more likely to vote for me."

Alice nodded. Millie had settled herself gingerly on the couch in the living room, holding herself so stiffly that Alice suspected she was afraid that the apricot-colored sectional sofa would swallow her. When Jessica waved the remote at the television set to turn it on, Millie gave a gasping shriek, and when Stavros buzzed up to let Alice know that the food had arrived, Millie gave a despairing moan. She didn't move from her spot on the couch, and she refused to try even a nibble of the pizza. All she did was poke at the cheese, say, "Gooey," and close her mouth up tight.

"Get it together," Jessica muttered. "You can't be freaking out like this at our audition."

"I am not freaking out. I am freaking in," said Millie. Jessica rolled her eyes. Alice thought of the things that soothed her when she was anxious or sad. Would a shower or bath help Millie, or would the idea of a man-made rainstorm in a glass box only scare her more?

"Millie," she said. Millie's head snapped around. Her eyes were wide, and her lips were trembling. "Do you want to take a bath?"

Millie considered, then nodded. Alice led her to her parents' bathroom, which had a deep soaking tub the size of a small wading pool. Pots and glass jars of bath salts and gels lined the ledge of the tub. Millie took a deep sniff and smiled for the first time since she'd arrived in the city when she saw that one of the little jars had an "Out of the Woods" label, which meant it had been made by the Yare and sold on-the-line.

"Our balsam body scrub was in a magazine," Millie said. "That is what Old Aunt Yetta told me. We got so many orders it took us months to keep up."

"That's good, right?" Alice asked.

Millie nodded and looked at the tub. "In our village," she said, "we have one big wooden tub." She held out her arms to indicate the tub's size. "On Sundays, every family boils up its biggest pots of water and carries them to the tub, until it is full. And then all the littlies go in for their scrubbing."

Alice imagined it, a half-dozen Yare bobbing in the steamy water like furry soup dumplings. "Do they like it?"

Millie's face crinkled. "They are hating it, every time. Yare do not like to be wet. They do not like the feel of water in their fur, and they do not float." She looked ruefully at the taps, maybe remembering her own failure to swim across the lake. When Alice turned on the taps, Millie asked how the water got all the way up here, to the top floor, and when Millie reluctantly pulled off her boots, she asked why the floor felt so warm.

"It's heated," Alice said.

"A wonderment," said Millie. "Your world is so full of wonderful things." Her words were cheerful, but her voice was bleak.

"Are you okay?" Alice blurted. She hadn't meant to ask. She'd meant to stay angry at Millie, to remind herself that Millie had abandoned her, in favor of fame and

Internet clicks and Jessica Jarvis. But Millie looked so pathetic, so lonely and so scared, that Alice couldn't stop remembering all the times she herself felt that way and had no one to comfort her.

"I am not," Millie whispered. She looked up, and her silvery eyes were filled with tears. "I am here, in the big city, and it is my dream come true, but all I am is afraid." She bent her head, her eyes turned toward the water that was filling the tub. "And you are feeling angry. And that is all my fault."

"I'm not angry," Alice said, the words coming out of her mouth before she could think about them. The truth was that she did feel angry, but her whole life, whenever she'd been mad or sad or jealous or envious or disappointed, she had learned not to say so, to smile and deny it and say that she was fine. Girls and women weren't supposed to feel those things, she'd learned, and if they ever said they did, they were punished, told, "Young ladies don't behave that way," or "Stop being such a baby."

Millie looked at her. Alice finally said, "Yes. I am angry. I feel like you don't like me anymore, and I didn't do anything wrong!" She hung her head and muttered, "It's not my fault I'm not pretty like Jessica."

Millie, who had been sitting on the ledge of the tub,

stood up and crossed the room, taking quick, hopping steps over the heated floor, and took Alice's hands. "Is that what you are thinking? That I like Jessica because she is pretty?" Her voice was getting higher and higher. "Do you think so little of me? That I am choosing my friends because of how they look?"

Alice frowned. Now that Millie had said it out loud, she realized that it was not a very flattering assessment. "You never want to spend any time with me," she said. "You barely talk to me. You were my friend, and I never even had a friend before, and when I thought that I was one of you—that I finally, finally was going to have a place where I wouldn't feel like such a freak—you wouldn't help me. You wouldn't even listen. All you cared about was this stupid show."

She waited for Millie to deny it, to tell Alice that she was wrong or exaggerating; that she was being silly or just imagining things. Instead, Millie gave a slow, solemn nod. "I am sorry," she said. "You are right. I have been"—she paused, inhaling slowly, before pronouncing judgment on herself—"a badfriend."

Alice couldn't keep herself from smiling a little. "It's two words, you know."

Millie did not seem to have heard her. "You did not

do anything wrong, and I think you are strong and lovely. But you are right. I did not listen to you. I . . ." Alice heard Millie's voice wobble. "I forgot about you, because I was trying so hard to be having what I wanted, and I saw that Jessica would help me, and I did not listen to you. I should have listened to you. I should have tried to help. And so I am badfriend." Her hands were balled up into fists, and she was hitting her chest, not too hard, but with enough force that Alice could hear the blows. "I did not listen to you. When you told me about the bad boy. When you said you might be Yare. When you asked me to help. I thought only of my own self. I didn't listen, and I didn't believe."

"It's all right," Alice said, but Millie was shaking her head.

"It is not being all right. Not! Not! Not!" she said, punctuating each "not" with a little punch. Then she crossed her hands at the wrists and held them out to Alice. "I am sorry," she said, her voice slow and somehow formal. "I was wrong. I was a badfriend. Alice of the No-Fur, will you do forgiveness?"

"I will," said Alice, taking Millie's hands and trying not to giggle. "I will do forgiveness."

"You are my only true No-Fur friend," Millie said. "My best friend of everyone. I am sorry if I behaved like I had forgotten." She went to her little bundle of clothing and pulled something out. "You see, I am packing the sweating-shirt you gave me, on the very first night we met."

Alice felt her throat get thick with tears.

"I wear it when I am afraid," Millie said. "I wear it because it makes me think of you and how you saved me and how you are brave and that I can be brave too."

"I'm not brave," said Alice.

"Oh, but you are," said Millie. "Think of all the new schools you have been to. All the new towns. Everywhere you went, you made a place for yourself."

Alice began to say that it wasn't true, that she'd never had a real place for herself until the Experimental Center, but Millie wasn't through.

"You stayed and stuck. Even when it was hard and you were lonely. Even when that bad boy had people chasing after you."

Alice smiled, remembering how she had run, and how Jeremy and his mob and the television crews had discovered not a Bigfoot lair but a hundred students and teachers who all announced that they were freaks.

"I tell myself," said Millie, "that if I could be the tiniest bit as brave as you, then maybe tomorrow will be a-okay."

"I know you'll be great," said Alice.

"Will you come with us to the audition?" Millie asked. "I will be braver if I know that you are there."

Alice had planned to call the clinic first thing in the morning and go there while Millie and Jessica were at the audition. She decided that the call could wait.

"Yes, I'll come," she said, and felt the warmth she remembered rising in her chest when Millie hugged her, that half-forgotten feeling of having swallowed a drop of sunshine. *My friend,* she thought. *My friend is here with me.*

# CHAPTER 17

*Jeremy*

THE BUS FROM STANDISH LEFT AT SIX IN THE morning. Jeremy was lucky enough to get out of the house before anyone woke up and to get a window seat with an empty seat beside him. Thanks to the GPS locator that Dr. Johansson had somehow activated in Alice's phone, he could see that she was still in her apartment on the Upper East Side, probably sound asleep.

At eight o'clock, just as the bus was groaning its way up the ramps at Port Authority Bus Terminal, Jeremy saw the Alice dot start to move, heading downtown, then stopping at a spot the map informed him was Carnegie Hall.

*She's with Millie,* Jeremy thought, feeling a lump swell

in his throat. But maybe that was okay. Mr. Carruthers was looking for Millie, that was true, but they were looking for her at the Jacob Javits Center, blocks away, in a completely different part of town.

Jeremy walked up Broadway, thinking that he'd keep an eye on Alice, make sure nothing happened, and wait for her to text him her next location.

It was easy enough to hide himself in the noisy crowd of would-be contestants and onlookers and fans who'd gathered all around Carnegie Hall, where a banner announced, "*The Next Stage* Auditions Start Now!" Some carried posters with things like "America Loves the Amazing Marvin" and "Go for Your Dreams, Serena!"

When he finally spotted Alice, she was with two other girls. One of them was another student at the Center. Jeremy recognized her from the night of the failed Bigfoot hunt, when she'd reluctantly told the world that she had a tail. The other one was Millie, who was wearing a sweatshirt with the hood pulled down low enough to cover her forehead, and the collar zipped up almost to her lips. She and Alice were walking along, unnoticed. Mostly, Jeremy suspected, because everyone who saw them was looking at the tail-girl, who looked extremely glamorous and very grown-up in high-heeled shoes and a short skirt and lipstick. "That's Millie from the videos!" he heard someone murmur, and someone else said, "She's the one to beat."

He wasn't sure he'd be able to talk his way through the doors, but luck was on his side. When a troupe of a dozen school-aged jugglers—along with their parents, their trainer, their manager, and their tutor—arrived just after noon, Jeremy slipped in with them and got waved right through the door. When the jugglers turned left, following a sign labeled "Dressing Rooms," Jeremy turned right. After a few dead ends and apologetic waves at harried-looking people with headsets and clipboards, he found his way to the auditorium and found a seat amid dozens of anxious parents, spouses, coaches, and piano teachers, many of them trying to sneak pictures of their competitors (in spite of the "No Cell Phone Use Permitted" and "Absolutely No Recording" signs that *The Next Stage*'s crew had put up on the walls).

He was sitting six rows from the front, and five rows behind the judges. There were dancers and jugglers and a ventriloquist, and then, finally, the judges called, "Millie Maximus!" and Millie took the stage. Millie was wearing a frilly white blouse that covered her neck and her arms all the way to her wrists. There were white gloves on her hands, a gray knitted winter hat with a pom-pom on her head, and something—leggings, or tights, Jeremy wasn't sure what girls called them—covering up her legs. Her body was entirely covered, every bit of what would have been skin on a normal person hidden. And her face . . .

Jeremy stared at her. She'd done something to her face. There was no more fur there, between the high neck of the blouse and the brim of the hat. Just cheeks and a nose, a mouth and chin and forehead, all the features a regular girl had. The only evidence that Millie was something other than human was her silvery-gray eyes, slightly too large and too shiny to be human.

"Hello," she said as she stepped into the spotlight and lifted one hand in a small salute. Even from a distance Jeremy could see that her hand was trembling. As he watched, the tail-girl, wearing a short black skirt and a black-and-white top, came to stand beside her.

Two of the judges turned toward the third. *Benjamin Burton,* Jeremy thought. He was the boss, the producer and creator of the show, the one who usually told the competitors how awful they were, only his manner was so elegant and his voice so beguiling that sometimes the singer or dancer or juggler wouldn't even realize that they'd been insulted or dismissed. Jeremy had never seen the man at a loss for words, but now he was silent and immobile as he stared at the two girls.

Romy Montez looked down at the sheet of paper, then up at the stage. "Millie Maximus?"

"That is me," said the girl, the furry girl who was now furless. *A glandular condition,* she'd said, but of course Jeremy had known better. Only now, a prickle of doubt worried at his heart. Where was her fur? What if he'd gotten it wrong?

"And who are you?" Romy asked the other girl.

"My name is Jessica Jarvis," she said. "And we can explain."

"Let's have it," said Benjamin Burton, who'd finally found his voice. "Quickly, if you please." He sounded the way he always did, speaking with the same clipped, sarcastic voice that viewers in America had gotten used to over the past four years, but Jeremy thought he heard something new underneath that cynicism. Surprise? Excitement? Maybe even a touch of fear?

"I am having shyness. Th-that is, I'm very shy," Millie stammered. Now it wasn't just her hands that were shaking; her voice too. Jeremy could even see her knees quivering underneath their layers. "I love to sing, but I do not enjoy to be on camera. So I got my friend Jessica to do lip-syncing. I sang, and she stood in front of the camera, so that it was her you'd be seeing." Her speech finished, Millie took one step backward, then another, and looked over her shoulder, longingly, at the darkness in the wings. Jeremy peered in the same direction and caught a glimpse of curly reddish hair. *Alice,* he thought, and felt his breath whoosh out of him, knowing that she was here and that she was safe. He could watch and make sure nothing happened, and follow her to the clinic.

"If you don't like being on camera, how do you think you'll manage on the show? You do realize," Romy Montez said politely, "that we are televised nationwide?"

Millie stopped walking backward. "I am working on my confidence, sir."

"Sir," said Julia Sharp, who sounded like she might have been giggling.

"And what about you?" Benjamin Burton asked. "You. Other one." He gestured with his pen, having apparently forgotten Jessica's name. She was happy to remind him.

"Jessica Jarvis. I'd like to be considered in the junior spokesmodel category."

"She's not entered," murmured Julia Sharp.

"This is highly irregular," Benjamin Burton said. He was on his feet, his ever-present sunglasses off his face and in his hands, staring at Millie with the strangest expression, a combination of surprise and something else, something Jeremy couldn't name, something that looked a little bit like longing.

Before Benjamin Burton could say anything else, Jessica whispered to Millie, who took one more quick glimpse backstage, then walked forward, into the spotlight. Her shoulders dropped. Her chin lifted. She pulled off her hat, and her long, silvery hair rippled as she shook her head gently from side to side. Jeremy leaned forward, aware that he was witnessing a kind of transformation, listening to the crowd murmur. Millie might have felt that she was "shyness" at some point in her life, but she seemed perfectly assured as she stood, her hair seeming to pull down all the light in the room, until Jessica was barely even visible. Millie moved smoothly as she took one last step forward into the spotlight, opened her mouth, and began to sing, unaccompanied.

"Something has changed within me / Something is not the same."

Her voice was quiet at first, but so pure and sweet that everyone in the crowd leaned forward, waiting for the next notes.

Millie stepped forward until she was almost at the

edge of the stage. Her silvery hair gleamed; her eyes seemed to capture the gazes of everyone watching.

From down in the orchestra pit, a piano picked up the melody. Millie's voice was strong and clear. She sang the song like it was her very own story, as if every word had been written just for her. Her hands were in fists at her chest, and her head was held high.

As she swung into the next verse, and the stringed instruments and the horns began to play along with her, the audience was perfectly silent, rapt and motionless.

She turned to look offstage. "Alice, come with me," she said. Jeremy sat up very straight, the hairs on the back of his neck bristling. He knew the line was supposed to be "Glinda, come with me," as Elphaba, the green "wicked witch" who sang the song, addressed her friend and rival. But Millie had changed it and put in Alice's name.

And that was as far as she got. There was a scream, then a thump, and then the sounds of a scuffle off to the side of the stage. Millie's head whipped around.

"Alice!" she screamed.

The audience started murmuring. They sounded dazed, like they'd woken up from a dream. "Alice? Is that what she said?" asked the woman, a juggler's mother, on

Jeremy's left, while a little girl climbed on top of her seat for a better look. "What's wrong?" she asked. "Why'd she stop singing?"

Millie turned to face the judges, and her furless face was pale. "I'm sorry!" she called, and ran off into the darkness.

"Thank you for the opportunity!" blurted Jessica Jarvis, and ran after Millie.

Jeremy got to his feet, grabbed his backpack, and vaulted over the row of seats in front of him and into the aisle. He ducked around a bouncer who tried to grab his shoulders, slipped between the legs of another one, and then ran up the stairs and onto the stage.

"Hey!" yelled Romy Montez, who had gotten to his feet.

"What's going on?" screeched Julia Sharp, who was cringing in her chair.

Jeremy felt like his insides were turning into ice as he looked backstage and saw what some part of him must have known he would see. Two men in dark suits and sunglasses, one on either side of her, each with a big hand under her arm, were pulling Alice out a door and onto the sidewalk.

Jeremy raced after them out into the chilly, gray afternoon. Across the street, with its engine running, was a familiar white van. His friend Skip Carruthers sat behind the wheel. *Of course we won't hurt her,* Skip had told him, and Jeremy hadn't entirely believed him, which was why he'd given Carruthers misinformation and told him it was Millie, not Alice, who'd be in the city that weekend, and that she'd be at a science-fiction convention, not here. But none of it had mattered. In typical Jeremy Bigelow fashion, his best efforts had only made trouble for people he cared about. The Department of Official Inquiry had gotten its Bigfoot, and Jeremy had led them right to her. *And, let's not forget,* his mind added, *you betrayed a friend.*

Feeling helpless and furious and sick and ashamed, Jeremy ran. The men who had their hands on Alice were dragging her across the street, getting ready to shove her into the van. Millie and Jessica were closing the distance, but Jeremy could see that they weren't going to reach her in time. "Hey," he shouted, knowing that yelling would do absolutely no good. He yelled anyway. "Hey, Skip!"

Skip Carruthers's head turned. He looked at Jeremy . . . except that wasn't right. He had his sunglasses on, and he seemed to be looking straight past Jeremy, through Jeremy, as if he'd never seen Jeremy before in his life, as if Jeremy were a stranger who didn't matter at all.

That dismissal echoed every other time he'd been ignored and overlooked by some grown-up, starting with his parents and continuing with every coach or teacher or choir director or Boy Scout troop leader who'd ever known one of his far superior brothers. It filled Jeremy with rage, and the rage gave him a brief burst of what felt like almost superhuman strength.

He raced across the street, hearing horns blatting and cabdrivers shouting, feeling a car's bumper brush his thigh as it screeched to a stop. He caught up to Millie and Jessica, then ran past them, reaching, his fingertips touching Alice's hair.

He was so close . . . but "close" only counts in hand grenades and horseshoes, like his papa Frank used to say. The men had hooked their hands underneath Alice's armpits, and they were wrestling her into the backseat. "It's the kid," one of the men said in a dismissive voice, and the other man gave Jeremy a contemptuous look.

The first man's leg shot out sideways, catching Jeremy in the belly, knocking the air out of him, and sending him to the pavement on his knees. Before he fell, he saw the man sitting in the backseat of the van. Dr. Marcus Johansson, of the Standish Children's Museum. A phone—probably the one he'd been using to track Alice—looked as tiny as a matchbox in his giant hand. His expression was grave.

"You!" yelled Jeremy. "You lied to us!"

Alice must have heard him or seen Dr. Johansson too, because suddenly she stopped struggling, and her body went limp. It caught her kidnappers by surprise, and as they struggled to keep their grip, Jeremy saw a woman jump out of a car parked on the side of the street and sprint toward the van.

"Alice!" she shouted.

The men in suits who had Alice weren't looking behind them. As they turned, the woman came racing right at them, her sneakered feet flying over the pavement, her hair, the same reddish-gold shade as Alice's, flying out behind her.

"Let her go!" she yelled.

One man kept hold of Alice as the other began, "Ma'am—"

But that was all he managed. The woman didn't even slow down. She jumped over Jeremy, dropped her shoulders, bent her knees, and slammed all of her weight into the sunglass man's belly, like a rugby player tackling an opponent. The man, startled and caught off guard, fell backward into the street, right in front of a city bus, which honked and then braked to a stop.

"Help!" Alice shrieked as the one man left holding her

tightened his grip. He lifted Alice off the ground, preparing to throw her into the van. Jeremy shoved himself forward, head butting the man's knee. The man didn't fall, but he stumbled, losing his balance for just a second, and then the redheaded woman was there. She jumped in front of him as the man, still off balance, tried to get a better grip on Alice. The woman wrestled her free. A little white car came screeching up right beside the van. Jeremy saw a small, white-haired woman at the wheel.

"Hurry!" Jeremy heard the driver shout.

The red-haired woman opened the back door and pushed Alice into the backseat. Millie tumbled in through the other door. Jessica stood in the street, like she wasn't sure what to do, and in her instant of hesitation, the doors slammed shut and the car zoomed off, zigging in front of the bus, zagging in front of a cab, becoming briefly airborne after hitting a pothole, then barreling through a red light and vanishing around a corner.

Jessica turned around, thinking that she'd run back across the street and get some help, but then the men in the suits, perhaps thinking that they needed something to show for their day's work, grabbed her and tossed her into the backseat.

"Hey!" Jeremy shouted as the van drove off in the

direction of the white car. He was starting to turn around—to go somewhere, to tell someone—when he felt heavy hands on his shoulders and heard a furious voice in his ear.

"If I discover that you had anything to do with that, *anything at all*, I will have you made into a mince pie."

Jeremy turned his head and saw *The Next Stage*'s most famous judge looking like he wanted to tear someone apart.

"I didn't," Jeremy said, swallowing hard, wondering if Benjamin Burton had any idea what he'd seen, any knowledge of the Bigfoot world. It didn't seem likely, but, Jeremy supposed, anything was possible. "I promise. I was trying to help." He stared at the space where the car and the van had been. Then he turned back toward Benjamin Burton. "Those guys . . . they were from a government organization . . ."

"The Department of Official Inquiry. Yes, yes, I know." Benjamin Burton put one hand between Jeremy's shoulder blades and marched him back across the street, into Carnegie Hall. They passed the auditorium and walked down a flight of stairs, then along a dim underground hallway. Whenever they walked by a window, Jeremy would look outside, hoping he'd see Alice again or Skip

Carruthers or the little white getaway car. But, of course, the New York City street looked the same as it ever had, the same as it probably always did, the sidewalk filled with pedestrians and joggers and dog walkers and strollers, the street crammed bumper to bumper with buses and taxis and cars. It was as if the day's drama had never even happened at all.

"Come on," said Benjamin Burton's deep voice. "You're going to tell me everything. And then I'm going to tell you how to set this mess right." He led Jeremy down one flight of stairs, then another, into a basement.

"I will," said Jeremy. "I promise."

He followed Benjamin Burton into the darkness, feeling his heart pound as, far above them, a door slammed shut.

# CHAPTER 18

## Alice

ONE MINUTE ALICE HAD BEEN STANDING backstage, trying to make herself inconspicuous in a pool of shadows next to the curtains, watching Millie first struggling to explain herself, and then getting ready to sing. On the way down to the audition, Millie hadn't been able to stop touching her face, stroking and poking and even pinching at the smooth skin, until Jessica said, "Cut it out!" Then she'd looked at Millie curiously. "If you've got stuff that makes the fur go away, why don't you use it all the time?"

Millie didn't answer, but Alice felt her shudder. Alice

had been the one who'd watched Millie breathing deeply, clearly working up her nerve before uncorking the vial and taking a sip. She'd been the one who'd seen her friend hunched over and shuddering; she'd been the one to hear the moans Millie made as her fur seemed to suck itself into her body. For a minute all Millie could do was lie there on the bathroom floor, looking even smaller than she usually did, her unhealthy pallor announcing that her skin had never seen the sunlight.

"Did it hurt?" Alice asked, feeling stupid.

"Hurts," Millie whispered, and pushed herself slowly upright. "I do not know how my father can do this over and over."

"Maybe it's different for him," Alice suggested. "Maybe the potion's too strong for you." But Millie had shaken her head.

"I think it's supposed to hurt," she'd said. "I think we are supposed to know who we are and that we should not be changing it." She'd touched her arms, her neck, her cheeks, then shuddered. "I don't like it," she whispered. "I am not feeling like myself."

Then Jessica had bustled in with her arms full of clothing. For the next thirty minutes, Alice had listened, amused, as Jessica had tried to cajole Millie into a dress—"so cute!"—or a pair of jeans—"very on trend!"—and Millie had either refused or somehow ruined the appearance of the outfit by adding scarves and hats when Jessica had her back turned.

Finally, Millie had emerged, swathed in her layers, with a hoodie covering her head and body and leggings beneath her long skirt.

The morning doorman called them a cab, and they'd gotten to Carnegie Hall, where the auditions were being held, in plenty of time. As the first group was called, Alice stood beside her friend, touching her arm or her shoulder, as Millie trembled and touched her smooth face and snuck peeks at the crowd. Millie had said she wished she could be as brave as Alice, and Alice hoped that her presence was giving her friend strength.

She'd held her breath when Jessica and Millie had gone onstage. For a minute she'd been sure that the judges would kick them both out for breaking the rules. She had been so proud when Millie had started singing, so proud of how she'd sounded, and when she'd said Alice's name, Alice had almost started crying. But before Millie could finish, there had been hands on her shoulders, hands underneath her arms. She'd screamed and tried to run, but the men grabbed her, saying, *Just come with us, don't make any noise, we don't want to hurt you, we just want to talk.* The men had managed to get her outside, out of the theater and into the street, in spite of her struggling. She thought that she'd heard Jessica and Millie chasing after her, and even Jeremy's voice, and then a strange woman had come out of nowhere, flying across the street like a football player or an avenging angel. She'd wrestled Alice away from the men and shoved her into another car, a car that was, even now, speeding up the West Side Highway in the direction of New England, with . . . Alice blinked. Her rescuer was behind the passenger seat. Alice was in the middle. Millie was on the other side of the backseat, and Miss Merriweather gave her a cheerful wave from behind the steering wheel.

"Hello, dears," she said.

Millie looked at Alice with wild eyes. Alice touched her hand, then looked past Millie, through the windows. The doors were locked; the car was zipping along at close to eighty miles an hour, and it was being driven by a woman Alice knew to be an agent of the Department of Official Inquiry, the arm of the government that was after the Yare.

*Oh, we are in trouble,* Alice thought. *We are in so much trouble.*

"Don't worry," said a familiar voice. "She's one of the good guys."

"A double agent, I believe the kids are calling it," said Miss Merriweather. But Alice barely heard. She was staring at the woman beside her, the one who'd saved her, the woman whose clothing and hair were entirely unfamiliar but whose low, cultivated voice was instantly, undeniably recognizable.

Alice swallowed hard. She squeezed her eyes shut. Then she opened them and made herself look . . . and see.

"Are you all right?" her mother asked.

Alice could only stare. Felicia, in a long-sleeved T-shirt and sneakers and sweatpants instead of the skirts and jackets and heels she always wore, could have been a different person. Her hair, which she religiously straightened each morning, was a mess of curls—*a familiar mess,* Alice thought—and her skin, without makeup, was the same shade as Alice's, right down to the constellation of freckles that dotted her cheeks and her nose.

Her mother's eyes narrowed. "What?" she asked. "What hurts? Did they twist your arms?"

Alice shook her head. Her mother nodded. It was a brisk nod, not the kind of slow, assessing gesture that Alice was used to, from a woman who had nothing on her schedule but lunch and a massage and a Pilates class and nothing on her mind but when the spring fashions would arrive. Without lipstick, her lips were pink and chapped, and without her perfume, she smelled clean and faintly sweet, like soap and fresh-cut grass and honey.

"All that Pilates actually came in handy," Alice's mother said. She reached over, wrapped her arms around Alice's shoulders, and pulled her close.

Alice let herself lean into Felicia's body. She thought of all the nights she'd dreamed about finding her real parents—how her mother would pull her into her arms, just like this, and cry over having lost her, and promise that she'd never let her go. Now, it seemed, it was happening. She'd found her real mother, and it had been her real mother all along.

She opened her mouth. "What," she began, and then, "How?" Complete sentences, it seemed, were beyond her.

Miss Merriweather's dimpled smile flashed in the rearview mirror. "Hiding in plain sight, dear," she said.

"I don't understand," said Alice.

Her mother stroked Alice's hair. "It's complicated," she said. "And I've been wanting to tell you forever! But before I do . . ." She took Alice's hands in her own—her mother, who, it seemed, had never liked to touch her—and stared into Alice's eyes. "I need to tell you that I'm sorry."

"Sorry," Alice repeated.

"I never wanted to send you away. Not ever." Her mother's voice was solemn. Then her expression became rueful, and her mouth moved into an unfamiliar smirk. "I never wanted to spend my entire life wearing girdles and doing juice fasts and going to charity balls either, but it was the only thing that I knew would throw them off our scent."

*Not your scent,* thought Alice. *Our scent.* "Are you Yare?" she asked. She heard Millie give a frightened squeak. She knew that she had broken one of the main rules, possibly the only rule of Yare existence: Never tell the No-Furs about the Yare. She waited for her mother to look puzzled and ask what Alice was talking about. Instead, Felicia shook her head.

"Not me, honey," she said. She stroked Alice's hair with a touch as gentle and as loving as anything Alice had ever imagined. "Your father. Not Mark. Your real father."

Alice blurted out the only two words she could think of. "What happened?"

And then, as Miss Merriweather drove them, first east, then north, Felicia told her.

"My name wasn't always Felicia. It was Faith. Faith Nolan. And I didn't always live in New York City. I grew up on a farm in Vermont. We kept cows and sold the milk to our neighbors, who turned it into cheddar cheese, and we grew apples that we sold at farmers' markets and to other neighbors who made cider. I wish I could show you pictures," she said. One of her hands was still patting Alice's hair gently. "I looked so much like you do when I was a girl. Same hair. Same freckles. Same everything."

Alice looked at her mother, who was still skinny underneath her sweatpants. Felicia sighed and ran her free hands along her torso, over her hip bones. "It's a disguise," she said, and continued.

"I was so happy on the farm. I had two older brothers, and I grew up chasing after them, always trying to keep up. We'd climb apple trees in the orchard, and skip stones and catch frogs in the pond."

Alice nodded, even though she was having a hard time picturing her elegant mother as a skipper of stones, a climber of trees, and a frog aficionado.

"At night our mother would read us stories in front of the fire. A half hour, every night, before we could watch TV. We'd complain about it, or we'd pretend to, but it was the best part of the day." Felicia smiled, remembering.

"The only problem with two older brothers was that they were very protective. They wouldn't let a boy come near me. The whole time I was in high school, not a single boy ever asked me to the movies or to one of the school dances, because they were terrified of Jack and Henry. When I left for college, I fell in love with the first guy I met." Her mother's gaze had turned inward, like she was watching a movie playing in her mind. "He was tall, with dark hair, and he was kind and smart and thoughtful and interesting. Not like anyone else I'd ever met. He knew everything about the woods, about building shelters and foraging and how to survive in the wilderness. He knew which plants you could eat and which ones were dangerous, and where to find every swimming hole near campus. But then there'd be things he'd never heard of, television shows or bands or even just things that had happened in the world. But I wasn't sophisticated enough to realize just how different he was, and it wasn't like I'd watched that much TV or been out in the world so much myself. And even if I had noticed, I don't think I could have ever guessed the truth."

She reached for a bottle of water in the seat-back pocket, unscrewed the cap, then replaced it without drinking. "He'd leave bouquets of flowers outside my dorm room door. Every morning, flowers." She smiled, remembering. "He'd take me camping, and he'd build a lean-to out of branches and start a fire with a flint. Whenever I asked him how he'd learned to do those things, he'd tell me that he'd been an Eagle Scout. He wasn't a college student—I thought he was at first, because he was the same age as the rest of us. When I realized he wasn't enrolled at the university, I thought he was a townie, one of the guys who lived in town and worked on campus. I didn't realize. I mean, how would I?" Felicia uncapped the bottle of water again and drank down half in a single swallow.

"So he was Yare." That was Millie's piping voice; Millie, who'd been listening to the story as closely as Alice had.

Felicia nodded. "We were in love," she said. Her voice was cracking, as if all of that high-society smoothness had been scraped away. "We were going to get married after I graduated, and have a little farm of our own."

Alice felt dizzy as the car wove through traffic, settling into the fast lane and racing along on a road that ran along the Hudson River. Her mother on a farm? Her beautiful, fashionable mother, raking out stalls and milking cows, picking apples for cider, weeding gardens? The mother Alice had known all her life would have hated that as much as she, Alice, would have loved it.

"When I found out I was pregnant, I was happy. Surprised but happy. I knew what he was by then. He had to tell me, if I was going to have a baby, and we'd have to figure out how to tell his Tribe and make sure it would be safe." She smiled, then sighed. "It was a shock, but I still loved him. We wanted to be together."

She looked down into her lap, where her fingers were worrying at the water bottle's cap. "And then they found me. The Department's men. They'd been after him for a while, I guess. He'd forged some papers so that he could get a social security number and a driver's license, and they found out that he wasn't who he said he was. They grabbed him, right off the street, but he got away." Her head bent even lower. "And then they got me." Her voice was low and dull. "They told me that Jamie wasn't human. That my baby would be a monster. They said they would take me to a safe place where I could deliver my baby and that then they would take it away, and I could get on with my life."

Alice closed her eyes. *A monster.* She'd heard kids calling her that, and worse, for her whole life. And now there was a government agency, a bunch of officials, maybe even scientists, saying the same thing.

"So you gave me away," said Alice. Her voice was small and mournful. Felicia took her hands.

"Never," she said. Her hazel eyes gleamed with tears, but her voice and her hands were steady. "I loved you from the minute I saw you. And I knew that I would never let them take you. I knew that the only way I could have you and keep you safe was if I found a way to turn into someone else." She sniffled, then raised her chin in a familiar, haughty gesture that Alice had seen a thousand times.

"I gave birth to you in a hospital in Vermont. The Department had men with me, all the time, right outside my hospital door, all day and all night. When you were five days old, I told them I needed some privacy, so I could feed you." She smiled, remembering. "I got dressed, and I got you dressed. I ripped the sheet from my bed into strips, so I could tie you against my chest. I put everything I could carry into my backpack, and I climbed out the window. Out of the window, around the hospital, and into town. I used all the money I had to buy a tent and a lantern—and diapers, of course, and a baby carrier—and you and I went hiking. All the way from Vermont to New York, following the path that Jamie had told me about."

Alice was trying to picture it: Felicia, who exercised only in regimented increments, usually under the instruction of a personal trainer, and always in color-coordinated, stylish athleisure wear, clumping through the woods in hiking boots and a flannel shirt with a baby strapped to her chest.

"Thank goodness you were such an easy baby," she said. "A few times, the men were so close I could hear them talking around their campfires, and I'd just sit and feed you, and then pray you wouldn't cry. But you never did." She sniffled. "Jamie told me where he'd come from and where to find his Tribe. I gave you to his brother and his brother's wife, and I promised I'd be back for you as soon as I could come." She looked down at her body with regret. "By then I'd already lost enough weight that I could almost pass as a New York society lady. I just needed a new name. And a husband." She smiled faintly. "Mark was an old friend of my brothers'. He'd always had a crush on me, and I'd never been interested. He was working in New York, so I went back to the city and found him, and I told him that I'd marry him but that there'd be a few conditions."

"So I was a condition," Alice said.

"You were my darling," her mother said, and pulled Alice's head against her shoulder, cradling her, holding her tight. "And so Faith Nolan became Felicia Mayfair, a fancy Upper East Side lady with a brand-new name. I straightened my hair." She touched her hair gently. "And I never ate anything." One hand strayed to her flat belly. "It took them years to catch on."

Alice wanted to hear about that—about how the Department had caught on and what had happened next—but she had other, more pressing questions. "When did you come and get me?"

"As soon as I thought it was safe. You were nine months old. Mark and I were married, so I had my new name. Mark told everyone that I was an old family friend. His family had a place in Vermont, near where I'd lived, but different. Very fancy." A faint smile curled the corners of her lips. "Everyone assumed that I was rich, like he was, that I was a cousin of one of the families that lived in one of the big houses in the compound where Mark's family had their place. And, of course, by then I looked the part. So I went back and got you. And I loved you." Her voice was cracking again. "I loved you so much. It killed me every time I had to send you away, to every single one of those god-awful snooty schools. Every time I tried to straighten your hair or put you in clothes that you hated." She touched Alice's curls again, gently, fondly. "I don't think you'll ever forgive me, but I had to keep moving you around. It was the only way to try to disguise you, keep you safe."

Alice thought of all the different schools she'd attended, how her family never went to the same place twice on their winter and spring vacations, and how the one constant in her summers was her visit to her granny.

"I don't understand."

"They suspected," Felicia explained. "But they never knew for sure. I never let them get close enough to test your blood or start asking Mark questions. As far as they knew, I was just a rich society lady, and you were just a girl in boarding school or at sleepaway camp. I was trying to keep you safe. Safe meant hidden. And hidden meant . . ." One of Felicia's hands touched Alice's hair and stroked it gently, from her crown to the nape of her neck. "Hidden meant that you had to look like the rest of them. Enough so that even my parents . . ." Her voice broke. She sniffled, then started to cry. "I'm so sorry," she said. Tears ran down her cheeks and did not leave muddied trails of mascara and eye makeup. "I wanted to tell you a thousand times, and every time I had to send you away, it felt like I was taking poison. And now . . ." Alice followed her mother's gaze to the rear window. The white van was still trailing them, and it had been joined by two gigantic black SUVs.

"Not to worry," said Miss Merriweather, but her hands had tightened on the wheel. The little car whined as she stepped on the gas, pulling into the left-hand lane.

"Where are we going?" Millie asked.

"A safe place," said Miss Merriweather.

Millie moved restlessly in her seat. Alice leaned into her mother, feeling her soft sweatshirt against her cheek, smelling the sweetness of her skin, hearing the slow, steady beat of her heart. *Home,* she thought, and shut her eyes as Miss Merriweather steered the car toward some unknown destination. Beside her, Millie squeezed her hand. *I am home.*

# EPILOGUE

JEREMY BIGELOW WALKED THROUGH THE woods, the same stretch of pine trees and fallen logs where he'd spotted his first Bigfoot. Only they weren't Bigfoots, he reminded himself. They were Yare. He'd learned that, and much more, during his time with Benjamin Burton, before *The Next Stage*'s founder and chief judge put him on a train back home. He counted out fifty paces, then called out something reassuring. "I am your friend!" he yelled, trying not to feel ridiculous. Then he stopped and listened, his head cocked, his eyes shut. Nothing. He walked on.

In spite of everything Benjamin Burton had told him,

in that office in the subbasement of Carnegie Hall, there were still about a hundred things Jeremy didn't know. Like whether Skip Carruthers had been hunting for Alice all along, or whether they'd started looking for Millie, and Alice was just a kind of bonus prize, like putting a quarter in the gumball machine at the Standish Diner and getting two balls instead of just one.

"I come in peace!" he shouted, and shut his eyes again. Still nothing. He kept walking.

He hadn't told his parents about what had happened on his so-called field trip. If they'd asked how his day in New York City had been, he would have said, "Fine," but neither of them asked. When Jeremy came home on Saturday afternoon, his mother was closed up in her office, the rattle of her fingers on the keyboard suggesting that she was working on a new poem. His father was with Ben at some kind of tournament, and Noah was in his basement lab. Which meant that there was no one to stop him from putting down his backpack, taking the long, hot shower he'd dreamed about during the hours of Benjamin Burton's interrogation, and then gathering his binoculars, his compass, and his maps and walking into the woods, walking with direction and purpose, not just wandering, but, for once, knowing exactly where he was going and what he'd say—and hopefully find—when he got there.

"Do not be afraid!" he shouted . . . and did he hear something? The crack of a branch beneath a large, hairy foot? A voice? He paused, then yelled something that wasn't on the approved list of phrases that Benjamin had given him. "Benjamin Burton told me to come!"

He stood still. He counted slowly backward from one hundred. At forty-nine, a figure slipped out of the shadows and moved noiselessly toward him. Jeremy felt his heart pounding, rattling his ribs, making black spots dance in front of his eyes. He made himself hold still as the creature—a female, large, furry, and in a dark blue dress—came closer.

From the top of her head to the tops of her feet, she was covered in dark, curling fur. Her brown eyes were large and frightened. She was wringing her hands, and the fur on her face was soaked, as if she'd dipped her face in water or been crying. Something about her looked familiar: the shape of her eyes or her mouth; the way she held herself as she edged toward him. She stopped at about fifty yards away, poised on the balls of her feet, ready to turn and run.

Jeremy held out his open hands. "I'm a friend," he said.

"Please, sir," she said in a whispery voice that Jeremy could barely hear, a voice that tore at his heart. He'd imagined this moment, pictured it for so long, thought about how proud he'd feel, how triumphant. But now that it had happened—now that he, Jeremy Bigelow, had actually found a real, live Bigfoot—he only felt sad.

"I'm not a sir," Jeremy said. "I'm just a kid."

The Bigfoot stretched out her arms, beseeching.

"Please, sir kid," the lady said . . . and now Jeremy could hear, for sure, that she was crying. "Please help me find my lost Millietta."

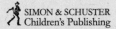